PRAISE FOR
Dreaming Anastasia

"Joy Preble has given readers an intriguing tale of magic, tragedy, love, and betrayal…Be prepared to fall into this story; your heart will ache for the characters and what they've suffered, especially Anastasia. Lovers of fantasy and romance will not be disappointed, and a sudden twist at the end will leave readers with eyes wide and mouths agape…*Dreaming Anastasia* will most definitely be gracing my shelves from now on."

—YABooksCentral.com

"A very entertaining and original story."

—The Book Lush

"The novel is cleverly written in alternating points of view (Anastasia, Anne, and Ethan) and takes you on a ride of paranormal fantasy, contemporary and historical fiction, with a little bit of romance. It's the perfect blend that will attract a variety of readers."

—Lori Calabrese, Examiner.com

"*Dreaming Anastasia* is a fun young adult fantasy that takes the reader back and forth from current-day Chicago to the time of the Romanovs, and throws in elements of a Russian folktale for added chills."

—MsBookish.com

"*Dreaming Anastasia* is a story of love and loss on many different levels. It was a wild, fun, and sweetly romantic ride."

—Galleysmith.com

"I really enjoyed this book. It made me want to research the Romanov family and the fairy-tale character of Baba Yaga…*Dreaming Anastasia* is easy to read and an enjoyable story. Thank you, Ms. Preble, for a great read."

—TeensReadToo.com

"Preble's blend of fiction, history, and folklore is spellbinding…I am smitten with this debut novel and its author."

—TheNeverendingShelf.com

"Once it gets going, it's impossible to put it down! The adventure is so irresistible that almost all teen readers will enjoy this book."

—MrsMagooReads.com

"This was a pretty awesome book."

—TheCozyReader.com

HAUNTED

THE RIVETING SEQUEL TO
Dreaming Anastasia

JOY PREBLE

sourcebooks
fire

Published by Sourcebooks Fire, an imprint of Sourcebooks, Inc.

P.O. Box 4410, Naperville, Illinois 60567-4410

(630) 961-3900

Fax: (630) 961-2168

teenfire.sourcebooks.com

Library of Congress Cataloging-in-Publication data is on file with the publisher.

Printed and bound in the United States of America.

VP 10 9 8 7 6 5 4 3 2 1

For all the mothers and all the daughters and for those who love with full and passionate hearts.

"I was much too far out all my life
And not waving but drowning."

—*Stevie Smith, from*
  "Not Waving but Drowning"

The Forest, Early Evening

Baba Yaga

THROUGH THE SKULL IN MY FIREPLACE, I WATCH HER. Does she know, I wonder? Does she sense my presence? It is hard to say. But I suppose it does not really matter. We are connected in ways she does not yet understand—ways that even I find curious. I am Baba Yaga, and she is Anne, and our destinies have mingled, twisted tightly together even before she found her way to my forest. Anne Michaelson—the ordinary girl who wasn't ordinary at all. The one who brought Anastasia out from my hut and captured the heart of a foolish man named Ethan. The one who weeps quietly, night after night, because she saved a girl who chose to die, and this does not sit easily on her heart. I would help her, I think, if I were not what I am. But as that cannot change, at least for now, I watch. I offer no balm. No words of comfort.

I am the glorious Baba Yaga. And while this is not a simple thing, it is what it is. I am the one who changes others. The Bone Mother. The Crone. For ever and ever, I have flown the skies in my mortar. Stirred the air with my pestle. Ground my enemies to dust or chewed them whole with my iron teeth and placed their heads on pikes outside my hut. I have come and gone as I pleased. Danced barefoot in my forest. Felt the sting of icy rain on my skin. Ridden fast through the woods with my horsemen. Taken lovers when I pleased. Reveled in the summer air. Laughed with glee as autumn approached. My season. The time of change. The wonderful approach of death.

But now there is something else. Something unexpected. Or rather, something I had forgotten to expect. It lurks in the water and watches my girl just as I watch her. Just as I watch it.

Water is not my true element. I am of the earth and the sky. I am of the fire. But in the seas and oceans, the rivers and streams, I am not at ease. I soar through the skies in my mortar. Nothing passes through my forest unchanged—not even this creature that floats below the surface of things, the one that has been haunting my girl. Honed to the bone, as I am. Skin pale as alabaster. Eyes dark with a hunger that verges on madness. Hair tangled and wild as her heart. Like me, she is not what she once was. But she is not what she wants to be either.

Then again, who really is? Even I have desires beyond my reach. At least for now. So she floats and waits, and so do I. Like all good stories, this one cannot begin until it is ready. However we come to our roles—air, water, earth, fire—we will fly, float, crawl, burn. It is, after all, our destiny.

And so I study the creature that watches Anne. A picture within a picture within the glowing eyes of the skull, licked by the flames of my fireplace. I stretch out my hands, brown and gnarled, etched with lines of my past, my present, my future. My cat, my *koshka,* his feline fur black as night, eyes yellow as bile, nips at my ankles. His sharp pink tongue flicks at a stray crumb on my hard wooden floor—the same floor that Anastasia used to sweep for me until it gleamed. Now the cup of hot, sweet tea that I drink—the one she used to bring me—is tinged with bitterness at her absence.

Does the woman in the water know that I am not so far away? Would she change her course if she did? I smile at the thought of it and see the glint of my iron teeth reflected in the eyes of the skull. If she wandered into my forest, I might grind her bones with my pestle. Crush what she is and reform it to my will. But she cannot cross over. She never could. She can only swim and hope and wait.

So I watch them. I stare into my fire. And realize that for all of us, there is no going back. We have all traveled too far, too deep.

Chicago

TUESDAY, 1:13 AM

ANNE

IN MY DREAM, I SIT AT BABA YAGA'S TABLE. ONE OF HER huge brown hands stirs something in the kettle hanging in the fireplace. The other creeps across the smooth wooden floor on its fingertips, a roughly crafted robin's-egg blue pottery mug hooked to its huge pinkie finger. This is gross and unsettling, and if I were awake, I'd probably say so. Detached hands offering people beverages is—generally speaking—rather icky. But I'm not awake. At least, I hope I'm not.

"Drink," Baba Yaga says to me. "If you want to control the power that sits in your veins, then choose to drink." The sleeves of her long, brown cotton dress flap emptily as her hands go about their business.

"No," I tell her. I shiver as I watch those empty sleeves. "I'm not yours. You have no hold on me, Baba Yaga. I'm not Anastasia. I'm Anne. Whatever you're offering, I don't want it."

"Oh, child," she says. Her mouth turns up in a hideous smile. Those iron teeth glint at me. The wrinkles in her dark face are etched so deeply that I wonder if they pain her somehow. It's as though they dip right inside her face. "You have no idea what's coming. No idea what you're giving up."

"I don't care," I tell her. "Whatever it is, I don't want it."

She's still laughing at me, her gravelly voice filling my head, when I wake up, my camisole soaked with sweat. I tell myself to breathe—just breathe—and lie there in the darkness under my ceiling fan until my heart stops pounding and the cool air takes the heat from my skin.

I sit up, fumble on my nightstand for my cell phone. The blue glow makes me blink as I flip it open and scroll to Ethan's number. My fingers hover there. Press? Don't press? Tell him? Don't tell him? It's a routine I've been going through night after night now that the dreams are back. I know I should call. *Let me know if you need me,* he always says. He checks on me once a week. Lately, he asks, *Is there something going on? You need to tell me, Anne.*

And maybe because he doesn't press me, doesn't call me out on what I'm sure he knows is a lie, I keep it to myself. I think about the few times that we kissed—that first time in the rain when Anastasia went back to die, and some others before he left. Tentative kisses that spoke of something more to come. The feel of him, the musky smell of him. Those crazy, ridiculous blue eyes. But then he left. And if he's coming back, he hasn't said. What kind of silly girl would I be to think those kisses meant the same thing to him? Better to move on. Better to keep things to myself.

So I don't tell him that things are getting weird again. Maybe they've never stopped being weird. If I tell him the truth, then I'll have to admit that the magic inside me hasn't let up one bit. And since this scares the hell out of me, it's a lot easier to lie.

But right now in the dark, with my heart still erratic, I imagine myself fessing up. *Funny thing, Ethan. Those powers you said would go away now that Anastasia didn't need saving anymore? Well, they haven't. I'm juiced up to the max most days with this stuff lurking inside me. But Anastasia's dead for real now. So what use is this magic to me? And why aren't you here to help me figure things out?*

Maybe that's why he left in the first place. Not to find himself or wander Europe. I mean, I get *that*. He was immortal for so long, and now he's not. He needs to know what that means. But maybe his journey took him that far, and now he's just done. Easier to bolt than to commit to the craziness again. Or to a girl he's known for just a few weeks. No matter how much they've been through together.

But I'm having these dreams again, and Baba Yaga hasn't let me go. I'm as much her prisoner as Anastasia ever was—I'm not stuck in that creepy hut, but I end up there night after night anyway. If it's not real, it feels real. And if I've learned one thing about all this magic business, it's that those two things are pretty much the same.

I don't know what she wants. Okay, that's a lie. I don't want to know. Whatever it is she thinks I can do or wants me for or hopes I'll stumble into—I don't want any part of it. And who else can I tell that to except Ethan? But then I remember that I've told him that before. Only it didn't really matter. When you're destiny girl, you don't get a lot of choice.

This is what I ponder while I sit here in the dark in the middle of the night. This and the fact that I probably bombed some of my final exams last week, and that summer's beginning, but I'm not exactly in a summery mood. Outside my window, some early-rising bird squeaks out a chirp. Just one lonely little *eep*, and then it's gone. Phone still in my hand, I walk to the window. The cool glass feels good as I press my forehead against it.

9

"Liar," I say to myself. "Go ahead. Blame everything on him."

Because here's the real truth: as much as I hate the chaos that Ethan Kozninsky brought with him when he smashed into my life last fall, I don't hate him. Not at all. And I won't say that I love him. But I won't say that I don't either. What I will say—just not to him, and definitely not to Tess because she'd get all judgy even though she's my best friend and certainly has had some major lack of judgment of her own—is that I can't get him out of my thoughts. Dreaming or waking, he's always there somewhere. I've told myself that's ridiculous. But telling it to myself doesn't make it true. Since he's been away, I've felt empty and alone and incomplete. And no matter how much I do to push away those feelings, they just keep coming back.

Serious neediness. Not something to make a girl feel proud. So I toss the phone on my nightstand, climb back into bed, draw my knees to my chest, and hike the covers up to my chin. It's not just the dreams anymore, I know. Or my more-than-slightly-conflicted feelings for one absurdly handsome, blue-eyed Russian. It's what I saw just now when I peered out into the darkness of our supposedly boring little Chicago suburb. It's the other thing I haven't mentioned to Ethan…

She was out there again, barely noticeable in the flicker of water from the Spauldings' sprinkler that comes on in the middle of the night. Just like last night, when she was leaning against the oak tree a few houses down during that thunderstorm. The same woman who'd stared at me silently a few weeks ago as she sat at the edge of the duck pond near our house, her tattered lilac dress soaked, her hair a mass of wild black waves. The woman who sometimes has a fish tail and sometimes has legs. The one who seems to be stalking me.

I close my eyes. I won't sleep, but at least I'll rest. If she's out there still, I won't go look. If this is all starting again, I don't want any part of it.

Only I'm pretty sure that once again, I don't have a choice.

New York

WEDNESDAY, 1:45 AM

ETHAN

THE SUBWAY PLATFORM AT 79TH STREET IS ALMOST deserted as I step off the train. I walk briskly up the stairs and head east, stopping only to pull out a cigarette, turn my back to the breeze, and cup my hand as I light it. I take a deep drag and blow out the smoke. It hovers in the humid New York summer air like a misty veil. One of the neighborhood bars is still open. I contemplate a beer. Or better still, a vodka. But I head to the hotel instead, nod at the doorman as I step inside and wait for the elevator. If I drink tonight, I'll drink alone.

It's taken me too long to come back to the States. Too long to come back to Anne.

In the room, I pour two fingers of Stoli in a glass, flip through the channels on the television, find nothing to distract me, and sip some more. The liquor takes the edge off. But only a little.

Do you need me to come back? I'd asked her a few weeks ago. There'd been a long pause on her end of the line. And when she'd told me no, I knew she was lying. I'm not linked with her the way I used to be. The magic I'd both loved and hated has almost left me. No need for it now that Anastasia is both freed and dead—which was not the outcome I'd imagined back when I was really eighteen.

But still, when I'm quiet, when I concentrate, I can sense Anne's emotions. Something's happening again, and she's not telling me what it is. I should push her for a response. In my mind, I do. I imagine hopping a plane, returning to Chicago, and figuring out the rest of this with her. So why have I waited? Why did it take me so many months to arrange to come back? Why, even now, have I made it across the Atlantic only to New York—close but not close enough?

Even the Stoli doesn't make the truth any easier. But here it is. It's not a simple thing to accept your life back from someone. Anne Michaelson—she of the auburn hair, brown eyes, and prima ballerina posture—gave me just that. I know she mourns for the girl she couldn't save. But Anastasia was beyond saving. I—it turns out—was not. I'm starting over at eighteen. For better or for worse, that's the way it is. The past is not erased, but the future's a lot different.

But how do you find equal ground to love someone when this is how you've begun? How do I get beyond that debt? It's selfish and small and foolishly male. And it's the truth. How can I know for sure that anything we feel for one another is real? That it's not colored by the past? By peril and danger and the loss of the girl we both tried to save? Isn't it better to just let Anne be? She has no tie to me now. Our lives are no longer linked. Just because I get to start over doesn't mean that she has to start over with me.

But what I think and what I feel are two different things.

I drain the glass. Pour another. And try once again to sort it all out.

Chicago

Thursday, 1:45 pm

Anne

"Aren't you going to open it?" Tess waggles the envelope with the Kennedy High School return address and my name peering out of the little see-through waxy strip in the lower right-hand corner. She had snagged it from the pile of mail on my kitchen counter when she came to pick me up—something I've only just now discovered.

"No." I fish a Diet Coke out of the cooler settled between our two bright yellow lounge chairs, unscrew the cap, and take a swig. On the other side of our neighborhood pool, a girl who looks about thirteen adjusts the bottom of her lime green bikini and looks up hopefully at Ben Logan, the lifeguard. She's smacking her gum so loudly I can hear it even from over here.

"But you have to know." Tess pokes the envelope at me again in her persistent Tess way. *I'll take it from her,* I think. *Be like everybody else who just ended junior year and open the letter so I can find out my grades.* Of course, I could have checked online too. But I didn't, and Tess knows it—just like she knows the things that happened last October.

"I don't have to do anything." I swallow some more Diet Coke. "They're *my* grades. I don't have to look at them if I don't want to."

"Then *I'll* open it."

I grab the envelope from her hand. And lacking any better plan, fling it into the air. It floats around for a few seconds, then the breeze catches it. Just like that, it's floating in the shallow end. I watch as the water soaks it.

"You're crazy." Tess shifts in her lounge chair and shoves her Oakleys back on her long blond hair. For a second, I think she's going to dive in after my report card.

"Leave it."

She gives me her squinty-eyed Tess look. But she doesn't get up. She just blows out a *humph*ing sound, flops back on her chair, and drops the Oakleys over her eyes.

In the shallow end, the woman in the frothy, lilac-colored gown gliding across the bottom of the pool darts up, grabs the soaking envelope in one very pale hand, and takes it back down with her. She smiles at me, and I think she even winks, except it's hard to tell, what with her being underwater and all. She kicks gracefully a couple of times and heads for the deep end, winding around two little boys playing Marco Polo. If they notice her, they don't show it. Neither does Tess.

Lifeguard Ben—who also happens to be my boyfriend and is thus sensibly ignoring the flirtations of the girl in the lime green bikini—doesn't see her either. Although unlike Tess, I'm pretty sure he wouldn't believe me if I told him.

Lime bikini girl, having failed to get Ben's attention, climbs the diving board steps, walks to the edge of the board, then executes a double flip and cuts neatly into the water. She barely misses a head-on collision with the woman in lilac, who's now settled on the bottom of the pool, her dress fanning out in waves around her as she opens my envelope, slides out the paper inside, and nods her head over my semester grades. She grins at me, baring her teeth in a way that's even more unsettling than any of the rest of it. This time only a fish tail peeks out from the tattered hem of her lilac dress.

Tess sighs. "Spill."

She's said that to me before. Back last fall, when Ethan and a not-so-dead Russian princess named Anastasia and a crazy witch named Baba Yaga turned my pretty ordinary world into a crazy mess.

Tess was there when it all happened. When I discovered that I had power. And a destiny. And a really nutty great-great-whatever-grandfather named Viktor who also happened to be the illegitimate son of Tsar Nicholas and had found a way to live forever. He'd recruited Ethan to his mystical Brotherhood and convinced him that they were saving the Romanov family. But after he had used ancient magic to compel Baba Yaga to save and hold Anastasia, the only one Viktor was really interested in helping was himself: eternal life for the Brotherhood guys as long as Anastasia remained in the witch's forest. Only Viktor never counted on Ethan finding me, the girl the prophecies said would be able to free Anastasia.

Somehow after all of that, school didn't quite do it for me.

"Coach Wicker's world history final," I explain to Tess. "I couldn't answer the essay."

"Oh?"

"Let me quote." In the deep end, the woman perusing my grades shakes her head. If I'm not mistaken, she even wags one long, pale finger at me. "Discuss the series of events that led to the assassination of the Romanov family in 1918."

"I see your point. But weren't there other choices? I helped Neal study for that one." Neal Patterson is Tess's boyfriend—the same Neal she's broken things off with two different times now. Tess is persistent in every area of her life. "He said there were two other questions to pick from. You didn't have to answer that one."

I shrug. She's right. I didn't have to answer it. I could have answered the question about the downfall of the Roman Empire instead. But by then, everything had sort of dribbled out of my brain.

In the deep end, the woman holding what is most likely my failing grade on the world history final—disappears.

I flick my gaze over to Ben, sitting in all his lifeguardy goodness on the stand, his red life preserver board slung over his shoulders. This is a new thing, Ben and me. About two months new, to be exact. He's smart and sweet and on the cute side of handsome. Sandy blond hair that's cut short but not buzzed, brown eyes a little darker than mine. He just graduated a few weeks ago and is headed to U of I in the fall to major in economics: Ben Logan, who's eighteen years old for his first time. Who, unlike a certain mysterious Russian, isn't actually closer to one hundred. And who has never been part of a mystical Russian Brotherhood that was supposed to protect the Romanovs. Ben has never been whammied by ancient magic to stay young and hot-looking until I finish his mission for him, rescue Anastasia and let him become mortal again and start over from where he'd stopped. Tess has both questioned and applauded my motives for going out with Ben. As she so delicately put it, *You know, if you'd only give in and hook up with water stud instead of moping about old Russian blue-eyes, then maybe you'd be fun again. Did you ever think about that? He's just what you need. Fun. Sexy. And seriously normal.*

Most days, I think she's right. Like right now, when Ben glances back at me—just me—even though he's supposed to be scanning the pool to make sure everyone's safe. He smiles his sweet Ben smile, and I smile back and feel all warm and tingly and think about what a fine kisser he is. And then I feel guilty—the kind of guilty a girl feels when she knows that a guy likes her way more than she likes him. Not that I don't like Ben. I do. But the liking is diminished by the knowledge that I'm using him because he makes me feel normal. And the more the dreams continue and strange aqua women in lilac stalk me in the neighborhood pool, the more attracted to Ben I feel… which is followed by more guilt.

Ben gestures with his shoulder toward the kiddy pool area. One of the other guards has called in sick today, so the kiddy pool with its frog slide is currently closed. Most of the little kids prefer the spacious shallow end of the main pool anyway. I glance at the clock on the storage shed wall by the Coke machine. It's almost Ben's break time.

"Gonna meet Ben by the frog slide." I slide the bottle of Diet Coke back in the cooler and hoist myself off the lounge chair. The pavement feels warm under my feet. But my arms are prickled with goose bumps even though it's in the low eighties and fairly humid. It's mid-June, and even Chicago heats up—at least occasionally—by this point in the summer.

Tess lifts her Oakleys briefly. "Now that's the spirit. You and lover boy go wade in the baby pool for a while. See if that perks you up. Maybe you can let him give you a little mouth-to-mouth resuscitation or something."

Sometimes, ignoring Tess is the only solution. So I do just that as I cross the hot pavement to the kiddy pool and wait for Ben on a bench in the shade. The huge frog slide—kids climb up the back side of the frog and zip out of its mouth—blocks my view of the rest of the Aqua Creek complex. I scan the empty baby pool—no woman in lilac. Maybe she didn't notice me leave my lounge chair. Maybe she just prefers deeper waters. Relieved, I close my eyes.

"Hey, Sleeping Beauty." Ben ruffles my hair affectionately, then flops down on the bench next to me. His skin smells of suntan lotion, sweat, and chlorine—like a personal embodiment of summer. He's wearing his navy lifeguard board shorts, flip-flops, and basically nothing else. It's a good look on him. He leans in and kisses me lightly on the mouth. Ben's not big on public displays of affection—at least while he's working.

"Hey."

He kisses me again, this time on the tip of my nose, then drapes one arm over my shoulders and pulls me close. I rest my head in the crook of his arm, feel packed, toned muscle against my cheek. His thumb rubs over my collarbone.

I wonder, not for the first time, what Ben would say if I told him how less-than-normal I really was. Would he still want to take me for pita and greasy French fries at the Wrap Hut or snuggle up next to me behind the frog slide if I told him that I know how to put a warding spell around someone's house? Or that Ethan and I used a magic lacquer box to enter Baba Yaga's forest? Or that a persistent mermaid in a lilac dress keeps swimming in my general proximity?

How about if I told him that I was there when Ethan's friend, Professor Olensky, was murdered last fall because he tried to help us rescue Anastasia? Or that it was my own crazy ancestor, Viktor, that killed him? Would he still want to go bowling later?

Ben purses his lips, which I've learned is his serious look. "You trying to lose weight or something? Because you don't need to, you know," he says and pokes a finger gently into my side. "Do you know I can feel all your ribs?"

I overlook the rib comment—mostly because it's true. I *am* thinner these days, but it's hard to eat when you're haunted by a persistent mermaid. And other things.

"I'm off at four, remember," Ben says after a few beats. "You're working today too, right? We'll do something after."

This is another part of why I'm with Ben. So many guys like to play the whole unavailable game. It's one of Tess's biggest issues with Neal. He pretends he doesn't know her schedule, or he blows her off to go out boozing with his buddies and tells her that she's making a big deal out of things when she reminds him that they had plans. But Ben's not like that. He listens when I talk and shows up when he says he will and even calls me before he goes to sleep just to say good night.

"After is good. But it'll be a little longer than that. Mrs. Benson has me scheduled from three until we close at eight."

Mrs. Benson is Amelia Benson, owner of the Jewel Box antique and estate jewelry shop, where I'm a part-time salesgirl for the summer. It's the shop that my mother helps manage—the same one that got pulverized last fall during the whole disastrous Anastasia rescue effort and has now been reroofed and restocked. Not that anyone seems to understand that's what happened, of course, or that a witch called Baba Yaga caused the destruction. People's memories seem pretty selective these days.

"I'll meet you at Java Joe's a little after eight," I suggest.

"You can buy me something with whipped cream." The whipped cream reference is my feeble attempt at making light of the weight thing.

"Hmm." Ben arches an eyebrow and smiles his cute smile. I'm sensing that the whipped cream reference has sent his boy brain to more interesting places than just fattening me up.

"I'm thinking venti mocha latte, Ben. Not whatever you're thinking."

Ben looks mildly disappointed. Back at the main pool, someone blows the safety break whistle. Ben unwraps himself from me.

"Gotta run, babe," he says. "Duty calls. Have to do a pH check before the kids all crash back into the water."

He's all business then, striding away. I start to follow him, only some mom in a black suit with one of those skirts that's probably supposed to hide her thighs but doesn't steps in his path. She starts a mild rant about *why, why, why are there no peanut butter crackers in the snack machine* because that's her son's favorite. Safer to hide on my little bench behind the slide.

Only it's not.

In front of me in the kiddy pool, the woman in the lilac gown slips down the mouth of the green frog slide and settles herself gracefully in its spacious lower jaw.

My heart goes thump. We stare at each other for a few beats. Me and my own personal mermaid, eyeball to eyeball. That's what she is, by the way. Not that I understood, at first. But it's amazing what I've learned in the wee hours when I can't fall back asleep after yet another crazy dream. Eventually, it was easier to just stay awake, fire up the laptop, and figure out what was stalking me. And so I did.

Rusalka. Russian mermaid. We haven't ever spoken, so I don't know if she's actually Russian—but given who I am and what I've seen, it's not that much of a stretch. Rusalka. A formerly human girl who somehow died tragically. Or got betrayed by the man she loved and *then* died tragically. Or whatever, blah, blah, blah, and then died tragically.

Emphasis on the *tragic*. And the dying.

According to every website I went to, she's supposed to be haunting whatever body of water is handy near wherever it is she died. Only right now, I think she just has to haunt *me*.

"I know what you are," I say quietly. I'm pretty sure that I'm the only one who sees her right now, but no sense gathering a crowd. My life is messy enough without everyone at the Aqua Creek Water Complex, including Ben and Tess, thinking that I talk to myself.

My mermaid smiles and runs a thin hand through her long, dark, wet hair. Shakes her head. Droplets of water fly around her, little wet sparkles in the patches of sunlight sneaking through the fabric canopy overhead. "Are you so sure you understand what I am?"

"Yeah. But you need to swim around someone else. Whatever it is you think you want from me, I'm not your girl."

She tilts her head and smiles at me. "Do not be so sure of that."

"Oh, I'm sure. Absolutely positive. I am *so* not the person you need."

"Help me," she says.

This startles me. "Help you what? You know, I don't even have to talk to you. I can choose to tell myself that you're not real."

Mermaid woman shakes that long, snaky, black hair.

Droplets of water splash against my legs. Even though I try not to, I shiver.

"You helped Anastasia." She says it so quickly and matter-of-factly that at first it doesn't even register. When it does, I just feel angry.

"Anastasia's dead. You're part of the supernatural crew. Figured you'd have known that."

"What if the Romanov girl still isn't dead?" is how the rusalka answers me. "What if she didn't actually go back to die?"

"Impossible." I shiver again, watch her stretch her pale arms in the cramped confines of the slide. "Been there, done that, bought the T-shirt. You know. Or maybe you don't know, you possibly being a figment of my imagination."

"Things are not always what they seem, Anne. You look at me, but you do not see what you need to see."

My heart pumps a little harder as the sound of my name echoes around me. So much for hoping that she had the wrong girl.

The rusalka—if that's what she is—tips back her head and catches a few stray drops of water on her tongue. Her skin is pale as skim milk, blue veins running the length of her bone-thin arms. "You saw Anastasia disappear. But that doesn't mean she died. Not like me. Although I suppose not unlike me. I'm here and not here. Everywhere and nowhere. Breathing and still drowning. If I can be as I am, then why not your Anastasia?"

"She's not *my* Anastasia." I stand up and edge toward the slide. I can feel my pulse in my throat. "She doesn't belong to me. And you're wrong. She made her choice. She went back to die. And I helped her."

The rusalka smiles at me again. Her teeth are white and

shiny and a little bit too sharp. "We all have our stories. Yours is no more tragic than the next girl's."

She makes a sound that I think is supposed to be a giggle, only it's a lot creepier. Then she's behind me, lounging casually on the bench I've just vacated. Tendrils of dark green seaweed dot her hair. The smell of her rises up and surrounds me—water, salt, and something I can't quite identify. The ocean, maybe.

"Well, then," I tell her, "if I'm so ordinary, then maybe you should just backstroke on out of here and leave me alone."

I sound a lot braver than I feel. Being brave, I've learned, isn't really all it's cracked up to be.

"He cares for you," she says as though she hasn't heard me. "But it's not easy. It never is for men."

"Whatever." I'm not even sure who she means. It could be Ethan. Or it could be Ben. My lifeguard, Ben Logan, with normal brown eyes, who's probably back on his guard stand on the other side of the pool and doesn't see crazy Russian mermaid women floating in the deep end like I do. Who'd never ask me to help him save a princess. Or turn my life upside down and then leave.

"Things are coming." The rusalka's voice—low and soft—yanks me out of my thoughts. "You need to be ready."

"If that's an ancient prophecy, you can keep it to yourself. Tell whoever it is that I'm not available. The world's a big place. Someone else will help. You just keep asking around."

"Perhaps Anastasia wasn't the only one who needed help. Perhaps there is more you need to know." Still stretched across the bench, mermaid lady sits up on an elbow and rests her chin in her hand. She watches me with eyes as gray as storm clouds.

"Wouldn't be the first time." I ignore the extra beat or

two my heart has taken and wave my hand in her general direction. "Shoo."

"Secrets within secrets, Anne. Stories within stories. Like Anastasia's pretty little doll. You know how it goes. You know the circle of it. It holds you, even if you pretend it does not. You must pursue this." She means Anastasia's *matroyshka* doll— the one I used to help send her back. The one that repeats its figure, smaller and smaller, each tucked within each other. The image of it in my head makes me sad—Anastasia choosing a fate we all wanted her to avoid.

"I don't have to pursue anything. And you need to just swim back up the slide or slither down the drain or whatever it is you do. Plus, how is it exactly that you know my name? It's not like I know yours. Or want to, honestly. No offense."

My rusalka sighs. Something that looks like sadness flickers through her dark eyes. She smooths her hands over her ripped and sodden lilac dress. "I know what I know. I am who I am. So here is what you must know. You have more to do. The witch is not done with you. And neither am I."

And then she's gone. She doesn't slip back into the kiddy pool or melt into the puddles of water that have dripped off her hair. She just stops being there.

"What the hell are you doing back here? Did I just hear you talking to someone?" I whip around to find Tess looking a little concerned and a lot annoyed.

"Talking? Well, I…" So what do I tell her? She's my best friend, and if I can't tell my best friend that I'm being stalked by a Russian rusalka, then honestly, who can I tell?

But if I tell her, then I have to admit it's really happening. I'll have to do something about it. And right now, that's about the last thing I need. But she's looking at me with the wrinkled-brow Tess look, the one that says she's going to pursue this like a pit bull until I tell her the truth.

I begin. "Something weird is going on," I say, which is certainly an understatement when it comes to my life.

"Weirder than you talking to the air?" She links her arm with mine, and we walk back to our chairs. I'm still sort of shivery and my hands feel clammy and I can see that Tess registers this. The furrow in her brow gets a little deeper.

"Well, I—" A few yards away, at the entrance counter, Ben waves cheerfully to me. I guess he's rotated to check-in duty.

I wave back, then brace myself for whatever it is that Tess is going to ask and I'm going to have to deflect somehow because I just can't do this all again. I can't, I can't, I can't.

Only Tess isn't paying attention to me anymore. She's looking beyond Ben to a figure that's standing just outside the Aqua Creek Park fence, his arms folded across his chest. He's wearing jeans and a short-sleeved, black T-shirt. His eyes are very blue, and his thick brown hair is just a bit too long. When he sees me, his face breaks into a smile that's a little less sweet and a lot more ironic than Ben's. Even from here, I can see that he's got a day's worth of stubble on his very strong chin. It looks good on him. He's also clearly a little bit older than the last time I saw him. This looks good on him, too. I'd wondered about that. After all, immortal hotties don't become mortal hotties every day.

And even though Ben is now just a few feet away from me, everything inside me sort of pulses toward the owner of that ironic smile.

Wrong, wrong, wrong! I tell myself. *This way leads to trouble. Those*

blue eyes. Those chiseled Russian cheekbones. That tattoo on his back, just at his left shoulder. They'll get you in trouble, Anne. What if he was the best kiss you've ever had? He's trouble. Nothing but. Aren't you supposed to be pissed at him for staying away so long? For never pushing for the truth when you told him you were fine each time he called? Didn't you learn your lesson last fall? Do you seriously need reminding?

Tess is now pulling me toward the entrance, and thus Ben, at a pace that can only be described as race-walking. "Holy crap." She yanks on my arm for emphasis. "Is that who I think it is?"

"Who?" asks Ben, now in earshot. "That guy over there? You two know him?"

Of course we know him. His name is Ethan. And he's come back.

Thursday, 2:10 pm

Ethan

S HE'S THINNER. IT'S THE FIRST THING I NOTICE. SHE'S still as beautiful as she was when I left her. And then I see the boy—this lifeguard walking toward me. He's with Tess, I think. That makes sense. Only as soon as I think it, he places his hand on Anne's shoulder—casual yet proprietary—and I know I'm wrong. Something else that Anne hasn't mentioned each time she and I have spoken. Something I didn't expect.

In my head, I cross the distance between us. I pull her close, kiss her, tangle my fingers in her hair, and I tell her that I was wrong to leave. That I'm back now, and I'm staying. I don't tell her I think she's in danger. Or that I know she's been keeping things from me and I've been choosing not to ask. I just hold her tight and kiss her again.

"Ethan!" Tess's voice is as loud as I remember it. "Took you long enough to get yourself back here. How come? No planes from Europe to Chicago? Besides, couldn't you, like, just—"

"Tess." Anne elbows her. "Enough. Ben hasn't met Ethan yet, remember?"

The four of us stare at each other. *Is she happy to see me? Has she missed me like I've missed her? And exactly who is this guy with his arm still resting on her shoulder?*

The hell with it, I think. And then somehow, we're hugging. She's moved toward me, and I've moved toward her, and she's in my arms. Not just in my thoughts, but right here in the sunshine. Her hair smells like rainwater and peppermint, and I bend to kiss her—lightly on the lips—when the wave of images jolts me: a blur of faces I can't make out. The sound of voices murmuring. Another voice weeping. A scream. Colors—reds and blues and blacks. The unmistakable feeling that I'm underwater. And then something more. For a second, it's like the first time she and I collided: that moment last fall when I touched her arm and knew she was the girl for whom I'd been searching. There's an electric surging. A spark.

Just a flash, then it's gone. My stomach clenches. I hadn't thought the connection between us would still be so visceral.

Anne's bare arms are still looped around my neck. The fragrance of her is still everywhere. "Um," she whispers in my ear, "we've got to talk about this. About a lot of things, actually."

"I know," I whisper back. "It's why I'm here."

I wince inside as the surprise of that registers in her eyes. Did she expect otherwise? I've kept my distance, telling myself that's for the best. I've confused her life enough, haven't I? Still, what I've told her isn't the entire truth, and I'm sure she knows that.

"Oh." She's no longer whispering, and I'm sensing this is not a good thing. Nor is the heat I feel coming from her hands, which are still resting on my neck. "I should have known, shouldn't I? That you wouldn't come back unless you thought there was something going on."

"I'll explain," I say quickly as she yanks her hands from

my neck and steps back a few paces. "When we can talk. We need to—"

"Took you long enough to get your ass back to the states, Ethan," Tess interrupts me. "And by the way," she grabs the boy's hand and pulls him with her to stand next to me and Anne. "Ethan Kozninsky, Ben Logan. Ben, Ethan."

Ben holds out his hand. It hangs there in the air a beat too long until I finally reach out my own hand and shake his. His grip is strong. Mine is stronger, though less than it used to be—mortality tends to have that effect—something else I've realized while I've been away.

"Old friend of Anne's." I realize that I'm squeezing his hand just a little harder than I probably should.

"Family friend," Anne adds quickly. Tess snorts, and we all stand there uncomfortably. I realize I'm still shaking Ben's hand and let go.

The family part isn't a lie, I suppose. Viktor had been my friend, and he was Tsar Nicholas Romanov's illegitimate son and Anne's great-great-grandfather. He'd offered himself up to the witch so she would stop destroying everything in sight once we had rescued Anastasia but were unsuccessful in breaking the spell that compelled her to protect a Romanov. Tricky business, that ancient magic.

"So is Tess right? You were in Europe?" Ben asks after another awkward pause. "I'm going during my junior year at U of I. I'm majoring in econ, and they've got a study-abroad program where you can work at The Hague for a semester. Learn finance. Kick around Europe while you're there. I backpacked for a couple of weeks last summer with my cousin, Josh, but I don't think you really learn a place until you've lived there, and I—"

"Slavic studies fellowship. I've been in Prague, mostly. A few months in St. Petersburg." Interrupting Ben Logan mid–travel monologue seems preferable to listening to more tips about maximizing the European experience. I've maximized it, and then some. Over many decades.

"Oh, yeah," Tess chimes in. "Ethan's got the whole Slavic folklore thing nailed. Don't you, Ethan?"

"Ben!" One of the other lifeguards gestures from the check-in desk. "I need you to guard the deep end at shift change, remember? So what are you doing out there?"

"Crap." In one impressively slick motion, Ben slings an arm over Anne's shoulder. "I gotta get back."

"I'll see you later," she tells him. "Java Joe's. Eight o'clock. Extra whip on my mocha, okay?"

Ben hesitates, and for a moment, I think he might question the "old family friend" story. But instead, he puts his other arm around Anne, pulls her to him, and presses his lips to hers. She kisses him back, and he grins at me over her shoulder when he breaks the kiss before she does. Clearly, Ben Logan is a fan of slick moves.

"Oh, my God," Tess says once Ben is out of earshot. "What was he going to do next, Anne? Pee on the ground and mark his territory? Good thing Ethan here isn't too much magic guy anymore. He could have zapped him or something. Maybe turned him into a newt or a toad or—"

"Give it a rest," Anne says dryly. "Seriously."

"I'm just saying. The testosterone is pretty thick around here."

Anne ignores this and turns to me. "Ben's my boyfriend. My really, really sweet, normal boyfriend. So let's make things clear. Everything that's happened? That's not stuff Ben needs to know about."

Is there some gentle way to tell her this might not be possible? But I don't have to find one because Tess interrupts—no surprise there.

"Ben's gonna find out eventually, Anne. Personally, I don't know how he's missed it. You're a mess, you know?"

Tess shifts her gaze to me. Her tone is fierce. "She hasn't been telling me most of it." Tess crosses her arms over her chest. "But I'm her best friend. She doesn't have to tell me. Stuff is going on. I know it. I can't see everything she sees, but that doesn't mean I don't know. All that power—I don't believe that it's gone."

"It *is* gone," Anne insists. But her eyes had told me something different only a few seconds earlier. "Give me a break, Anne," Tess snaps.

"Is that true?" I rest my hand gently on Anne's arm. "You have to tell me."

"I don't have to tell anyone anything. And besides, there's nothing to tell."

Tess rubs her arms as a brisk breeze picks up around us. "What about that day in English class right before school let out? And don't look like you don't know what I'm talking about. Brett Sullivan—stupid, muscle-bound idiot—knocks my pencil off my desk so he can take a peek at my boobs when I bend over to pick it up, only when I lay it back on my desk, it somehow rolls off, bounces on the floor, and stabs him in the ankle. Then I look up, and you're smiling. You think I believe that just *happened*? That pencils have a mind of their own?"

"Wonderful." Anne turns and starts walking back to the pool. Tess and I have no choice but to follow. The breeze has turned into a wind. Anne's auburn hair is blowing behind her. "That's what you think, huh? That I've got magic power left inside me that I could do *anything* with, but I'm using it to manipulate number-two pencils? You really think I'm that lame?"

"She stabbed someone with a pencil?"

"Oh, great, Ethan," Anne says as the three of us reach the pool entrance. Her brown eyes look darker. "You're back like what, five seconds, and already you're talking about me like I'm not standing here?"

"Well, did you?" She still hasn't answered about the pencil.

"You two are amazing." Tess shakes her head. The wind picks up even more. Someone's towel lifts from a lounge chair and tumbles across the concrete into the shallow end. "And by the way, Ethan, in case you haven't figured it out, what with the jet lag and everything, your girlfriend can do more than poke jerks in the leg with pencils. I'm pretty sure she can make the wind blow when she gets pissed off—not that she's going to admit it. But just so you know—it's scaring the crap out of me!"

"I'm not his girlfriend." Anne stalks past us. She seems headed for the far side of the pool, where lifeguard and European traveler Ben has just climbed up the guard stand and seated himself.

"Anne, wait." I put a hand on her arm. "We need to talk about this. You can't just walk away like nothing's happening."

She glowers at me. Isn't she even a little happy to see me? I've learned a lot over my many years, but obviously female logic isn't something I've managed to master.

"I can do whatever I want to. You went to Europe. I can go to the other side of the pool. And you"—Anne flips her gaze to Tess—"need to stop having such a big mouth about everything. It's no big deal. I'm fine. Everything's fine. I mean, look around you. It's a lovely day. We're at Aqua Creek Park, remember? Swimming pool. Suntan lotion. Kids playing Marco Polo. What could possibly happen at—?"

The shrill sound of a whistle breaks through the air. My pulse picks up a few notches. On the guard platform, Ben stands. The whistle on its chain, its sound still echoing in the air, flops back against his chest. He hesitates only a second, scanning the water. I track where he's looking in the deep end. Nothing's there.

"Going in!" Ben shouts. He dives, straight and clean, into the deep end of the pool, and pushes through the water to the bottom. And unless I'm mistaken, he begins to wrestle with something that only he can see.

"Ben!" Anne screams. "Ben!" She races to the edge of the pool. My brain forms a single word. *No.*

"No!" I yell. "Don't!" I stop thinking—just kick off my shoes, push Anne aside, and dive in after Ben. Another lifeguard hits the water as I do. It's freezing—colder than it should be.

On the bottom of the pool, Ben's struggling. He's tugging fiercely at the invisible something, trying to pull it toward the surface.

I reach him first, grab his arm and try to yank him up from the bottom. Whatever he's got pulls him back. The other guard pulls at Ben's other arm, but neither of us manages to budge him.

Seconds pass, then more. What breath is left in my lungs burns, and I know I can't stay underwater for too much longer. We pull at Ben again, harder this time. I catch a glimpse of his eyes, and I can see the confusion—not fear, really, which impresses me, because at this point, he should be afraid. But I know that any second now, he's going to realize that he's trapped, and he's going to panic.

Then I see her. Just a glimpse, a shadow. A woman? Her arms draw Ben to her. Her long fingers pull at his hair.

Above us, somehow, I hear Anne shouting. "Let him go! Please! Let him go!" And then she's in the water too, and my lungs are bursting with the need to breathe.

The woman at the pool bottom lifts her head. Storm gray eyes stare at me. There's something about her, I think, although it's hard to think when all I want to do is kick to the surface so I can breathe. A few months ago, this wouldn't have been a problem. I was immortal then. But now I'm not. I try again to free Ben from her grasp when suddenly, she speaks.

"Only you," the woman says. I don't know if what I'm seeing is real, and it should be impossible for me to hear her clearly underwater, but I still do. She reaches out one bony finger and points at Anne. "Only you truly dare to swim with the rusalkas. Go to her, girl. You need her. She'll grind you with her pestle and pull you out whole and make you what you are not. Then you can come back to me. The Death Crone, girl. Go to her. Only then can you heal. Only then can you do what you must."

With that, it's gone. All of it—the woman, the cold, the wind that's been whipping waves in the pool. The three of us drag Ben to the surface. We all hoist ourselves out of the pool, and Ben coughs up a few lungfuls of water.

"There was a woman." Ben coughs some more. "There was a woman down there."

"Ben, buddy." The other lifeguard bends over him and rolls Ben to his side, where he coughs some more. "There was no one down there. But the suction was wicked. The filter, maybe. I don't know, man. I think the pool equipment is malfunctioning. We need to close the pool. Get someone in here to look at this. God, Ben. Why the hell did you dive in? There was nothing there."

Ben sits up, shakes his head. "But there was. I—I thought there was. It was the weirdest—"

"Jesus, Ben!" Tess tosses a towel at Anne, who's sitting between me and Ben on the pavement, her face drained of color. "What were you thinking?" She flops down on the ground next to Anne. "You okay?" she asks her.

"I'm—I don't know." Anne pulls the towel around her and looks away from Tess to Ben. "There was—she was…I don't know." Anne pushes up to stand in one graceful motion. "Ben," she says. "Oh, Ben."

She flicks a quick glance at me—anger? Confusion? Fear?—and kneels next to Ben, reaches for him. He leans into her embrace. A variety of emotions wash over me, the strongest being the wish that he wasn't holding her.

"Did you do something?" Tess is standing in front of me, scowling. She pokes a finger at my chest.

"Lower your voice." I move away, and she follows me. "And no," I add once we're over by the Coke machine. "Is that what you think?"

"Of course it's what I think. If it wasn't, I wouldn't be asking you."

"You think I got Ben to leap into the pool and almost drown himself? And you think this *why?*"

"Why? After last fall, you have to ask me that? You're the one who got her into all this in the first place: witches and trapped princesses and crazy bad guys. You're the one who almost got her killed like half a dozen times, the one who opened the door to everything that's been going on since and then left her here for me to pick up the pieces."

"I talked to her every week."

"And she lied to you for most of them." Tess says this as though it's the plainest of facts, but the words feel like stabs, mostly because she's right. *Have I really not listened carefully enough to Anne these past months? Did I just not want to know?*

"Like I was saying before Ben almost got dragged down by whatever the hell it was in the pool." Tess's tone shifts to something a little less even. "All that energy or power or whatever it was that you zapped Anne with to save Anastasia? It hasn't gone away. Oh, she'll keep telling you it has. But it hasn't. In fact, I think there's more of it. I think she's full of stuff she's not telling you or me about."

I glance behind me at Anne and Ben. As though Anne feels me watching, she turns, meets my gaze, then looks away. Ben coughs some more, spits water onto the pavement.

"I didn't do this, Tess."

"Maybe not," she acknowledges. "But you started it all. Everything was fine before you started following her around. And now it's not. So don't even try to deny that part, Ethan."

"There was something down there." I don't mean to tell her this, but I do anyway. "It was only a flash. A shadow. But I saw it. A woman, I think. And then there was a voice. Did you hear it too?"

"I'd have told you if I did." Tess flips that long blond hair behind her. "But I bet Anne did." She sighs, seems to push all that flaring anger down a few notches. "I hate this. Watching her. It's like when her brother died. She got all quiet then too. That's just how she is—private like that. But I guess you know that. Or if you don't—well, you should."

"Of course I know it." *Only if I did, then I should have pushed more for the truth, rather than accepted Anne's silences. But I didn't.* "And for the record, I didn't start all this. It would have happened whether I was there or not. She was the one, Tess—the girl who could save Anastasia. I was just the person who figured it out."

Tess is quiet for a moment. This unnerves me almost more than the rest of it. In my thankfully limited experience, Tess has never been quiet.

She looks at me, her expression intense. "Ethan—what made Ben jump into the pool?"

"I don't know. But I'm going to try to find out."

Tess pokes a finger at me again. "I'm holding you to that." Her voice lowers to almost a whisper. "She feels responsible, you know. For Anastasia's death. Probably for that rotten Viktor, too. That's what I think, anyway. I guess that might not be worth much to you, it being my opinion and all. But that's how I see it. And now this thing with Ben is going to make it all worse."

She places her hands on her hips and seems to wait for me to disagree with her. My jeans and T-shirt continue to drip pool water.

"So that shadow woman," Tess asks. "What exactly is it that you thought you saw?"

The answer rises from me quickly. Like the tales of Baba Yaga that I'd once thought were just stories, another tale comes to mind: one that the women in my village had told when our neighbor's nineteen-year-old daughter had drowned in the river a few days after her lover had died of influenza. She was pregnant, and he had promised to marry her, and then suddenly, he was gone. She grieved and grieved, and then one day, her father found her floating, her hair wild around her in the water.

"Rusalka," I say. "Russian mermaid."

"Ru-what? Don't just say that like I'm supposed to know what you're talking about. Mermaid? Like Ariel in that Disney movie?"

I smile in spite of myself. "More malevolent. Less cheery singing. Definitely less cheery outcome. Women who've been wronged. Sometimes murdered. Always near a body of water. They transform sometimes. That's how the legends go. They become this other thing—this water creature. In some stories, they find release. In others, it's more—um, permanent. But I've—well, I've seen things. They're real. Rusalkas exist."

"Terrific. You know it might be easier if you made us a list, Ethan. You know—crazy Russian folklore shit that's going to appear, freak us all out, and try to kill someone's boyfriend. That kind of thing."

"I'll consider that. So he really is her boyfriend?"

Tess raises an eyebrow. "Yup. So this mermaid thing—is it dangerous?"

My silence is my answer. It's broken by the sound of sirens. Someone's called an ambulance or the fire department.

"Ben has been really good for her," Tess says. "So while you're screwing things up again, you remember that."

"I'm here to help. That's why I came back." It sounds as foolish coming out of my mouth as it did in my head before I said it.

Tess laughs. "Right," she says. "So start helping."

THE FOREST, EARLY AFTERNOON

BABA YAGA

THROUGH THE SKULL IN MY FIREPLACE, I WATCH ANNE. The one who is mine but not mine. The one who is not gone from me. I had not known what losing Anastasia would feel like: the pain of it; the wrenching bitterness.

The loss of that one girl has weakened me. Changed me. I had not known that I could be other than I was. But I have learned that there are things beyond what even I know.

Maiden. Mother. Crone. These are what I am. What I have been. Goddess, but more than goddess. And now—something else. The emptiness of it creeps into me, worms its way deep inside and holds fast, even as I struggle to shake it loose.

"Ben." Anne hugs the boy on the ground tightly in her arms. "Oh, Ben. I was so afraid."

"Me too," he tells her. "I don't understand what happened. I saw her, Anne. I saw her. You did too, didn't you? Tell me I wasn't seeing things."

She does not answer, only pulls him even tighter, and her thoughts float out to me as mine sometimes float to her. She feels responsible for what happened. For what might have happened. This much I can see. Does she love this boy whose life almost disappeared in front of her eyes? I believe she wants to.

But Ethan is back. Love does not always obey logic. It is as I am—impossible to predict. It can empower as much as it can destroy. It can hull us empty, or it can fill us with great joy. But we cannot know which is our destiny. Not even I can know for sure.

I lean closer to my fire and try to warm myself. I study the face of the man who has been my prisoner—the one who offered himself in place of my other girl. My Anastasia. He let her free. Does he know that she chose death? I have told him, but he is quite stunningly mad these days, and so I do not know if he has heard me.

"Mother," he whispers to me. "Baba Yaga." And sometimes, when the madness digs deeper, "Darling."

When Anastasia was in the hut, things were different. She swept and brought me sweet tea and pretended not to understand what I was. In her bed, she hid the doll that her mother had given her, the one that spoke to her. She believed that it protected her, and I let her have this thought. Perhaps it was even true sometimes. Like love, magic is a strange and mercurial thing. Its strength comes from the object and the user, but also from the giver. Anastasia's mother gave her that doll, and so the wishes and dreams and hopes she had for her daughter came with it. Potent magic. More powerful than this man who now shares my hut could ever believe. I could *make* him believe, of course, but I see no need. The truth would not set him free.

"Yaga," he calls to me. It is my name, and names have power. Viktor knows this. He knows many things. But he has never known what I truly am.

Had he come to me like Anastasia, when the magic was at its height, when I was compelled to take a girl against her truest will, as well as mine, things might not have gone so badly for him. Anastasia suffered here, but she did not age. That magic has not been so kind to Brother Viktor.

I look at his face now, and I laugh. Time—as always—follows its own rules here in my hut. Once, long, long ago—so distant that I can barely see it now—I was human. Or at least, closer to human than I am now; than I have been for a very, very long time. I ran through meadows, wove flowers through my hair, felt the earth's power beneath me. I was beautiful then. My hair flowed long and thick. My eyes were bright, my hands small and smooth, my body young and firm and strong. And I thought I would be young forever.

When he offered himself to me—a Romanov in blood but not in heart—Viktor too looked different than the man I see now, crouched by the fire, his hair matted, his eyes rheumy, his face lined so deeply that were there a mirror in the hut, he would scream if he saw himself. But there is not. Still, he runs his hands over his face. I know he feels the change, and I know it frightens him. And in those moments, I feel a bitter kind of pleasure.

"Yaga," he says to me now. "My dear Yaga. What will we do today?"

Because the possibilities are many, I ponder this. And because I can, I concentrate, feel the power surge inside me as my right hand releases, drops heavily to the wooden floor of the hut, then crawls—huge and brown and wrinkled—on its finger tips to this man whose gaze skitters from the fire to the hand to my face.

"No," he says softly.

But I do not listen. Instead, I smile as my hand strokes his hair. I see him shudder. I concentrate and move the hand to his cheek, run one finger across those deep grooves. He bites his tongue so he will not scream, and somehow, in my own mouth, I taste the copper tang of it.

"If I find a way to let you go," I say, "what will you do?"

For a moment, my hand still on his cheek, his gaze clears. He was, after all, a powerful magician. Not as powerful as I am. Certainly not as powerful as those whose magic resides in me: The Old Ones. The ones who came before. The ones who changed me, who made me what I am now.

"If you don't let me go, what will become of you, Yaga?"

The question lies between us. My hand moves from his cheek, slithers over his shoulder and down his back, scuttles back across the smooth wooden floor and up my dress, and re-attaches itself to my body. My arm tingles, tiny prickles of sensation. In the fireplace, the skull gleams brighter, its bleached bones almost sparkling. In its eyes, Anne strokes the hair of the fragile mortal called Ben. Ethan watches them, his blue eyes missing nothing. His heart, I fear, is missing everything. And deep in the water, so deep that none of them can see her, the rusalka swims and smiles. I know she is there. I just am not sure what she wants—or what she will do to get it.

Here in my hut, I know that if I do not free this man I've held captive, his presence will weaken me further. He is a Romanov, yes. But he is not the Romanov who is supposed to be here. That one is dead—or if not dead, not here nevertheless, and that is all the same to me. It is not his magic that weakens me. It is my own. The Crone's magic. Virgin. Mother. Hag. The girl awakened my middle nature. Mother. And it was that which almost destroyed me. The grief of giving her up clawed at my insides. Burned me from within.

I do not harbor those feelings for Viktor. Only rage—hot and red, or sometimes black as night, an oily rage that slicks about the hut like a presence. I cannot kill him, and I cannot love him. He is linked by blood to my two girls, Anastasia and Anne, and blood is powerful. The first night he was with me, I dreamed of slaughtering him where he lay, cowering and whimpering like a mewling infant, the smell of fear so strong on him that I could almost see it rising in waves. I hated that I had taken him, that he lay on Anastasia's bed, clutching at the red and blue cotton quilt she had used, that his skin touched something that had touched hers. *Impossible.*

That first night, I rose from my chair, fetched a knife from the table. I would not send my hands alone to do this business. I would do it with a whole body. This man had tricked the tsar's youngest daughter, had tried to kill Anne. What kind of man uses a seventeen-year-old girl for his own power? What kind of man tries to kill another innocent girl to keep that power? I raised the knife. I felt only calm. Only peace.

Viktor watched me. He was in his prime still. The youth he'd killed for had not yet abandoned him. If there was fear in his eyes, I couldn't find it. "Can you do it, Yaga?" he asked me. His tone was even. His breathing calm. "If you want to kill me, then kill me. Don't toy with me. We are old friends, you and I. Perhaps it is only fitting that you are the one to do it."

I didn't believe him, of course. Some men are willing to die for what they believe in. Viktor believed in nothing but himself. And men like that don't court death. Even ones like Viktor, able to trick me into doing his bidding. Able to compel me to save a girl who in the end, wanted only to die.

I had thought that nothing more could surprise me. But I was wrong. I am the Death Crone, but I am more than that. And in that moment, perhaps because I sensed he wanted me to choose death, I chose to keep it from him. I set the knife on the table. I let Viktor live.

But that kindness has weakened me. I am, after all, not human anymore. I gave that up a long, long time ago. The price was steep, but I did not understand that then. Now, like my hut, I obey a different set of rules. The Crone in me understands, but the mother and maiden suffer when I destroy. It is a precarious balance, harder and harder to manage with each passing day.

We talk about this sometimes, Anne and I. At night she comes to me, a dream but not a dream. Real enough for both of us. We walk in my forest, and we talk. I try not to frighten her, but it is my way, and thus impossible to avoid. We speak of magic and life, of love and loss. Of the things that foolish girls do. She does not ask to see Viktor. And I do not offer. Sometimes, I catch her thinking about Ethan. Sometimes, I catch her grieving. She has much to grieve. I invite her to drink of the stream near my hut. So far, she has declined.

And now there is the rusalka. Once more, forces are ready to collide—just as they were when the time came for Anne to claim her power and free Anastasia. I know this in my deepest self. I wait for it. But I fear it, and this is strange because I have conquered fear.

At my feet, Viktor smiles. The madness has returned. In the skull in the fireplace, Anne strokes Ben's hair. Ethan talks to the one called Tess, the one whose friendship shines like diamonds.

"Come to me," I tell my captive.

Still smiling, he does as I command.

Thursday, 3:33 pm

Anne

My head aches. Ben almost drowned. Ben almost drowned, and Ethan is back, and whatever this thing is that keeps following me around has finally figured out a way to keep me from ignoring it. It's talking to me. Ethan could hear it, and it tried to grab Ben. I don't know why it let him go, and I don't know what it wants from me. I only know that I've been pretending for months that none of this is happening, but now I can't pretend anymore.

"Let me take you to the hospital," I tell Ben over and over. It's all I can think to say. I would drive him to the hospital, and they'd check him out. They'd tell me that he was okay, and then maybe I could forget the rest of it. Only he won't go—even though the paramedics came in the ambulance because someone had dialed 911 while we were pulling Ben out of the water.

"I'm fine." He raises his hands in a stopping motion. "God, Anne. Calm down. It was weird, but I'm fine. I mean, it's not like it's your fault. Why the hell did you jump in there anyway? Carter had my back." Carter is the other guard on duty. "He knows what to do. Shit, Anne. You're not even that good of a swimmer. Why would you do that? Plus, what's the deal with your friend? Not that I didn't appreciate it, but what the hell?

He dives in fully clothed? Who is this guy, anyway? He looks sort of familiar. Did he go to Kennedy last year or something? It's like I've seen him, but I don't know where."

"Ethan. His name is Ethan. He's a friend of our family." It sounds just as lame the second time as it did the first. But what else am I supposed to say? *Yeah, Ben, you're right. I'm a big fat liar. You probably did see him last fall—right before the crazy witch chased us both out of the courtyard and my life turned upside down. Only for some reason, almost everyone seems to have blocked all that out. Like it's just too hard to believe, so you don't.*

We're standing in the little lifeguard office near the entrance to the pool. Ben had closed the door, but I can hear the muffled sound of Carter talking to someone outside—maybe one of the paramedics because they haven't driven away yet.

"Anne." Ben's voice is low and serious-sounding. He pulls me to him. He'd put on his white Aqua Creek T-shirt, but I'm still just in my swimsuit, and I can feel the familiar warmth of him, which makes me happy. He'd been so cold when we'd dragged him from the pool. His damp hair smells of chlorine.

Suddenly, I feel like crying, and because I'm not sure why, I tip my head up and kiss Ben on the mouth. Kissing Ben always makes me feel safe—just me and Ben together, as close as possible. Everything focuses on just that, and I stop feeling like the world is caving in around me because of huge scary stuff I can't control. I feel safe. I feel normal.

"You feel amazing." Ben's hands are in my hair then, and on my skin, and our tongues are tangled together. *You almost died*, I keep thinking. *You almost died, and somehow, it was my fault.* I'm pretty sure this is not what Ben wants me to contemplate while he's slipping his hand under the top of my bikini and

I'm letting him—in fact, encouraging him. This is the problem with being me. I could let Ben feel me up all day long, but it's not going to change the fact that a Russian mermaid almost killed him. Telling Ben the truth isn't going to happen anytime soon either.

Ben's hand wanders in the other direction, flicks around my bikini bottom. I flick it away. It wanders back.

Two things occur to me. One is that if I don't object a little more obviously—correction, if I don't object even subtly—I'm about to have guilt sex with my boyfriend on the fake wood desk in the Aqua Creek office and possibly end up with lifeguard applications plastered to my back. The other is that even while Ben's hands are exploring all sorts of interesting places, and even while I'm still freaking out mightily about the whole mermaid thing, I'm still thinking about Ethan.

This is definitely one wild swing of emotions, even for me. "Not here, Ben."

Ben seems to feel that here is just fine.

"Seriously, Ben. There are people out there."

"And we're in here."

I swat his hands away a couple more times, and he finally gets the message, which is a relief, since I might still be terrified, but I'm not stupid.

"Let me drive you home," I insist. "They're closing the pool for the afternoon, Ben. That's what Carter told you, remember? So let me drive you home before I go to work. Please, Ben?"

Ben is quiet then, but he blows out a breath, and I take it as a yes.

Ethan and Tess are standing by my car. They look like they've been arguing. This doesn't surprise me. Someone—Carter, probably—had given Ethan dry shorts and a T-shirt to replace his soaked clothes. I try not to notice how low the shorts hang on his hips. I fail.

Tess all but leaps on me. "I need to talk to you."

"Gotta take Ben home."

"I'll call you." This comes from Ethan. Ben tightens his grip on my hand, and I see him frown.

I tell Tess I'll talk to her later. On the positive side, no Russian mermaids float into view—although that possibly might have cut the tension between Ben, Ethan, and me. Possibly not.

"Why does he need to call you?" Ben frowns again as he settles into the passenger seat of the Jetta that I'd gotten for my seventeenth birthday.

"Don't know. It's no big deal, Ben." Except clearly, it is.

Ben's tone gets a little edgier. "So you're sure there's nothing else I should know about this? He seems sort of shady."

My lips twitch back a laugh. Of all the adjectives I'd use to describe Ethan, shady probably isn't one of them. Ben's brow furrows. He scowls at me.

"Something you're not telling me? Seriously, Anne. The dude looks like he's hiding something. Don't you think?"

"No," I tell Ben firmly. "I don't think that at all."

Having dropped Ben off, then gone home, showered, and changed into a denim skirt, layered tank tops, and my black "Yes, I'm a salesgirl in a vintage jewelry shop" cardigan, I sit in the back room of the Jewel Box, attempting to do my job, still totally clueless about what—if anything—I should do, other than tell more lies like the ones I just fed to Ben.

I slip a price tag around one link of a chunky turquoise bracelet—stones the size of small eyes embedded in heavy twists of gold—and listen to the chatter coming from the front of the store. We're getting ready for a private show, and this involves arranging boxes full of pieces with special tags and signs. It's costume jewelry, mostly—stuff from the 1950s and 1960s—but real pieces too, like the blue twists of flapper beads from the 1920s, long necklaces that catch the light and swing against you when you wear them. It's boring work putting tiny jewelry tags on necklaces and bracelets and then cataloging them on the Jewel Box worksheets, but boring is okay right now—more than okay.

"Are you sure you don't mind working in the back, dear?" Mrs. Benson had asked when I'd walked in the door almost twenty minutes late, hoping she wouldn't notice. "I suppose I can continue to manage up here alone. But I do enjoy your company. Your mother could arrange the pieces tomorrow, you know."

Her voice was nothing but polite, except that I know she's angry. At me for being late, obviously, and at my mother for taking the afternoon off without enough notice, which is something she's been doing a lot lately and something Mrs. Benson has chosen to ignore. At least to Mom's face.

My mother hasn't been the same since my brother David died of cancer almost three years ago. She goes out for hours and doesn't tell Dad or me where she is. I actually followed her a couple of times once I'd realized that no one was going to do something about her frequent disappearing act. She doesn't go far—usually just for a long walk or to a matinee at the little movie theater about a mile from the Jewel Box. But she's dropped enough weight that she's wearing a size double-zero, and even then, her clothes hang on her. She'd gotten better, but after last fall, when the Jewel Box roof collapsed on her, she wasn't better anymore.

My dad pretends not to notice. But maybe that's because while I was standing next to my mother—all doped up on painkillers in the hospital emergency room—he was still at the front desk, filling out paperwork. So he didn't hear her whisper that she wished she was dead so she could be with her son. Only I did.

I don't talk about this stuff with my dad because I don't think he wants to hear it. I don't tell Ben, even when we're kissing and we're pressed together close enough that I feel—if not safe, at least like a regular girl, and not one with a destiny. Most days, I don't even tell Tess, although I know she'd listen. It's the stuff I thought I might tell Ethan, because somehow, I thought he'd understand. Only then he left, and everything felt different.

But it surprises me that Mrs. Benson lets my mom's behavior go. She's usually not one to hold her tongue about things that piss her off, except that I guess with my mother, it's different, since it was Mrs. Benson's store roof that smashed into her when Baba Yaga followed us back from the forest.

Not that either my mother or Mrs. Benson seems to remember that this is what really happened. They both think it was a freak thunderstorm and possibly a tornado. Neither of them remembers the crazy Russian lacquer box—the one that's currently shoved under my bed—that held the key to Baba Yaga's hut. Only *I* do. It's part of a long list of things that I've chosen to keep to myself. Things like: 1) Witches are real, and so, it turns out, are Russian mermaids called rusalkas who try to kill your boyfriend; 2) My mother and I are both descended from the Romanovs through the tsar's wacky evil illegitimate son; 3) Tess is absolutely right. I haven't lost any of the power inside me. In fact, it's only gotten stronger. And the dreams of Baba Yaga have too.

"Careful with those stones, dear," Mrs. Benson's deep voice booms behind me. The bracelet slips from my hand and falls with a heavy thud onto the carpeted floor. I add *silent* and *sneaky* to my mental checklist of things that annoy me about my boss.

I bend quickly and scoop the bracelet from the floor. Mrs. Benson plucks it from my hand. "Sorry, dear. Didn't mean to startle you. I had no idea you wouldn't hear me come in." She arches an already perfectly arched eyebrow at me and seems to be waiting for some kind of response. Unfortunately, I don't have one.

"Turquoise is pretty sturdy," she says after a few uncomfortable seconds. She taps one of the turquoise nuggets. "But the prongs are delicate. And no one wants to buy damaged goods."

I ponder that tidbit. Seriously, I rarely know what to say to this woman. I love the stories behind the jewelry, love that everything in the store was owned by someone else at some point. But the whole place makes me uneasy these days.

Maybe it's because I watched it get smacked to smithereens by lightning that day I brought Anastasia back. Maybe it's because this is where my mother first handed me the Russian lacquer box that turned out to hold the key to Baba Yaga's hut. Maybe it's just Mrs. Benson—frosted, blond, chin-length hair never out of place, nails always manicured, pin-thin in her wardrobe of gray pantsuits, white blouses, and tasteful scarves that she always fastens with an antique cameo pin. The perfection of it just bugs me somehow.

Still, when she offered me a summer job, I snapped it up. Tess wanted me to teach beginning ballet with her at Miss Amy's, where we've both taken dance since we were toddlers, but I took the Jewel Box job instead. I told Tess it was because it pays more—only that wasn't the entire truth. Mrs. Benson is, in fact, paying me more per hour. But I'm here because it's easier. Neither Mrs. Benson nor my mother chooses to have much conversation with me at all; Mrs. Benson because that's just how she is, and my mother because that's just how she is these days too.

At Miss Amy's, I'd see Tess every day. She'd poke and prod at me and dig out the stuff I'd rather she not know. The stuff I think she's safer not knowing. Stuff I'm just not ready to say—even to myself sometimes. Just the other day, she asked me if I loved Ben—and what kind of crazy girl doesn't love a boy like Ben, who's cute and smart and tells her over and over that he loves her? Who am I these days that I have to lie about something like that?

"I'll be more careful," I tell Mrs. Benson. "I'm sorry I dropped it."

"So—your mother." Mrs. Benson sets the bracelet on the work table and flicks at an imaginary speck of dust with one exactly oval nail. "What appointment did she have today?"

I shrug. "Don't know. She doesn't run her schedule by me for approval."

"Dear girl, I'm sure she doesn't. But perhaps you should pay better attention anyway."

"I—what?" I'd been looking at the bracelet, but now I meet Mrs. Benson's gaze. Her eyes are a really vivid green with these little flecks of gold. Both of them are fixed on me more sharply than I'd like. What's the deal with this woman today?

"Anne, dear, I'm worried. Your mother has been with me since I opened this shop. Seven years now. I count on her, you know. She knows this business as well as I do."

"She took the afternoon off. That's all I know." *And if you want to bitch at someone, bitch at her, not me. Because personally, I'm sitting here willing my hands to stop tingling so I don't melt this stupid bracelet when I tag it. Or maybe get my inventory pencil to poke you in the eye.* Then *maybe you'd have something to talk about with my mother when she finally shows up. "Laura, dear, do you know that while you've been off moping, depressed, and on the verge of an eating disorder, your darling daughter has developed powers she can't control? Why, just this afternoon, she burned a hole in my Alfred Dunner slacks. It was horrendous."*

What I actually say is, "But I'll see what I can find out." I know I don't really mean it, but she nods her head and graces me with a toothy smile, so I guess it's what she wanted to hear.

I'm turning my attention back to the inventory sheet when the images slam into me like a wall of concrete. The rusalka. Mrs. Benson. My mother. Ben. Viktor. Anastasia. Their faces rush at me through a haze of color. A wave of nausea rises in my throat. "Steady, girl." Baba Yaga's voice echoes in my head. At least, I think it's in my head. "Swallow the fear. Do not let it control you. You are stronger than that."

"But I'm not," I say to her as the vision clears out of my head. Like always, it's been quick. Just *zip-zap*, and it's over. No wonder I'm such a master at pretending it hasn't happened.

"Not what, dear?" Mrs. Benson asks. Her expression is as bland as always. Clearly she hasn't just been treated to my ride down the rabbit hole.

"Um," I manage. My voice sounds as tight and knotted as my stomach feels. "I'm not done."

"Oh, dear, I know you're not done. Why, you've barely started. But don't worry. You'll get there. I have the utmost faith in you. You are your mother's daughter, after all."

Huh. That clears things up.

In the front of the store, the bell tinkles, indicating that someone has walked in the door.

"Oh, my. Look at me." Mrs. Benson straightens her already perfectly affixed cameo locket pin on her perfectly knotted floral pattern scarf. "Standing here chatting with you when I should be out there greeting our customers, silly woman that I am." She bustles out to the front of the store.

Baba Yaga is wrong. I'm not strong. I don't want to be strong. I don't want to worry about saving anyone. That's the thing I've realized lately too. Sometimes, you have to be more than what you want to be. Especially when right now, I can still see myself in the water pulling at Ben's arm, still remember how the rusalka and I locked eyes, and for just a second or two, I felt what she felt.

It was like it used to be when I dreamed I was Anastasia. For those few seconds underwater, I was me, but I was also her: this woman who didn't want to be what she was. Who was so overcome by loss that when I felt it, my grip loosened from Ben's arm, and my brain filled with the thought that she might pull him even deeper—which was impossible, since she was already on the bottom of the pool. She needed him. She wanted him. She had no choice. These were thoughts that came to me right before I heard her speak. Right before—

"Hey." Ethan, dressed in a different pair of jeans and a navy T-shirt, his hair dry and bangs brushed neatly to the side, stands in the back doorway, looking at me with those ridiculously blue eyes.

Everything inside me gives a little quiver. This does not make me happy. *Stupid blue eyes.*

He walks to the far side of the little room, picks up a folding chair, sets it down next to me, and lowers himself into it. Even sitting, he's taller than I am.

"You should really lock that better," he says.

"And you should tell me why you're really here. What is it that you plan on doing now that you're back? Besides saving Ben from drowning and stuff like that?"

He rests his hands on his thighs and seems to consider the question. "I was telling the truth to Ben about the Prague fellowship. I'll be finishing my studies in Slavic Folklore at Northwestern."

That knot tightens in my throat again. He's following in Professor Olensky's footsteps. This shouldn't surprise me. "You didn't tell me."

Ethan shrugs. It's hard to read the expression on his face.

"How's Ben?" His attempt at changing the subject needs a little work.

"Fine. He's home. He's supposed to be resting. I doubt that he is. Speaking of which, you were supposed to just call me, remember? Not come to my work."

Ethan looks at me. I look at him. I should tell him to go.

I really should. He's nothing but trouble. My trouble. Like a stalker mermaid who tried to kill my boyfriend.

I should call Tess. Or Ben. Or check on my mother's whereabouts, since, according to Mrs. Benson, this should be a priority for me.

But none of that is what I feel like doing right now.

"Oh, the hell with it." Feeling more than a little disloyal to Ben, I reach under the table and grab my purse. Whatever's going on, Ethan's part of it, and in any case, I'm in no mood to tag more jewelry. "C'mon. By the time she misses me, maybe we'll be back."

"Do you want me to say that this isn't like you?"

"No."

"I'm going to say it anyway. This isn't like you."

That said, he follows me through the back door of the Jewel Box.

Thursday, 4:10 pm

Anne

So, now where?" I buckle myself into the leather seat of Ethan's black Mercedes sedan. It's the same car he had last year, and I wonder who's been taking care of it for him, although I don't ask.

"Back to the pool." He shifts the car into gear and starts to pull out of his parking space. "It's where the rusalka appeared. You've seen her before this. I gathered that much. But she hasn't done anything like this before, right? So we need to go back there. See if she—"

"Wait." Like everything that Ethan has brought into my world since last fall, this is going too fast. "You can't just drop into my life and start giving me orders. It isn't going to work like that this time, Ethan. It can't. I won't let it."

He steps on the brake, and we sit there, half in, half out of the street. A Lexus SUV maneuvers around us, and the driver honks his horn—a sharp blast. Ethan's gaze is on me, though, not the traffic.

"Oh, my God, Ethan. Let's not get mushed while we're deciding what to do! Besides, I just snuck out on my job, which is definitely not going to win me any bonus points with Mrs. Benson. Or Ben, for that matter. So if we're going somewhere, we need to go. But we'll decide all that together. Okay?" I don't have a plan if he disagrees. I only know that just because he's back doesn't mean that I'm going to let him call the shots. About anything.

We stare at each other for another few seconds before he shifts his attention to driving and heads out into traffic. We hang a right on Lake Street, drive another block in silence. He really does look older now—not a lot, but it's noticeable. The mortality thing is sticking. This is what I'm thinking when, in my skirt pocket, my phone begins to vibrate.

"Did you seriously just cut out of work?" is what Tess whispers to me when I answer.

"You know this how? And why are you whispering?"

"Because I'm in the back of the stupid jewelry store, having just walked in to see you on my way to Miss Amy's to teach spoiled five-year-olds how to tap dance. Your boss told me you were cataloging crap in the work room. Only I'm standing here alone. So unless you're freakin' invisible, I'm assuming that Mr. Stealthy is up to his old tricks and that's who you're with. Am I warm?"

"Shit."

"You can say that again—only not too loud. Your boss is up front selling some god-awful bracelet to a woman with shellacked helmet hair. Any second now, I'm going to have to explain to her why I'm back here and you're not."

"Oh, my God, Tess! You're going to have to tell her something!"

"So it was fine for you to sneak out with Ethan, but now *I* have to tell her something?"

"Well, yes. I mean, you're there and all—and now it's just too complicated. You're good at this. You'll come up with something."

There is an ominous silence on Tess's end.

Then she says, "And if I do, where exactly are you? Because don't think I'm going to let you go off with him alone. I did that before, and you're wicked crazy if you think I'm going to do it again."

Tess has not used her old favorite, *wicked*, in a long time. This is my clue that she has shifted into pit bull mode and will track me down by any means possible if I don't tell her where I'm going.

"We're headed back to the Aqua Creek pool."

"I thought we weren't going there," Ethan comments sort of testily from the driver's seat.

"Hush. Let me finish telling Tess."

"Tess? Anne, you have got to be—"

"My way, remember?" I narrow my eyes at him, and I guess he gets the message because he sighs and keeps on driving in the general direction of the pool.

"I'll figure something out," Tess mutters in my ear. "And then you need to pick me up in front of the Wrap Hut. I am *so* not letting you drive around with the Russian hunk of trouble without me."

I contemplate telling her no—but only for a second. "Sounds like a plan," I say instead. "We'll be there in a couple of minutes."

"You owe me, Michaelson. And you better be careful. You know I don't trust the guy. Now all this stuff with Ben and crazy Russian mermaids and—"

She stops mid-sentence, but it's too late. She's been talking with Ethan behind my back, and I've caught them. I glance over at Ethan, but his eyes are on the road.

"Hey," I say to Tess. "I didn't tell you about that last part. I mean, I was going to, but—"

"Like I said, Anne, I don't trust him. But he knows stuff. So yes, while you were holed up, macking on Ben or whatever, I talked to Ethan."

"I would have told you, Tess."

"But you didn't. You *haven't* been telling me. And you know it."

We both digest that.

"I'm going to make up some story for your boss," Tess says eventually. "If you've got all that power now, you could at least have put some spell on her so she wouldn't ask any questions. But no, you just leave. You'd think you'd at least embrace this a little bit, use it for something more than poking asshats in the leg with number-two pencils."

She clicks off before I can respond. I glance over at Ethan. He glances back at me.

I'm thinking fast about what should really happen here. We could just double back, and I could get out of the car and tell Ethan to leave. He would, I think. Does he want all this anymore? He doesn't have to be part of it. He's mortal because of me, and he left so he could figure out what he wants. Does he know that I've got magic flipping around inside me like dozens of out-of-control ping-pong balls? Maybe that's the reason he's back. Or maybe it's not. Maybe only I feel this crazy dangerous pull—like we're part of each other on some weird cellular level. But maybe for him, it's different.

Last fall, I figured it was just the adrenalin from all the danger we were in. Maybe it still is. I only know that when I see him, I want to be with him—even when some other, more sane part of me tells me this is ridiculous and dangerous. And that I already have Ben, who—as boyfriends go—is absolutely perfect in every single way.

But the stupid truth is that nothing with Ben ever feels as intimate as just standing next to Ethan—which is crazy, since I still barely know him. Not like Ben, who's even memorized my work schedule. Not like Ben, who just almost died.

This is getting me nowhere, especially because the truth is that I need Ethan's help.

"Tess is going to meet us. We need to circle back and pick her up at the Wrap Hut."

"So I gathered."

"And you two just need to get along. End of story."

"Any other orders I need to follow?"

"I'll let you know."

"I imagine you will," Ethan says. "I imagine you will."

Thursday, 4:45 PM

Ethan

W HAT'S CARTER DOING?" TESS PEERS THROUGH THE
fence at the lifeguard who'd dived in after Ben.

"Looks like he's still closing everything down." Anne moves closer to Tess. The three of us are standing half hidden in the bushes that flank the back part of the fence. Behind us, the ground dips slightly. There's a small stream at the bottom, and on its other side, over a wooden footbridge, is a subdivision of ranch-style houses. We've parked on a side street there and walked the quarter-mile or so to the pool.

We watch as Carter stacks some remaining lounge chair cushions in the storage tent and lowers and fastens the flaps. No one else is in sight. The police and firemen have gone. The other lifeguards too, it seems. We wait in silence until he finishes and approaches the gate. He pauses and looks back at the pool.

"Move." I edge the girls back behind the bushes.

"Bossy." Tess scowls at me.

"Shh." Anne elbows her.

Tess elbows her back. "I am shushing. There's no way that Carter can hear us from over there anyway."

Well, he can if she keeps talking at that decibel. I have a fleeting thought about my favorite café in Prague—the one I was sitting at only last week, drinking black coffee and eating chocolate torte. Alone. And not necessarily unhappy about it.

Eventually, Carter locks the gate and disappears out of view into the parking lot. The pool stays quiet. No sign of the rusalka.

"What now?" Tess asks. "Climb over the fence? Just stand out here like three idiots? Do you guys even have a plan?"

I reach into my pocket for my pack of Marlboros and remember that I've quit smoking. Or rather, that I'm attempting to and mostly failing miserably. I leave the pack in my pocket.

"Has it ever spoken to you before?" I direct my question to Anne. "The rusalka?" We haven't established much, but at least on that point, we're in agreement. We know what Anne's been seeing and what tried to hurt Ben.

"No." Anne edges closer to the fence. "I've seen her three or four times, not counting today. The first time, she was sitting by the duck pond near my house. You know, Tess—that little one with the willow trees all around it. I was jogging with my dad. He stopped to tie his shoe, and I saw her. Her hair was wet— that's the first thing I noticed. All that long, dark snaky hair."

"Gotta take your word for it," Tess says. "'Cause let me remind you—I'm not seeing what you're seeing."

Anne ignores the interruption. "I don't think I even had time to process it, really, because then my dad stood up and looked straight at her. And I realized that he didn't see her, only I did. Which was about to freak me out when she disappeared. Just like she did today over by the slide. She just wasn't there anymore. I think that first time, I wondered if I'd just been seeing things. That's how sudden it was."

"You didn't tell me." I try to hold Anne's gaze, but she looks away from me and back to the pool.

She shrugs. "You didn't ask."

"Well, that's just ridic—"

"We should go in," Anne interrupts me. "Carter's gone. The place is deserted. If we want to look around again, let's go. Otherwise, I'm just going back to work. Or to Ben's."

"Wow," Tess begins. "You two—"

"Save it," Anne tells her. "It'll give both of you something to talk about the next time you're talking behind my back."

She doesn't wait for either Tess or me to respond. She just turns and walks away, heading up the side fence toward the front gate.

"Boy," Tess says as we follow behind Anne. "You really piss her off, don't you?"

It seems pointless to disagree.

We reach the gate just as Anne places her hand over the padlock. "Let me try something." Her voice is hesitant, but her eyes flash with excitement. "I—"

"Is it locked?" Tess asks. "Maybe there's a—"

I hold up my hand. "Shh."

"What is it with you two always telling me to—?"

I put my hand on Tess's shoulder. "Quiet. Wait."

Anne closes her eyes. I feel a slight buzzing, a stirring of the atmosphere. Without thinking, I close my own eyes and concentrate with her. It takes more for me these days. The shift to mortality has dulled the edges of my magic. The power has been slowly slipping from me, each day surprising me not by how much less I have, but at how much I miss what I once believed I didn't want.

Still, the feel of it pulls me. There's an excitement as the power draws inward, readies to push out and do my will. "*Ya*

dolzhen," I say without thinking. The old words slip from mouth. *Ya dolzhen.* I must. *Foolish,* I think. Foolish to waste what magic I have left on such a simple task. But foolish things sometimes feel good. Too good.

"Hey!" Anne's voice registers her surprise. My eyes snap open. She's felt it too—my power slipping into her, mingling with her own. Like those times last fall: when we used magic to open the door in my loft while Viktor's whirlwind threatened to destroy us; when I stood with her on Tess's front lawn, guiding her through a basic protection spell. My magic and hers, dancing inside both of us, intertwined and potent. Only this time, her power is stronger. And so—I realize as I stand there—is what I feel for her.

"Don't do that," she says. "That was seriously weird, Ethan. It was like you were…well, don't do that," she repeats.

"Look," Tess says. If she's aware of the odd intimacy of the moment, she doesn't acknowledge it. She points to the padlock. It's hanging open. The metal looks darkened—singed. "You're a hoss, Anne. That was wicked awesome. So just exactly how long have you been able to lay your hands on a padlock and get it to open?"

"I know we probably could have just picked it or something, but I just wanted to—whatever. It's open. I opened it. So now we look around, right?" Anne directs the question to me.

Like before, she doesn't wait for an answer. She just pushes open the gate and walks in toward the pool.

Thursday, 5:20 pm

Anne

So," Tess says to me a few minutes later as she, Ethan, and I stand at the edge of the pool. The water laps lightly against the stairs in the shallow end. "See anything? Feel anything?"

I feel sort of silly. Kids sneak in here all the time. Ben is always bitching that in the mornings, when he opens up, he'll find empty beer cans and cigarette butts and the odd roach clip or two left behind from some after-hours round of partying.

But sometimes whatever it is inside me just—well, needs to be used. It builds up, and if I don't use it, I get sort of jumpy until I do. I haven't told Tess this. Or Ethan. Mostly because it makes me sound like a supernatural junkie or something.

"No," I say. "I don't see or feel anything. If mermaid girl is here, she's not showing herself." I wince inwardly at how confident I sound—all joking and secure—which is definitely not how I feel.

We poke around the pool area some more. Tess plops down cross-legged at the edge of the deep end for a while, staring intently into the pool like she's doing some kind of meditation. Ethan and I scope out the bathrooms. I peek up the slide at the kiddy pool. Nothing. Nada. Zip.

Figures. You want to see supernatural stuff, and it gets all shy. "Hey!" I say to the rusalka, who's gone all invisible on us. "Come out, come out, wherever you are!" Still nothing.

We let ourselves out the front gate. I've trashed the padlock beyond locking, so we leave it hanging there. Carter will probably get yelled at for leaving it open, but that will be about it.

I pull my cell out of my skirt pocket. It's been buzzing up a storm since we got to the pool, but I've been ignoring it—which, let me say, is not something I'm programmed to do—but if we're headed back, I guess it's time for a little damage control. Or at least for me to figure out how cranky Mrs. Benson really is that I've cut out on her like this. Tess's story, that Miss Amy had taken ill and I was the only one who could help her with the beginning tap class, probably sounded as contrived to Mrs. Benson as it did to me when Tess relayed it as she'd climbed into the car. "You totally owe me," she'd said. "Especially since I had to lie to Amy, too, about why I wasn't going to be there to teach my class."

I thumb through the missed calls, then press voice mail. Two messages in, it's clear that I'm in big trouble. Mrs. Benson has chosen the passive-aggressive method of dealing with my unplanned exit from work. She's called my mother, who has uncharacteristically surfaced from wherever she's gone this afternoon.

My mother's voice message consists of, "Where are you? Call me. Amelia is really pissed at you. I can't believe you're screwing up this job after she was nice enough to give it to you." Actually, she used a more colorful phrase than *screwing up*. Once she decides to be a less-than-model citizen, her language is one of the first things to go. Especially when she's angry.

My father has left two messages: one asking me where I am, and the other asking me if I'd heard from my mother.

There are also two texts from Ben, the last one confirming that we're still meeting at eight. Both of them end with *xo*.

I text Ben back, *See you then*, adding my own *xo*. We walk toward the footbridge to the Birnam Woods subdivision that spans the little stream. I wonder, not for the first time, how many residents ever think it's sort of odd to name a housing development after the forest in *Macbeth*. But it's not like there's a ton of *For Sale* signs or anything. Everyone seems just fine living on Inverness Lane and Dunsinane Street. Maybe if they kept getting visited in their dreams by a witch named Baba Yaga, they'd think twice about buying a house on a street named after a play in which just about everyone dies and the three witches mess with Macbeth's head until he goes crazy. Or maybe not.

This is what I'm thinking about when I see her. I stop so suddenly that Tess, walking too close behind me, smacks into my back. Ethan, walking on my right, stops too. I feel this happen rather than see it because I can't really focus on anything but the woman in front of me. My heart leaps into my throat.

"What?" Tess's voice is shrill, I register that much. "What do you—? Oh. Hey! I see her! This time, I see her! This is totally amazing. I actually—"

"Careful." Ethan takes my hand and holds it so tightly that I almost yelp—except that my throat's so tight with fear that no sound comes out.

The rusalka stands with her back to us on the far end of the wooden footbridge. Tiny droplets of water fly in the air as she combs her pale fingers through her dark hair.

"Tell me what you want," I ask her. "Why do you keep following me around?"

"Stories within stories, Anne." The rusalka stays where she is and turns her head ever so slightly as she speaks. "You're a smart girl. Not like me. You'll figure it out."

Right.

"*Kak vas zovut?*" Ethan's still gripping my hand, but he moves us a few steps closer to the rusalka.

I don't know what's said, but I know it's a question by the inflection of his voice. I also know he's speaking Russian, which makes sense if this really is a rusalka, and so far, I have no reason to believe otherwise. Possibly, I think, I should learn more than what I've taught myself from the *Lonely Planet* Russian phrase book I picked up a few months ago.

"What did you ask her?" I whisper.

"Her name. We need to know who she is. *Kak vas zovut?*" he calls to the rusalka another time. She still hasn't turned around. "Your name. Please."

"She's the crazy woman who tried to kill Anne's boyfriend." Tess glares at Ethan. "Isn't that everything we need to know?"

"No." Ethan's voice is a harsh whisper. "Names are crucial. Identity is crucial."

I expect Tess to argue with him, but instead, she says, "Like in fairy tales? Like with that Rumpelstiltskin dude? Once the girl knew his name, he destroyed himself. You mean like that?"

"Well, yes."

"You know," Tess says, "you don't need to sound so surprised, Ethan. It's not like I don't know *anything*." She advances another step closer to the rusalka. "Hey! If you've got a problem, maybe we can help you. But not if you keep trying to drown people. And you need to tell us who you are, like Ethan just asked you. What's your name?"

"It is what it is," the rusalka says, "the name my mother gave me. Just as I gave my child her name. Just as all mothers do. Innocent names. Names to protect. Names to heal. Names of strength. This man you are with—he tells you correctly. And yet you choose not to listen, and he chooses not to see the truth. These are perilous faults, ones I understand all too well. What we love can be lost in an instant. What we name can still be taken from us. You must all listen carefully. You must see what there is to see."

Tess starts to move closer still, but I grab her arm. Then we're both shivering violently as the temperature of the air around us plummets. I'm freezing—as cold as I'd been in the pool. Colder. The only thought standing out in my head is this—I need to see the woman's face. Why won't she turn around? I've talked to her, and she's followed me. I've seen her more than once. So why won't she show me her face?

She doesn't turn. She just flicks her head in a gesture that seems to say, *Follow me.* So we do. We cross the bridge and walk behind her along the far edge of the stream until it widens out into a pond. The air warms up some. The rusalka edges closer to the pond. Her dress trails behind her, the hem coated in mud, with tiny bits of twigs and brambles clinging to the wet sludge.

Fear and frustration morph inside me into what feels more like anger. "Just turn around!" I shout at her. "Let me see you, and then we'll talk."

"If that's what you want," the rusalka says. She walks to the pond's edge and steps into the murky green water up to her ankles. Farther out, the pond is deeper—deep enough to canoe or swim. Or drown.

"Yes." I edge my way down the grassy incline after her. But the black sandals I'm wearing have slick soles. I stumble, and only Ethan's grabbing my arm keeps me falling. But it doesn't keep me from gasping. Because when the woman in lilac finally swivels gracefully, I see that, impossibly, it's not the rusalka whose face smiles at me. It's my mother.

The lilac gown is gone. My mother stands in the Birnam Wood pond, brackish water lapping over her feet. She's wearing black, slim-cut jeans, a white tee, and a snug-fitting, short denim jacket. The tops of her black ankle boots—the ones she bought last weekend in Nordstrom's—peer out from the water. Her hair is pulled back into a tight ponytail. The rusalka had eyes as gray as storm clouds, but my mother has brown eyes like mine. They study me as I force myself to stop screaming. *It's not real,* I tell myself. *It's not real. It can't be real. It's stupid, crazy magic just like everything else. It is* absolutely *not real.*

"You're not my mother," I tell the person in the water. "You aren't fooling me." I can barely get the words out because my voice is shaking. All of me is shaking. *It's not real*, I tell myself again.

The woman with my mother's face smiles sadly at me. Her thin shoulders sag just a little as she stands there, and I see her move to straighten her posture. The motion is familiar and intimate, something my mother does all the time, probably without thinking. It's another habit she's started again since last fall. Every time I see her do it, my heart twists a little.

The woman who looks like my mother but isn't backs up a little deeper. The pond water begins to fill her ankle boots as they disappear from view.

"Don't believe it," Ethan says. His voice is steady, but still I can hear an edge of panic underneath. "It's a trick."

"Foolish man," the thing with my mother's face tells him.

Then she turns and wades into the deepest part of the pond so quickly that I barely see her slip under the water.

"No!" I scream. I know it's not real, and I can hear Tess yelling at me to stop, but I'm wading in after my mother anyway—wading up to my waist in the sludgy pond water before Ethan can grab me and pull me back. All I can see is the image of my mother disappearing in the water. It blends in my head with the image of Ben at the bottom of the pool. It doesn't look like swimming. It looks like drowning.

The rusalka resurfaces as suddenly as she went under, floating on her back, arms stretched out. Still as death. It's really her again, the lilac gown sagging beneath her, wild black curls dipping this way and that in the current. For one brief second, she raises her head, opens her eyes, and looks at me. "Please," she says. "Oh, please help me." And then she's gone.

Ethan drags me up onto the grass. "It wasn't real," he says to me over and over.

Tess just strokes my hair and tells me it will be okay.

"I don't know what she wants from me. I don't know how to help her." I realize I'm not sure which woman I really mean.

So I do what I've wanted to do since I first saw Ethan this afternoon. I sit down in the grass, my wet denim skirt heavy against my legs, and cry.

THURSDAY, 6:12 PM

ETHAN

I KNOW. I KNOW." ANNE HAS REPEATED THIS OVER AND over as we walk back to the car. "It wasn't really her. It's fake. It's magic. I get it. But why would she do that?"

Anne settles herself in the front seat as Tess climbs into the back of the sedan. None of us has a towel, so Anne and I are both still soaked from the waist down. Pond water drips from us onto the seats and runs onto the carpet.

"If she wants me to help her with something—whatever it is— why scare the crap out of me? Why show me my mother's face? What sense does that make, Ethan? No sense at all." She shivers.

She isn't crying anymore, but she wipes her nose with the back of her hand, dabs at her red eyes, then pulls down the visor and peers into the tiny mirror. "Wonderful. Now I can add looking like hell to my list of problems."

"You look fine." Tess leans forward between us and pats Anne on the shoulder. "But this is totally creepy. I mean, if it can make itself look like anyone, why pick your mother? No offense to her or anything, but if the rusalka wanted you to follow her into the water, why not make herself look like Ben? What's the deal? Only you would get a mermaid with some mother complex. If I'm going to be haunted, I want to be haunted by someone hot. And male."

"Thanks for the perspective." Anne squeezes some more water out of her skirt. "Sorry," she says to me. "Your car is going to smell like pond for a while."

I ignore the obvious. The state of my car is the least of our worries right now. "We just need to sort this all out, Anne. We need to slow this all down, go somewhere, and talk. I need to know everything that's been going on." I hesitate for a second and then add, "And so do you."

The words settle on all three of us as I jam the Mercedes into gear and pull out onto the street.

"Crap." Anne digs her phone out from the pocket of her soaked skirt. Pond water dribbles out as she flips it open. "Even more wonderful." She inspects the phone. "Yup. Dead. *God*, I hate my life right now. Seriously."

She pokes me in the arm with her forefinger. "Maybe I don't want to go talk this all out. You *do* realize that you're back for—what? An hour? And already my life is crazy again. And don't you dare say it's my destiny or whatever. Getting haunted by some Russian mermaid is not my choice of destiny. And neither is destroying yet another cell phone."

I smile at the last part. I remember how she'd used her phone as a makeshift weapon to help us escape from Viktor on the speeding, out-of-control El train.

"Oh, yeah," Anne says. She jabs my arm again, harder. "This is really funny, right? I have to use my minimum wage salary to replace my phone. Hysterical." She tosses her cell phone to Tess. "Dump that in my purse, would you? It's back there on the floor. Hopefully not wet. I'll see what I can do once it's dried out."

"Sure thing, boss. Maybe it's fixable. My brother dropped his into the toilet two months ago at some frat party, and he's still using it. But that's Zach for you. Speaking of which, I'm meeting him at seven. We're going to grab a burger somewhere and then go to the movies. You and Ben should come with." She pauses for one beat too many for the next part to be sincere. "You too, Ethan. More the merrier. You could get to know Ben. Because Anne and Ben—"

"Tess," Anne says. "Enough."

"Just saying." Tess edges up so her face is closer to mine. Her tone shifts from cheery to something a bit darker. "And here's what else I'm saying. Whatever's going on, Ethan, you need to figure it out. Isn't that what you told me at the pool? That you were here to help? Well, so far, you're not helping."

"I said, enough," Anne tells Tess once again. "This isn't solving anything. Go to the movies with your brother. I'll call you later." She turns to me. "And you need to drive me home. We can talk on the way."

"All right." Tess scowls. "But don't let Russian Magic Boy talk you into anything. Because the way I see it, you've got a dead phone, a boyfriend who got lured into the deep end, and a mermaid who wants you to think she's your mother. Telling you to be careful is like the understatement of the year."

"Do you remember the way to my house?" Anne asks after we've dropped Tess off at her car and I've taken her back to her Jetta, checking first to make sure that Mrs. Benson isn't watching out the back door of the shop.

"Think I can find it."

"Magic?"

"GPS."

Water still dripping from both of us, we leave it at that.

Thursday, 6:45 pm

Anne

M Y MOTHER'S VOLVO IS IN OUR DRIVEWAY AS I PARK THE Jetta, and Ethan pulls up into a space on the street. We walk up to the house together. This is not good.

"Maybe I should just run in. I'll change, make up some story about a cloudburst. I don't know." I wring another few drops of pond water out of my skirt. This is *so* not good. "I mean, you're soaked too. What are you going to do? Sit around my kitchen in your boxers while your jeans dry?"

"No." Ethan flushes slightly as he answers, and I feel some heat rise in my own face in response.

"Well, I didn't mean that—"

"Anne." My mother has walked out of the back door and is standing on our driveway, hands on her hips. She's wearing black jeans, a white shirt, a snug-fitting denim jacket, and her black Nordstrom's ankle boots.

My heart freezes in my chest. That's actually what it feels like. It's the same outfit—the one that the rusalka had on when she walked into the pond and made me feel that she was going in to drown.

"So," my mother says. "What in the world were you thinking today? You had better have a very good reason for why you left in the middle of your shift. Do you have any idea how embarrassing it was for me to get that message from Amelia? I get you this job, and this is how thank me? By—um, and why exactly is your skirt plastered to you like that?"

This is what gets the fear to subside and gets my brain to decide that it's actually Mom and not some supernatural something or other—her bitching at me. No crazy Russian rusalka would do that. I don't think.

"I was—we were—walking by the pond. You know, the one near Aqua Creek?" I hurry into my explanation, hoping she won't notice that I'm skipping the first question. If it was any other job, I probably wouldn't have to explain. She wouldn't even know I'd cut out. But it's her store and her boss, and I get that she's pissed. Even if she has no right to be, since she was supposed to be working too. "I guess the grass was wet," I go on, "and when I went to feed some bread crumbs to the ducks—well, I slipped and fell in and then—"

"I pulled her out before she did any real damage to the mallard population." Ethan finishes my sentence. I stare at him. Just a few seconds ago, he was actually blushing at the image of sitting in my kitchen in his underwear. Now he's smooth-talking my mother like a pro.

My mother looks over at him, startled. I guess she's been so busy griping at me that she hasn't noticed that I'm not alone. She narrows her eyes. I can see the wheels turning in her mom brain. My mother might be depressed and on the verge of an eating disorder, but she is still my mother.

"You're Ethan, right?" she says after the few beats of contemplation. "The boy whose father works for one of the oil companies?"

"You remember." Ethan smiles and holds out his hand. "It's wonderful to see you again, Mrs. Michaelson. Sorry I'm a bit soggy."

Mom shakes his hand. I shake my head. I'd forgotten that even though the world sees him as eighteen—or now nineteen, I guess, although I don't even know his birthday—he's been around a lot longer than that, at least when it comes to talking to parents. Who, of course, are a little closer to his real age.

"Ethan's been in Europe, Mom. But he's back now. He's going to be majoring in Slavic Studies at NU."

"Lovely," my mother says. This is her standard response when she's either not sure what to say or she's busy thinking about something else—which is probably more likely right now.

"And I'm sorry about work. I don't know—I just didn't want to be there. I know it puts you in a bad position, but I—"

"Wasn't there a—? Yes, there was. Amelia told me about it. I hadn't heard last fall; I think that's when I was in the hospital. But the other day, she mentioned something she'd heard from a friend of hers who lived in Moscow, I think. Or maybe it was Budapest."

"Mom. Get to the point. Please," I add since I'm already on pretty thin ice here.

"The Slavic Studies program at Northwestern. There was a terrible tragedy there, Amelia said. One of their best professors—his name starts with O: Olen or Olenowitz or something like that. No. Olensky. That's it. Professor Olensky. She says he was murdered last fall, right on campus in his office. Can you believe that? I don't know why it wasn't shown on the news more. Or maybe we just missed it. Things were so crazy then. But Amelia says that's what happened. It was a great loss for the program." She turns to Ethan, whose face has drained of color. "Had you heard of him?"

Ethan's silence lasts a number of long seconds. "I was acquainted with him, yes," he says finally. It's one of those moments that happens with him every once in a while—when the way he forms a sentence reminds me that he isn't really an American college student. Usually, it makes me smile when I hear him do that. It's sort of sweet, somehow. But right now, I'm not smiling.

But if there's one thing my mother is familiar with, it's grief. So it actually doesn't surprise me when she chooses not to push the conversation further. She just pats Ethan on the arm and says, "You must have been very shocked when you heard. It's hard to lose someone, especially when it's unexpected. I'm sorry, Ethan. I apologize if I made you uncomfortable. That was thoughtless of me."

Ethan swallows. "It wasn't thoughtless at all. You had no idea that I would have known him. He was a great man, actually. A really wonderful professor. I'd heard him speak in Europe last summer. That's how I got to know him. Um, well, the fellowship that I have—it's named after him. I'll be a teaching assistant under one of the adjunct professors."

"Well." My mother smiles at him. "You must be a wonderful student if you're already accepted into an advanced program like that. Your parents must be very proud of you."

I stand there praying that eventually Mom will run out of awkward things to say and give Ethan something he can respond to without mentioning, *Professor Olensky? Sure, I was there when he died. And you know who killed him? Your great-great-grandfather, who happens to be the illegitimate son of Tsar Nicholas*

Romanov. And my parents? Well, even if they hadn't been murdered by the Cossacks, they'd pretty much be dead now anyway since I'm over one hundred years old. Or something along those lines.

Luckily, none of this occurs. Unluckily, it's because Ben chooses this moment to pull into my driveway in his Saturn two-seater convertible and honk the horn.

"Hey," he says. He unfolds himself from the driver's seat and hops out, looking tall, blond, and cute in dark-wash jeans, a gray polo shirt, and flip-flops and—compared to the rest of us—acting pretty darn calm, considering that a mermaid almost killed him earlier in the day. "I tried to call you, but your cell kept flipping to voicemail. Then I called your work, but Mrs. Benson said you'd left early, so I figured I'd find you here. And here you are." He grins at me, then—because he's one of the things in my world that my parents actually do know about, and he feels at home around them—strides over, pulls me into a hug, and kisses me. He even flicks his tongue against my lips a little for good measure. Next to us, Ethan clears his throat.

A few seconds after that, my father, home from his law office and with no place to park in our driveway, pulls up behind Ethan's Mercedes and walks over to join us.

"What a day," he says.

"Well." My mother places her hand on my shoulder and pulls me back from Ben. "Now that your father is home, you can finish that little story you were telling me. I'm sure Dad will be fascinated."

Oh, yeah. I'm sure he will.

Thursday, 10:12 pm

Anne

I was going to wait until Saturday night, but I'm glad I didn't." Ben pats the silver, linked bracelet he's just clasped around my wrist. A small silver disc engraved *B&A* dangles from one of the links. "It looks nice on you."

He smiles his sweet Ben smile and waits for me to say something—probably something other than, *I really, really like you, but I think maybe I've been going out with you for all the wrong reasons, and now this bracelet is making things worse.*

We're in Ben's room, sitting on his bed, the bracelet box between us. There's a card too, which he signed, *Love, Ben.* He'd even drawn a little heart.

"It's beautiful, Ben. Really. Thank you." Just to make my mixed messages even more mixed, I lean in and kiss him, which feels safe and familiar but doesn't erase my thoughts of a certain, blue-eyed, annoying Russian.

Interestingly, Ethan seems to be in Ben's head too.

"So tell me again." Ben kisses me some more: tiny kisses down my neck that make me tingle straight to my toes. Ben is a great kisser. "How do you know Ethan? And why were you and Tess with him at the pond behind Aqua Creek?"

"Told you that. We went back to the pool. Tess left her

cooler, and we went back to get it."

"But you were supposed to be at work."

"I know, but Tess was still so freaked about what had happened to you, and I was distracted, and I just didn't want to sit there tagging jewelry all afternoon. So I wasn't exactly honest with Mrs. Benson. She'll get over it." *I'm not being honest with you either. And I have no idea if you'll get over it if you ever find out.*

"And Ethan?" Ben kisses my neck some more, but I can tell this is really bothering him, because normally, Ben is not a talker when we're making out. He's quite focused that way—especially at times like now, when we're alone in the house. Ben's parents—with whom he hasn't shared the pool incident because he thinks it isn't a big deal—went to a play in the city, and when they do that, they usually stay the night at their studio apartment off Lake Shore Drive, rather than driving all the way back out to the suburbs.

Tess thinks that this makes Ben the perfect boyfriend. He's not only cute and athletic, but he's rich and the youngest of four kids—the only one still living at home until he goes to college in the fall—and his parents pretty much leave him to do his own thing most of the time.

But right now, an interrupting parental unit would be just fine with me. As long as it wasn't one of *mine*, that is.

My conversation with my own parents hadn't gone any more smoothly than this back-and-forth dodging the truth with Ben. But how smooth can things go when you just can't tell the truth? Or rather, when you could tell the truth, except then your family would think you're crazy?

And maybe I am. Because what else other than crazy explains my attraction to Ethan? Ben is sweet and wonderful and perfect. He likes funny movies, and he's smart enough to have gotten accepted into the business school at U of I, and when I let him, he rattles on about things like Keynesian economics and why the recession is probably going to last a little longer. He's taken me out for Lou Malnati's pizza and to a Cubs game, and next week—if I make it to next week—we're going to the improv show downtown at Second City. He's the first boy I've ever seriously thought about having sex with—although right now, I'm glad we haven't actually done the deed because that would only make things worse.

Ethan, on the other hand, pops in when there's danger brewing. He brings craziness and mermaid attacks and witches and a princess I just couldn't help. He's absurdly good-looking, and when I saw the sadness on his face at my mother's mention of Professor Olensky, my heart ached for him. What I feel for him is impossible to categorize, even though I keep trying. Mostly, it's like he's part of me—that whatever he is and whatever I am are just somehow more whole when we're together.

You don't have a relationship with him, I've told myself over and over these past months. *You're like his work partner or something.* But that's not how it feels. I've been lying my ass off about so many things lately. Maybe it's time to stop lying to myself about how I feel—which, it seems, is not in love with Ben.

"Ethan's Ethan. God, Ben. Don't worry about it so much. You had a bad enough day. Let it be."

Ben dips his hands under my tank top and runs them along my sides, edges me down on the navy and tan comforter. "You smell good," he says. "Your hair smells like candy or something."

His hands are familiar, and the weight of him feels good against me, but I sit up because being honest about at least one thing feels better.

Ben looks at me carefully. "Carter says he remembers this Ethan guy. From last year. I told him he had to be wrong. But he says he saw you and Tess with him at Northwestern. But that's not what you told me."

My heart skips a beat. Northwestern. Shit. Carter goes to Northwestern. Why hadn't I remembered that? This is going from bad to worse. It's bad enough that I ended up in a shouting match with my parents. *Why don't you ask Mom why she wasn't at work either? Because you don't want to know about that, do you? So don't tell me what to do! I'm seventeen! If I want to screw up my job, it's really none of your business!* I'd screamed at my father before I'd stomped upstairs, changed into jeans and a black tank top, and walked out to Ben's car without looking back. Ethan, of course, had already driven off, after telling me quietly but firmly yet again that he really needed to talk to me later.

"He says it didn't occur to him at first," Ben continues, "but then something just clicked. He remembers because it was one of those days we kept having all those weird thunderstorms. The weather was really freaky for a couple of days, remember? And he says he saw you and Tess with the guy on campus. And that he might not have thought about it again except that he recognized you 'cause he used to hang with your brother. Says he would have said hello except he almost got hit by some huge bolt of lightning or something just as he saw you and Ethan running across Sheridan Road."

My skin feels hot and cold at the same time. Carter remembered me. Of course Carter would remember me because

Carter knew David. How could I be so stupid to forget that my brother had this circle of friends? Carter might not remember Baba Yaga flying at us in her mortar that day or a witch's disembodied hands flopping onto Sheridan Road—like everyone else, he seems to have blocked that part out—but he remembers me and Tess being there. And he remembers Ethan. Is there any way out of this conversation?

I know I should feel guilty about lying to Ben. I do feel guilty. So I try for some semblance of honesty.

"Well, yeah." I pause, fumbling for the right words. "I guess he's right. We were hanging out that day. We'd gone to the campus to visit a professor friend of Ethan's."

It's the wrong thing for me to say. In my mind, I see Professor Olensky's body lying dead on the floor of his office. And I guess because of that, anger mixes with my guilt. I'm angry with Ben for poking at this so much. But more than that, I'm angry with myself.

"I told you I knew him," I say. "I told you it's no big deal. I'm entitled to have things you don't know about, Ben."

This is totally unfair, and I know it. None of this is Ben's fault. He's perfectly right to think that something strange is going on. But if I can't tell him the truth, I don't know what else to do. It's not like there's some rule book for how to behave when the guy you're dating has no idea that you have magic powers, an all-access pass to a witch's forest in my dreams, and an undeniable crush on a guy who just finished a century of immortality. Not to mention a stalker mermaid pal.

"Yeah." Ben's tone shifts to something a little sharper. "You're entitled. That seems to be your story a lot lately." He rolls away from me, sits on the side of the bed, and places his hands on his thighs. I can see the muscles in his biceps tighten. I brace myself for him to say something else, but he stays silent.

"Ben. It's nothing. Really." I move to sit next to him, my leg against his. I reach up and touch the side of his face. The silver bracelet slides down my arm and the little *B&A* charm winks up at me.

I know I'm confusing things more, but I kiss him again because part of me really wants to love him—the same part, I guess, that wants Ethan out of my head because having him in my head makes me feel out of control. My body relaxes a little when Ben stays quiet and kisses me back.

Against me, his lips still pressed to mine, Ben shivers. This is how I realize that the temperature in the room is dropping. I open my eyes.

The rusalka is hovering in the doorway, her wild hair flicking tiny drops of water onto the hardwood floor. Tears well in her gray eyes. She shakes her head at me and smiles. "Oh, my sweet, sweet girl. So sad. Don't be. He is just a man. He will get over it. Men forget so easily. Not like us. Not like me. Have you figured it out yet? I have tried to show you as best I can. But it is hard. This body does not always do what I want it to. It has desires of its own. You understand that too, don't you? So sweet, my Anne. My dearest Anne."

My body floods with fear. The stupid, stupid magic rises into my fingertips. Ben yelps in pain as I yank my hand away from his cheek. On the smooth tan skin just at his right cheekbone, I see three angry red welts the size and shape of my three fingertips.

"What the hell?" He touches his hand to his face. But this is all he reacts to. He hasn't heard her speak like I have, and though he saw her at the pool—I now realize she must have wanted him to—when he whips around to look where I'm still staring, he clearly doesn't see anything but his door.

"Go to her," the rusalka says. "The Death Crone. Baba Yaga. Give in to it. She has your answers. Let her help you fix what is damaged. Let me have what I deserve. I cannot do it on my own."

"Leave me alone," I tell her.

And then, in a blink, she's gone.

"What do you mean, *Leave you*—did you just burn my face?" Ben pushes off the bed and walks to the mirror over his dresser. I follow him. We stand reflected, his faced burned, mine horrified. For a second, I see the rusalka reflected between us, black hair dripping, gray eyes huge like storm clouds. Ben pivots and looks behind us. "What the—?" he begins, but once again, there's nothing to see.

I reach out to touch his face again. If I've hurt him, maybe I can reverse it. It's something I've been trying, something I haven't learned to control yet. Not that I can control anything right now. But Ben pushes my hand away. The fear rises inside me again, and only one thing echoes in my head. *Leave now.*

"Shit, Ben. I'm sorry. I don't know—I'm sorry. Oh, God, Ben. I just can't—I need to go. It's better if I just go—better for you. I can't stay here."

I don't stop to let him respond. I just scoop my purse off the floor and run. Out of Ben's room, through his house, out the front door, and onto the street. My only thought is to run.

Two blocks from Ben's house, I finally stop to catch my breath. *Should I go back? Will the rusalka go after him if I'm not there? Or is it just me she wants?* I'm totally clueless.

I dig into my purse for my cell phone—my dead, water-logged cell phone that I need to replace. *Wonderful. Just damn wonderful.* I should go back to Ben—Ben Logan, who loves me and didn't ask to be a part of the weirdness that is my world. *I'll come up with something.* That's what I've become an expert at, isn't it? Lying to everyone. Covering up the stuff they just wouldn't understand or that I just can't explain.

I'm about to slam the phone onto the sidewalk—smash it to bits, like I've probably just done to my relationship with Ben. I hear Baba Yaga's voice in my head. *Steady, dear,* Baba Yaga says to me. *You are stronger than you think. But you must embrace your gifts, or they will destroy you.* And as though she's placed it in my mind, I see myself on the train with Ethan and Viktor, the other time I'd trashed my cell phone.

"Okay," I say aloud. "Okay. I get it. You don't have to drop a house on me." If Baba Yaga is listening in and gets the joke, she doesn't let me know.

I wrap my hand as tightly as possible around my poor little phone. The AT&T people obviously didn't have me in mind when they built this thing. And most people who know magic like mine probably use it for something other than burning their boyfriends and recharging their phones. Maybe once I figure it out, I'll write a user's manual to leave for the next girl who gets chosen for all this craziness. But right now, I just close my eyes and concentrate. The phone warms encouragingly in my hand.

A minute or two later, the result isn't much: a couple of bars and a half-charged battery. The head shot of Ben that I'd been using as wallpaper looks dim and foggy. This makes my stomach knot up even more than it already is. *I'll walk back anyway*, I think. *It's really what I should do.*

But it isn't Ben I call as my heart thuds faster than I'd like. I press in the numbers that I've memorized, even though I keep telling myself I should forget them.

"Anne?" Ethan's voice sounds tired and alert all at once.

I swallow. No fear. That's what Baba Yaga keeps telling me. "I need a ride. I hurt Ben. He's okay. But I need a ride. Please, Ethan. Can you come get me?"

"On my way. Where are you?"

I tell him, grateful beyond words that he hasn't hesitated in offering to come to my rescue.

I'm studying the prices on the specials sign at the 7-Eleven on Lake Street when he pulls up fifteen minutes later and gets out of the Mercedes. It's given me something to do other than obsessing over Ben or watching the various stoners choose their late-night junk food stash.

"So what do you think? Two ninety-nine a pound for Land O'Lakes American cheese? Or how about a blueberry muffin and a large coffee?"

"Hazelnut or mocha?" Ethan grins at me, but I can see the worry in those blue eyes. He's wearing faded jeans and a gray T-shirt, and his hair looks like he's shoved his hand through a few dozen times. But he's shaved the stubble from his chin.

"The muffin or the coffee?"

"Neither. I'm thinking the cheese."

We stand there in the fluorescent glow of the 7-Eleven sign. Two guys reeking heavily of marijuana wander up and begin a discussion about Slushie choices.

"I need your help, Ethan. I hurt Ben. God. I—the rusalka. I saw her again."

"I'm here. Just tell me everything, and we'll figure it out. No more secrets, okay?"

I don't know if I'm ready for that, but I nod my head anyway. I'm pretty sure he's got some secrets of his own. "Okay."

Ethan puts his arm around me. He doesn't ask me any questions.

"Raspberry's better than bubblegum," I comment to the taller of the two stoned dudes as I let Ethan clasp my hand in his and lead me to the car. "You won't be sorry."

The car still smells like pond, and thus, the rusalka. "Maybe I should just go back to Ben's," I say, more to myself than to Ethan. "What if he's not safe?"

"Is that what you want?" Ethan glances over at me from the driver's seat.

"Yes. No—no. Let's just go. Are you still in that same loft?" I feel silly that I don't even know where he's staying.

Ethan shakes his head. "I've got a flat in Evanston. I really am going to school, Anne. That part's true."

I don't ask him how long he's been back or exactly how someone in his position pays for things like rent. When you've been around as long as he has, I guess you figure these things out. Who knows? Maybe the Brotherhood had some kind of pension plan.

"Oh. Well, then. Let's go."

"You sure?"

"Positive," I lie. Once again, Baba Yaga's voice echoes in my head. *Embrace your gifts, girl. You must believe in what lies inside you.*

I don't know what this means or where it will lead or how it connects to the rusalka, but honestly, I don't see any other choice. Whatever answers I need, I'm not going to find them in the 7-Eleven parking lot.

I'm embracing, I tell Baba Yaga silently. I just wish I knew what.

THURSDAY, 11:42 PM

ETHAN

I BREW TEA WHILE ANNE ROAMS THE APARTMENT. SHE CALLS Tess, and after a whispered conversation, calls her mother and informs her that she's sleeping at Tess's. "Fine, then," she snaps into the phone. "Don't believe me. I am *not* spending the night at Ben's."

Anne flashes me a sheepish expression. The color rises in her cheeks. She isn't at Ben's. She's with me.

"Well," she says when she's finished the call, "looks like we're back to where we started." She gestures to the mugs of tea on my small kitchen table. We first talked over tea that day last fall, across from each other at the table in my loft, her face so pretty and earnest.

She takes a tentative sip of tea, then resumes pacing, mug in hand. "Could you stop being so calm? I'm freaking out here, Ethan. And you're serving tea."

"Would you rather have coffee? Water? Just tell me."

"I'd rather not be here. I'd rather not have just singed Ben's face with my hand and run out of his house like a maniac. I'd rather a lot of things."

"You did what?" I try to keep my voice even but fail. Foolishly, when she said *hurt*, I'd thought of something other than physical. "How? When?" I follow her into the living room. Our footsteps echo on the wood floor. *Carpets*, I think ridiculously. *I haven't bought any carpets for this room. I need to make it feel less empty.* This, I've learned, is what happens sometimes when a problem is too big to easily solve. The brain shifts to something more feasible.

The story pours from her—not all at once, but in waves. She sips the tea, although she tells me she doesn't want it, and later, she eats the sandwich I make her, even though she protests that she isn't hungry. I butter thickly sliced bread, add tomatoes and salt. She pulls off small bites with her fingers, eats as she continues to pace, coming back to the table now and then until she's finished it all.

"I keep dreaming about her—Baba Yaga. Only I don't think it's just a dream. I'm with her in her hut. I talk to her, and she tells me things. It's like—well, it's like she's confiding in me or something. Really weird. And Viktor's there too, I think, only I can't see him. And it seems to upset her that he has to be there. I think she'd kill him if she could; only she can't."

Anne paces some more, the mug of tea clutched in her hands. She sets it gently back on the table. "God, Ethan, this is what I haven't told anyone. Not you, not Tess. I mean, I guess you two are the only ones I *could* tell. But I haven't. And I'm sorry. The power didn't fade away after Anastasia went back to die. Or even after you left. It kept getting stronger. There were little things at first, things I could explain away. I nicked my thumb one day while slicing an apple, and then I wrapped my fingers around the cut so it would stop bleeding. But when I let go, the cut was gone. Not just healed over, but gone like it had never been there. Another time, I was having an argument with my mom while we were at Starbucks. My hands were around my latte, and all of a sudden, I could feel it boiling in the cup. I can't make people do stuff, I don't have a clue about spells or anything like that—not like you and the Brotherhood. But I can change the nature of things somehow. It's more than what you taught me I could do before. More than just warding spells or getting a padlock to open. There's something in me, Ethan. And I need to figure out what. And why."

I take Anne's hands in mine. They're warm against my skin. A thin silver bracelet slips down her arm; the round disc hanging from it taps lightly against my wrist. "Show me. You showed me today with the padlock. Now you need to show me this."

"I don't know if I can. I haven't consciously tried. Well, not much, anyway." Her cheeks color again. "Tess was right. I *did* poke Brett Sullivan with my pencil. But he deserved it. All that staring at girls' boobs—it gets annoying. So I figured it was as good a time as any to try things out. Although I have to say, I was pretty amazed that it worked." A tiny smile plays on her lips. It fades quickly. "God, Ethan—I hurt Ben, and when I pulled myself together to try to heal him, he just pushed me away. Maybe I could have done something. Maybe I could have—"

Heal. Something occurs to me. "Wait. In the pool, the first time, when Ben dived in. Do you remember what the rusalka said to you? I heard her speak too, you know. I don't think Ben, Carter, or Tess heard. But I did, and you did too, didn't you? What did she say, Anne? Do you remember?"

"She said," Anne begins slowly, "that only I could swim with the rusalkas. Which, let me say, is seriously creepy, because that means there are probably more of them, and personally, I think one's enough. She also said that I had to go to the Death Crone—to Baba Yaga—for her to teach me. She told me that only then could I heal. But it doesn't make sense. Heal from what? And what does Baba Yaga have to do with the rusalka? I mean, is there actually a connection? I—oh, wait a second. When I healed my cut and wanted to help Ben—do you think that's what she meant? Did she know that she'd startle me so I'd hurt Ben and then try to fix what I did?"

"I don't know. It's part of what we've got to solve. But it feels right. The magics Viktor taught us—they bent nature too. Only not like this. I can—or at least, I could—do certain basic tricks, as you know all too well. Protection spells. Magic that helped defend me. Basic wards and glamours and the like. Joining the Brotherhood gave me those powers."

"Plus the immortality." Anne gives my hands a light squeeze, then let's go and fingers her silver bracelet.

"Well, that came only after Viktor created the spell that used Anastasia. But none of it was automatic. I had to perform spells or concentrate to will it to happen. It didn't just—"

"It didn't just flow out of you." Anne finishes the thought for me.

"Exactly. So—if, theoretically, you gained your powers from me as a conduit to the Brotherhood's magic, then why is your power different from mine? Why can you do things I never could? Why is it getting stronger even though the magic's original purpose has been fulfilled?"

"You've been thinking about all this, haven't you? Be honest, Ethan. Why is it, really, that you're back?"

I knew that she'd ask eventually. Even so, as I walk to the

leather sofa across the room and Anne follows, I fumble for an answer that makes sense.

"A lot of reasons. The university established a fellowship in Alex's name. It felt like a worthy thing to continue his work. I've studied informally for years. The folklore, the literature, the art—they're what I grew up with, what I lived with. I speak Russian and English and passable Bulgarian and Czech. It seemed a good fit, a good next step—something a little more permanent after so much that hasn't been."

"So what did you do? Take your SATs? Add in a few AP courses while you were in Europe?" Her brown eyes sparkle with laughter—and possibly a bit of gentle mockery—in the soft light of the desk lamp.

I consider the proper response. "There are ways. You know that, Anne."

"Well, maybe for you. My college board scores aren't exactly where they need to be, especially since I've been a little, um, distracted lately. I'll be lucky to get into junior college next year, at the rate I'm going."

"This is taking us away from the point."

"Hey. You're the one who brought it up. I was just clarifying. So that's it? You came back to go to school. And what? You just decided to pop by the pool and see if I was around?" She rubs her hand over the bracelet again, and I notice the letters on the disc. *B&A*. Ben and Anne.

What I tell her is the truth, but not all of it. All of it would be telling her how I feel about her. *Can I? What about that bracelet on her wrist?* "I'm back because you need me. Because whatever it is that shifted power through me to you is still like an open line. I don't see what's going on with you, exactly. It's not that strong. But I feel it. I know you've been in pain. And I know you've been scared. I needed to leave. I wasn't lying last fall. You don't know what it's been like—how could you know, really? I needed to—hey!"

She slaps my face with an open hand. The *B&A* charm raps sharply against my cheek. "Don't you dare tell me that I don't know, Ethan." Anne's up from the couch before I can even fully react. "After all I've—after what we've been through, what I've seen, after what keeps happening? You can sit there all smug and tell me that I don't understand? That I don't get it? You're back here because we're just unlucky enough to have some supernatural umbilical cord connecting us now? But really, what? You'd rather be wandering around Prague or Moscow? Sitting in cafes smoking those cigarettes you think I don't notice are in your pocket, even though it's hard to miss since you keep putting your hand there like you want one? Ben almost died today, Ethan. And I should feel lucky that you chose this moment to grace me with an appearance? Well, I don't. I don't feel lucky at all. I just feel scared and angry and confused."

I rub my cheek, just happy that she hasn't bolted out the door. "I didn't mean to—"

"Well, you did. For someone who says he's all linked in to how I'm feeling, you are seriously dense, Ethan."

Truer words have rarely been spoken. My eye catches my reflection in the mirror over the desk. The slight, reddened imprint of her palm on my cheek glares at me.

"I'm sorry," I say, and I hope she knows I mean it. "I was out of line. I never should have said—"

"Whatever. I don't want to argue about it." She sighs. "And I'm sorry I slapped you." She doesn't look entirely sorry, but when I go to her, she stays put and reaches up slowly to press her hand to my cheek.

Maybe it's the silence that reminds me. Maybe it's just the touch of her hand. "Show me what you can do," I ask her again. "Please, Anne."

She pulls her hand away. "I don't know, Ethan. I mean, look at us. We're a mess. Plus, I can't always make it do what I want. What if I can't—?"

Gently, I place her hand back on my face. "Show me. Just show me."

She hesitates, then closes her eyes. Her face is very close to mine—so close that I can feel her breath against my lips.

"Hope you're ready."

I press my hand against hers. When the warmth seeps into my palm, I know it's begun.

Friday, 12:20 am

Anne

His hand stays on top of mine as I press my palm to his cheek. It's not much to heal—just the red outline of my hand. I'm embarrassed that I slapped him, that I let myself get out of control. I hate that it's Ben's bracelet that's caused the wound. But as I close my eyes, I see the tiniest of cuts just barely bleeding, right at his chin. My bracelet must have nicked him. So I slide my thumb down to cover that too, feel the slightest slickness against my skin.

"Don't move." I haven't done this to another person before, just to myself and my cell phone, although this is probably not the time to mention that. In my head, I visualize the slap mark on Ethan's face, the tiny sliver of a cut. Like a movie on rewind, I imagine the scene in reverse, the slap going back into my hand, the cut moving out and back into the bracelet. I visualize my will acting on what I've done: taking back the hurt, reversing the damage. My body hums as it happens, a pulsing buzz that's exciting and scary at the same time.

It doesn't take very long. I open my eyes. Ethan's hand is still pressed against mine. He's closed his eyes too, and when he opens them, I look into those two pools of blue. I'm not sure whether it's good or bad that this makes my stomach flutter. A lot.

"I think that's enough. Let's see." We remove our hands. I study his face. The red blotch of the slap is gone, the cut healed as though it had never opened. "Look for yourself." I point to the mirror.

"Why haven't you told me about this before now?" He touches his face again like he's making sure it's not a trick or something.

"I haven't really—well, it's new. I mean, I don't think I could do this last fall. I don't know. Should I have told you? Would it have made a difference?"

I see him ponder this. "It means something. We need to know what. Anne—we need to know exactly what you can really do."

His tone sounds serious, and this makes my stomach flutter some more. "I just showed you."

"You showed me a little. I think you can do more than a little." He steps back from me and then walks to the kitchen counter. He opens a drawer and pulls out a small paring knife.

"Whoa. What the heck, Ethan?" My heart knocks against my ribs. *How well do I really know him? And what exactly does he plan on doing with the knife?*

"I need to know more. I need to see exactly what you're capable of." He holds the knife in his right hand, turns his left hand palm side up, and before I can even protest, slices the fleshy part of his thumb. Blood oozes slowly as the wound opens. It's a deep cut, and the backs of my knees prickle as I look at it.

"What do you think you're doing?"

"Show me what you can really do. I don't heal instantly like I used to. I'm mortal. If I leave this, it will continue to bleed. If I don't attend to it, it'll get infected. I don't have that magic in me anymore. My body won't take care of this. So show me what you can do."

My impulse—part fear, part annoyance—is to resist. "No. What are you going to do, keep cutting yourself over and over to make me do a cool little party trick? And then what? I can do what I can do. I don't have to keep giving you demos. I called you because things were out of control. I don't know how this is going to solve anything."

Ethan sets the knife on the counter, walks back to me, and holds out his hand. Blood trickles down to his wrist. A couple of drops fall to the floor.

"Oh, come on, Ethan. Just get a Band-Aid, or a towel, or a—oh, whatever. Here." It's just easier to give in and do it before he bleeds to death. "You know this is really gross, right? I mean, I should put on a rubber glove or something. Oh, never mind."

I suck in a breath, then wrap my fingers around his thumb, pressing the wound to my palm. Once again, I close my eyes. At first, it's hard to concentrate. I'm feeling self-conscious and thinking this is ridiculous, and I'm definitely feeling like I'm betraying Ben. It's not like healing Ethan is some prime act of cheating, but somehow, that's how it feels. Baba Yaga's voice is still in the back of my brain, and the image of the rusalka turning into my mother hasn't quite faded either. Long story short—it's pretty damn crowded in my head. The fact that Ethan smells really good—sort of clean and musky all at once—isn't helping.

This time, I have to concentrate harder. My memory flashes on an image of Ethan standing behind me on Tess's front lawn in the shadow of a spruce tree—that night, I had asked him to teach me a protection spell. We stretched out our arms together, and it was the first time in all that craziness that I remember thinking that possibly there was something more to how I felt about him. *You need to feel the power inside you*, he'd told me. *You need to imagine what you want it to do.*

I think of this now as I attempt to heal the wound on Ethan's hand. In my head, I visualize the cut on his thumb, the molecules of blood flowing away, the skin cut open so that it no longer protects the precious parts inside. I'm not a poetic person—I've never written Ben a love note or made him a mix CD or baked him homemade fortune cookies with little love messages like Tess did once for Neal. But when I think about this process, this thing I've acknowledged and I'm attempting to embrace, that's sort of what it feels like. Poetry. When I think about what I'm trying to do, the words I hear in my head flow like a poem or a song.

That's when I understand part of what I've been resisting: when I use this power, I'm not just me. I'm part of something bigger, something that flows back to places I can't even imagine, people I've never met. I don't know this for sure. Like I've said, it's not like I've got an instruction manual or something. Baba Yaga—if my dream visits to her have been real, and I think they probably are—has only hinted at it. But somewhere in my bones, I think it's true. It's like when I dreamed as Anastasia—I was more than just me. What she felt and dreamed, I did too. The power that I'm using right now—it feels like that.

Everything in my head clears out. I feel my body pulsing, power flowing out of me and into Ethan's hand over and over. It is, I think, almost like sharing the same skin. The rush of it kicks my pulse into high gear. A wave of dizziness and nausea washes over me. I open my eyes to steady myself, and what I see causes me to gasp and Ethan's eyes to snap open.

"Ethan?" I tighten my grip on his hand so much that he winces.

Like they've done before, my hands are glowing—blue, then pure white, the color radiating out of them in little bursts. Only this time, the color transfers itself to Ethan. Or maybe it's coming from him too, and mingling back in me. It's hard to tell. Blue ribbons of energy swirl around us, and because it looks like the magic Viktor used to hurt Ethan as we barreled along on that speeding El train last fall, my stomach tightens with the memory.

And then something else happens. I don't believe it at first. But as my feet lift from the floor and I look up to see the ceiling a lot closer than I'd like it to be, I know it's real.

"Um," I manage, "are we, um, flying?"

"I'd say *hovering*." Ethan reaches out his free hand and pulls me against him. I don't know what he thinks this will do, but I manage to stop panicking long enough to appreciate the gesture.

It's hard to say exactly why my concentration chooses the next moment to fizzle. Most likely, it's a combination of blue sparks, exhaustion from the whole healing thing, the distraction of being mashed against Ethan's chest, and possibly also the fact that we're flying—correction, *hovering*—four feet or so off the floor. We shudder a little, then slam back down in a rush. Ethan lands first, and I flop on top of him. His head hits the floor with a loud *crack*. I'm still clutching his thumb.

"Ow! Shit!" It's a fairly mild response, and I have to give him props for his restraint.

"Sorry. That was—well, I don't know what that was." I catch my breath and let go of his thumb. We peer at it. The cut is totally healed, the skin completely smooth. "Well, at least that worked." My head hurts, and not just from the fall. I roll off him and lie back on the floor. I feel drained—like the magic has used me as much as I've used it.

"Sit up. You need to sit up. Your nose is bleeding. Let me get you something." Ethan hoists himself from the floor, rubbing his head. By the time I sit up, he's returned with a damp towel. "Here. You need to apply pressure." He hands me the towel while I collect my thoughts. Towel against my face, I push myself to stand. The dizziness hits again. I make it as far as the couch, then sink into the soft leather.

"What *was* that?" I put more pressure on my nose, then remove the towel. It's red with blood.

Ethan lowers himself next to me on the couch. He takes the towel from my hand, studies my nose for a second, then presses the towel back in place. "It's slowing," he says. "It should stop soon. And I don't know. We connected somehow. I—I didn't think I had much power left, but whatever I have, yours drew it from me. Like you were using it for fuel."

My response is a little muffled because the bottom of the towel is half over my mouth. "Fuel for what? Lifting us off the floor? That's just crazy, Ethan. I mean, so is the rest of this. But that's even crazier."

Ethan holds up his thumb, and we peer at it again. "But it worked. I'll admit it got out of control for a second, but now you know to expect that. And now we know what you can do. I made that cut deep. And it's totally healed."

I push his hand and the towel away and stand up, then flop down again. The dizziness hasn't gone away. I think about putting my head between my knees, except I'm fairly certain this won't help the nosebleed. This strikes me as rather ironic—I can heal cuts and make my cell phone work but can't seem to get my own nose to stop dripping. This makes me simultaneously tired and cranky. For months, I've worked very hard to pretend that none of this was still happening. Now, I'm sitting here on Ethan's couch just attempting not to hyperventilate.

"Don't. You need to keep pressure on it." He presses the towel against my face again, and again I swipe it away.

"So what now?" I ask him petulantly as I try to ignore another wave of nausea. Whatever this magic is that I can do, my body obviously isn't a real fan of it. "What am I supposed to do? Hang around hospitals? Apply to medical school? Become an EMT? Seriously, Ethan, what? Go on some talk show and demonstrate my freak-of-the-week abilities? Because you know what? I don't think this is all of it. The healing thing, I mean."

That I blurt this out surprises me—until this second, I hadn't even realized that's what I thought. "Do you? Do you really think this is just about healing magic? You know better than that, Ethan. If it was that simple, then why are you back? Why is a crazy Russian mermaid trying to get my attention? Why can't I stop dreaming about the witch? I thought whatever powers I had were supposed to just allow me to save Anastasia. So now I'm—what? A healer? You know what I think? I think you don't even know. And I hate that you did this to me. You came and found me, and nothing's ever been the same. My life was screwed up enough before you got here. But now it's worse."

"Anne," Ethan begins. But I don't let him finish.

"The rusalka told me that Anastasia might not be dead." My dizziness has eased, but when I say this my stomach flips.

Any number of emotions cross Ethan's face. Shock, I think. Sadness mostly. Worry. "You can't trust what she says. Like Baba Yaga. Not everything is the truth. Not everything is the way it looks."

"But what if she's right? What if it's still not over? We don't really know, do we? You just said it yourself. Not everything is the way it looks. So how do we ever know for sure? Maybe it's all connected. Anastasia. Baba Yaga. The rusalka. If we can't trust stuff to be true, then how can we ever know if we're doing the right thing? How can I"—here, I hesitate and then blurt out the rest of it—"trust you? I know you say I can. But how do I really know?"

The silence between us lasts a long time. Somewhere out on the lake, a few blocks away, a foghorn sounds. A tanker, maybe. Or some fishing boat heading out really early. Is the rusalka out there in the water? Watching some sailor she doesn't know? Or is she only watching me? I think about that moment at the pond, when she turned and I saw my mother's face. She'd melded so easily, as if her features were already similar on their own. It has to mean something, but I don't know what. Can I trust Ethan? I want to. I need to. I just don't know if I can.

"I came back because I couldn't stay away any longer." Of the things I'm expecting Ethan to say, this is not one of them. He sits very still as he speaks, his gaze still locked on mine. "Because everywhere I went—Prague, St. Petersburg, Moscow, Paris—I just kept thinking of *you*. I'm sorry about that. I'm not who you should be with. I thought if I left, it would make things better. But I—"

In the seconds that follow, I know two things. The first is

that he's going to kiss me. The second is that I'm going to let him. And when his mouth doesn't find mine quite fast enough, I lift my chin, hoping my nose really has stopped bleeding, and close the distance between us.

"Anne," Ethan says against my lips. "We'll figure this all out. I promise you. I won't let anything hurt you."

I allow him that last part, even though I know it's just not true. No one—not Ethan, not me, not Baba Yaga herself—can stop someone else from getting hurt. I'm hurting Ben right now by kissing Ethan. Even if he never knows. Even if Ethan and I never kiss again. I'm cheating on Ben, and I've been cheating on him in my heart for a while. Ethan is right. Not everything is the way it looks. Especially not me.

We kiss for a long time. I lean against him and link my arms around his neck and everything in me feels like it's centering on this one thing—kissing Ethan and letting him kiss me back. His tongue is warm as it explores my mouth. I'm thinking that I could kiss him forever. He pulls me even closer and strokes my hair, and I run my hands under his shirt, all the way up his back to where I know that lion tattoo is etched near his shoulder. His skin is smooth and warm, his hands still tangled in my hair. He kisses my forehead. He kisses my eyelids. I rub my fingers against that spot near his shoulder, imagine the tattoo as my fingers touch it.

He's ridiculously good at kissing, which probably shouldn't surprise me, since he's had a few years to perfect his moves. Only then I feel Ben's bracelet slide down my arm, and it occurs to me that I'm actually not able to kiss two guys in one day—correction, two days, since it's well past midnight—without feeling guilty and sort of scummy. This is not what certain parts of my body are expecting. But my brain chooses this moment to get bossy with the rest of me.

I ease my hands out from under Ethan's shirt, sigh, and push him away. He opens his eyes, only slightly surprised.

"I can't," I say. This sounds silly since obviously I can and just did. "I'm—well, Ben and I, we're…" *We're what?* I wonder.

Ethan reddens a little as I stumble around it.

"Oh," he says. "Idiot. Me, I mean." He clears his throat and looks uncomfortable.

"I'm glad you're back, Ethan. I'm glad I called you to come get me. I don't know what I would have done if—"

"It's fine. You're safe here," he tells me softly. "You did exactly what you needed to do." I know there's more unsaid between us, but those few words are enough. The tension in my body eases.

"I'm so tired," I tell him, because all of a sudden it's the truth. "I'm just so very tired." Exhausted is more like it. Fear, magic, guilt—it's easier, I think, to just close my eyes.

Ethan pulls me back into his arms. "I know," he whispers to me softly. "It's okay. Be tired." He kisses me again—a little tentatively, but I'm so wiped out that I don't protest this time. He strokes my hair as I nestle my head against his chest and keeps holding me as I drift off to sleep.

Friday, 3:03 am

Anne

You better not take the last slice." David slaps my hand away from the pizza box.

I smile. It's been so long since I've seen my brother. All I've had is just the slightest scent of Lucky that still clings to his comforter hidden in the back of my closet.

"Let your sister have the pizza." My mother's curled up on the couch, the remote in her hand. My father is sitting next to her, his arm looped over her shoulders. She leans over and kisses him.

"Gross," David says. "Get a room, you two."

Mom tosses a throw pillow at him, and David falls backward on the carpet, laughing.

He's got auburn hair like I do, and brown eyes like mine, and a long straight nose like mine too. He plays football, and his buddies hang around our house eating everything in sight and teasing me. Judd Angstrom and Drew Miller and Zach Geller—who plays center and once told me that I was really cute. I mooned about him for days after that, writing his name and his football number—55—on my social studies notebook over and over, sometimes with little hearts.

David's number is 18. I love going to watch him play. He's a natural out there on the field. Like he was born for it.

This is what I remember when I dream about my brother.

"You could see him, you know," Baba Yaga says to me. "If you wanted to."

"I do see him," I tell her. "He's right here."

Baba Yaga smiles, a huge grimace that shows off her iron teeth. "We see what we want to. Like I taught you. Ya khachu videt. 'I want to see.'"

"I don't want your spells."

"You are so very certain of this? It will not take much. The power is already inside you. You cannot give it back. Use it, then. Time shifts here. Bring him back to you. To your mother. Ease her sadness." She brushes my cheek with one enormous wrinkled hand. Her touch is oddly gentle, her skin dry as cracked leather.

On our family room carpet, David is still laughing. Worms slither out of the back of his head where it meets the carpet.

"You can't bring back the dead," I say.

"Don't." My mother's voice quavers on the verge of tears. "Don't say it. If you don't say it, then maybe it won't be true."

"There are worse things than death, Laura." Anastasia sits next to me on the floor. She's wearing the same white dress she had on the day I took her hand and walked with her from Baba Yaga's hut.

"How do you know my name?" My mother turns her attention to Anastasia.

"You're part of me. But hasn't Anne told you that?"

"Shhh. She'll tell her when she's ready. Won't you, Anne?" Ethan sits on the other side of me, his brown hair a little bit too long, his eyes the startling blue of the sky on one of those cloudless summer days. "But don't tell her about me. That will just be our little secret."

"You don't know what it's like to lose a child," my mother says.

"Oh, my dear woman." Baba Yaga hovers above us now in her mortar. The ceiling has expanded to accommodate her, opened up to the night sky. *"I beg to differ."* Stars wink around her. One. Then two. Then three. *"We all live as happily as we can. Then we move on. It is the order of things. Haven't we learned that?"*

"Hush, Yaga." The rusalka shimmers into view. *"Hush. You'll frighten the girl, and then she won't help me. You know the story doesn't have to go like that. Some of us don't move on. Some of us can't."* My nostrils fill with the smell of the sea. Salty. Ancient. Powerful. Her dark eyes look wild, and so does her long dark hair. Her arms are bare, her skin very white. She reaches out one pale hand and points it at my mother.

"Don't look at her," Ethan whispers in my ear. His breath is warm against my skin.

"You're all fools. You don't know what's coming. You can't see beyond yourselves. Only I could do that. But not even I can stop it." Viktor leans against Baba Yaga in her mortar. His hair is pure white, his face skeletal.

"You cursed him!" The woman with the wild eyes points her bony finger toward the sky. *"And then you cursed me! He doesn't know what you did. But I do. I know the truth. I won't forget. I can't. I gave her up. And look where it got me."*

She touches one bony finger to my face. Water surrounds us. We float together in an endless sea. Tiny fish dart around us. I feel them bump against me. Deeper and deeper, she pulls me under, the shafts of light above us dimming. The heaviness of it exhausts me. My hair fans out around me and entwines with hers until I can no longer tell where mine ends and hers begins. Even as I'm afraid, there is a familiarity to her—a connection as primal and elemental as the water in which we're swimming. But it all makes no sense. We swim deeper yet. The need to breathe fills every fiber of my body. I struggle against the impulse to open my mouth and swallow.

"Oh, for heaven's sake, Anne." Tess sits next to me now, her long

blond hair pulled into a tail. She's sipping something from mug. It smells like coffee. "You're dreaming. Wake up."

Still dreaming, I open my eyes. They're all gone. But the smell of the sea lingers.

The Forest, Early Morning

Baba Yaga

I T IS TIME," I TELL VIKTOR. "MY GIRL IS READY. SHE DOESN'T know it yet, but she is. All is aligned. Soon, she will understand. She will see what she has not. She will have no choice but to act."

Viktor stares into the fire, its embers reflected in the dark irises of his eyes. My cat, my koshka, sits at his feet, occasionally flicking at some stray crumb on the floor with his sharp, pink tongue. Viktor chuckles. It is an odd sound; he has not laughed much since he has been with me; certainly, his situation has not amused him. But today, he is his old self, at least for now. "Perhaps, Yaga. Perhaps."

It angers me that he questions my judgment, but I let him have his illusion, his false sense of security. Really, he is like a dog on a very long chain. Round and round the yard he goes, until he is choked back when he strays too far. It is the illusion of freedom. Sometimes, I have seen, it is easier to just let him believe. But today, the gleam in his eyes tells me that perhaps he is not fooled at all. It is no matter. He remains my prisoner, whether he understands his fate or not.

"She will do what she needs to. She will right what has been wronged. It is what she is made for. It is what is inside her."

"Yaga. Dear." With effort, Viktor stands up. His body is wrecked, his bones brittle. But his eyes and tongue—when the madness ebbs—are still sharp. "Even Ethan will realize the truth eventually. And when he does, he'll act. Do you honestly think he will keep his secrets from her then? When he knows for sure? He is what he has always been—virtuous to the bitter end. More virtuous than your girl, perhaps."

I point my hand at him, and the burn that travels across his skin makes him scream. I watch the red, scarring sizzle move up his fingers, travel the length of his arm under his tattered shirt, and spread over his chest. I pull back my power before the damage is too great. This is one of the lessons of keeping him captive: knowing exactly how long to sustain the pain before his body wears out. It is an art that I do not enjoy, but one I have perfected.

"You loved once." I settle into my rocking chair, pick up my mug of hot, sweet tea with one hand, and reach down to stroke my koshka's head with the other. "Or have you forgotten? Even I still remember what it is to feel that passion. But you—with you, I do not know. She is your blood. The blood of your blood. And yet you speak of her with such disrespect. She is the one who was strong enough to defeat you. Do not forget that. There is great strength in giving your heart to someone. Even I know this. And I gave up the right to love a long time ago. Have you forgotten the sacrifice the rusalka made? Have you forgotten why she made it?"

He does not speak. But he shrugs his gaunt shoulders, so I know he understands. It is time for me to intervene. All worlds are colliding. The outcome will be what it will be.

Because I can, I reach through my girl's dream and ease her pain. "You will remember," I say to her. "But later. For now, rest. You have the answers you need. You just need to understand what they are. It will come to you, my girl. But for now, just rest. Let your heart open."

"Ah, Yaga." Viktor smiles despite the pain still coursing through him—perhaps because of it. "You are a clever one, just as always. It is what has made you a legend. Stirring hearts like you stir that mortar of yours. Clever, clever woman."

"I have not been a woman for a very long time," I tell him. "But some things one never forgets. I cannot make her do what she might not on her own. But perhaps I can speed the process. I have waited long enough."

I turn from him then, stir the fire, watch the embers spark and burn. Watch my girl dream. And then I stir things just a little more.

Friday, 5:25 am

Anne

Anne. Anne! Wake up! You're dreaming."
Ethan's voice jerks me awake. We're still on the couch, and it's still dark outside. My cheeks feel damp. Have I been crying?

"What time is it? How long have I been asleep?" I rub my face, then run my hand over my hair. Even without a mirror, I'm fairly certain I'm not a pretty sight. It's entirely possible that I've drooled on Ethan's shirt.

"It's a little after five in the morning. Not quite dawn." Ethan rolls his shoulders and stretches. His stomach and chest are warm where I've been leaning on him. I move to sit up, but he pulls me back, encircling my waist with his arms. "You were crying. What were you dreaming?"

It's weird that I don't know what to tell him. When it comes to my dreams, I always know. That's been a given since this whole mess started. I didn't know I was dreaming as Anastasia, but I knew what I saw in the dream. No matter how freaky my dreams are, I always remember them. But not this time. It feels like I've got a word at the tip of my tongue, but I just can't figure it out.

"Don't know," I tell Ethan. "Baba Yaga, maybe? My family

too, I think. I woke up at some point, but I can't remember. I just know it was sort of scary, and I think it was sad."

"I should get you home." Ethan stretches again, yawns. "We can talk more later. Maybe write down what we know. See if there's a pattern to what's happening."

I run my hand through my hair again, and Ben's bracelet clinks against my wrist. The dream isn't coming to me, but everything else that happened last night returns in a big, stomach-dropping *whoosh!*

I came back because I couldn't stay away. Because everywhere I went, I just kept thinking of you. Ethan's lips on mine, his hands on me and mine on him. And that moment when I told him I couldn't do this. I feel myself flush a little, remembering the rest of it—the two of us lifting off the floor as my power meshed with his and the cut on his thumb disappeared. Me stumbling over my words, trying to tell him about Ben. Drifting off against him and waking up just now, still in his arms. I might not remember my dream, but I know how I feel right now in this moment.

Ethan goes on talking about what we'll do and how we might get the rusalka to come out again, but I'm not really listening. Everything inside me has gone sort of still because it has occurred to me that the last thing I want to do right now is talk. I shift to face him, quietly unclasp Ben's bracelet, and tuck it into the pocket of my jeans. Then I lean in and kiss him on the lips. "I don't want to go yet." I kiss him again. His lips taste sweet and bitter at the same time. I hope I don't have morning breath.

"I missed you too," I say, because I haven't told him this, not really. "I kept telling myself that I didn't. But I did."

Ethan studies my face, and my stomach goes *whoosh* again.

It's not entirely unpleasant this time. He takes my hand in his and kisses it. The gesture is so sweet that for a second, tears sting the backs of my eyes again.

My world has shifted a lot lately. When my brother died. When Ethan held out his hand that day in the library. When I held out my own hand and led Anastasia out of Baba Yaga's hut. The first time I kissed Ben—really kissed him, that is, even though I'm thinking now that he wasn't the person I was supposed to be with. It was still important. Still a shift from one thing to another. This moment right now with Ethan feels like that. Maybe that's what happens when you let someone into your heart—not just say that you like them, but really let them in. It's scary and risky, and right now, I know that I could be making a huge mistake.

"Anne, I—are you sure this is—?"

"Nothing's sure. Nothing's going to be." It makes me sound cynical and not a little jaded, but it's the truth. "You know that, Ethan. You *know* that."

He does know it, and I can see it in his face. How could he not?

"What about Ben?"

My heart jolts as I hear Ben's name. I wonder at how suddenly reckless I feel. Is that like me? Maybe it is. Maybe once you know for sure that things don't always turn out the way you want them to, that there isn't always a happily ever after, you just get reckless.

"I don't want to be with Ben. I want him to be safe. I don't want him to get hurt. I'm sorry that he's in the middle of all this, and I'm sorry that it's my fault. But I don't love Ben. And it isn't fair to pretend that I do."

"Ben loves you."

"Maybe. Maybe not. Ben loves the idea of me. Or at least, the me he thinks I am."

"You aren't any different. I know you think you are. But you're not, Anne. It's what I admire in you. You're steady, and you're honest. Even when you're not exactly telling the truth." Ethan leans very close. He kisses the tip of my nose. Runs his hand gently against my cheek. He dips his head and kisses the center of each of my palms. The wonderful sensation of it rockets through me. "You're beautiful," he says softly. "Perfect just the way you are."

I don't think either of those is true, but I like hearing him say it. We ease into another kiss. And then another.

It's different than kissing Ben—less familiar and, weirdly, more familiar at the same time. Ethan's lips are fuller. There's the faintest taste of tobacco when my tongue flicks against his—not bad, really, but definitely there. His arms around me feel as strong as Ben's, but his fingertips are slightly rougher as he pulls back from me to trace a finger over my eyelids and forehead, my cheeks and nose, lips and chin, like he's trying to memorize the feel of me. I do the same to him. I wonder if you really can learn to remember someone that way so that if age or time or something you're just not expecting takes it all away, your fingertips will still know, even in the darkness.

Which is all so crazily intimate and romantic that it stops me for a second, even though most of me had no intention of stopping anytime soon. In fact, my hands had honestly been sort of itching to peel that T-shirt off him and take a peek at the lion tattoo.

We both catch our breath, edge apart, and lean back against

the couch. And I guess because I still have thoughts of Ben, I ask, "Have you ever been in love?" The question sounds random as it pops out of my mouth, but it occurs to me that I'm sprawled on Ethan's couch contemplating all sorts of things, and maybe this is something I should know.

Ethan blinks. Those blue eyes register some definite surprise. I wonder if he's going to evade the question. But he doesn't.

"Ah. Well." He sighs. "Her name was Natasha. Tasha was what she went by. Tasha Levin. I knew her in London. It was about five years after the Revolution. I was living there for a while, renting a flat that I'd come back to every few months or so. She was Russian, like me—from a small town in what's now Belarus. By then, I'd finally understood the nature of what I'd become. The Brotherhood vows seemed sort of, well, restricting. Forever—or at least the possibility of forever—is a bit too long to go without…well…" He plucks up his lips in that crooked, ironic smile of his.

"And?"

"And I loved her. Tasha was a classically trained pianist. Her family had immigrated before the Revolution. Her parents had both died of influenza not long after. She'd stayed in England and had started her own small music conservatory. It was doing quite well—enough to support her while she earned a name as a performer. That's how I met her, actually. She was playing a Rachmaninoff concerto at a local hall one night, and I'd gone on a whim. I couldn't take my eyes off her."

I think about this as I listen to his quiet, even breathing and trace my fingers over his face again. I don't ask him what she looked like, but in my head, I see a tall slim girl with long graceful fingers and wavy brown hair that she weaves into a long braid to keep it out of her face when she's at the piano.

"We were together for three years," he says. "I wasn't always in London, of course. I was still doing what I thought I was supposed to—searching for the girl we needed to save Anastasia. It all still seemed so imminent then—that any second we'd find her. The Revolution, the assassination—they all were still so close in my mind, so vivid. Tasha thought I was traveling on business all those times, and I suppose that wasn't really a lie. But when I'd go back, we'd be together. And then one day—one afternoon—she'd planned a picnic for us. We were sitting on a blanket in a small park not far from where she lived. The sun was shining, and the weather was pleasant, and I honestly don't remember what we were talking about. But what I *do* remember is that she stopped in the middle of what she was saying and looked at me—really looked at me in a way that she never had before. And then, very slowly, she said, 'Do you know that you don't look a day older than that first day I met you?' There was more that we said to each other that day, but I don't remember that either. All I know is that a few weeks later, I left her note telling her that I wouldn't be back. Because what else could I do, really? That's how I saw it then. I couldn't tell her, and I couldn't stay and not tell her, so I left."

"That's it? You *left*? You really never saw her again?" I hate how shocked my voice sounds when I say it, but it's just so sad. And it's more than sad, but I don't want to go there. Could I leave someone like that, even if I knew I had to? What does it say about Ethan that he could do that, give up on love like that? Or did he just feel he really had no choice?

He's silent for a while. "Those were different times," he says eventually. "I was different. I—I truly believed that I was bound to some higher cause. That the path I'd chosen obligated me to certain sacrifices that were simply inevitable. So yes, I left. But I did come back, actually. I did see her. She just didn't see me. The first time was a few years later. She'd married and had a daughter by then. The last was not long before she died. She was eighty years old by then. I—well, I hadn't planned on seeing her. It had been a long time since I'd been in London, and I never imagined that our paths would cross. Except they did. The lobby bar of the hotel I was staying at had live music in the evenings. A woman in her late thirties or even early forties sat down to play that night. She had long brown hair in a braid that hung down her back. And she looked right at me and smiled. She looked so much like Tasha that for a few seconds, I couldn't move. Then an older woman walked in. And the woman at the piano rose and hugged her. 'Nana,' she called her. 'Nana, I'm so glad you could come hear me tonight.' The older woman had been Tasha. She'd grown older just like I should have, but couldn't and—well, that's my story. Have I taught you the word *zalupa?* Idiot. Dickhead. That's me."

I don't push him to tell me more, even though my mind is brimming with questions. What if he'd been honest with her? Wouldn't she have found a way to deal with it? But it's easy to say stuff like that when you have no idea if it's possible. I ponder telling him about Ben and me, about why I first liked him. But the story seems so small and so typical. Girl likes guy for all the wrong reasons. Guy likes girl. Girl's heart—and her wacky, uncontrollable super powers—lead her somewhere else. Breakup follows—still to be announced. The only thing I know for sure is that I can't judge Ethan on his choices.

Based on mine, I could also be considered a—what did he just say? *Zalupa*.

Instead, I surprise myself again and say, "When my brother died, I thought I'd break in two. I know I've told you about it some. But I—I'd walk into his room and sit on his floor and just cry until I didn't have any tears left. It didn't help that my mom just kind of checked out for a while. Oh, she still got up every morning and made coffee and talked to me while I ate my break-fast. And she still went to work at the Jewel Box. But sometimes, when I would tell her about my day, I knew she wasn't listening. Not really. It was like she was there and not there at the same time. My dad—well, he just kept on going, the same as always. I suppose he just didn't know what else to do. I mean, what else *do* you do, really? I guess he figured that my mom would just deal somehow. And he was sort of right, but not really. She just pretends a lot. I don't know if she'll ever truly get over it."

Ethan sighs and pulls me to him again. "She won't. You know that, right? It'll become easier—maybe. I suspect it has. But she won't get over it, Anne. Just like you won't. Just like I've never—"

"I know." Talking about it makes my chest feel tight. All things in our family seem to circle back to David. But Ethan reaches up then and strokes my hair, and I kiss him, and he kisses me, and then I'm happy when we stop talking for a while.

In fact, we're so busy doing things that don't include talking that it takes a few minutes for the sound of running water to register in either of our brains.

"Is that the shower?" My skin prickles in a way that lets me know this is not good at all.

Ethan presses his hand over my lips. "Shh. Let me listen."

But he's off the couch and headed toward his bathroom before I can say anything to be shushed about.

The hardwood floor is cold under my bare feet as I follow him.

"Stay behind me." Ethan's voice is low, and he holds up a hand to signal me to stop.

The shower sound is distinct. My pulse kicks into high gear as we reach the bathroom door—the one I'm sure was open earlier. My hands—the same ones Ethan had been kissing not long ago—tingle with a sudden burst of energy. Terrific. Maybe whatever has chosen this moment to take a shower in Ethan's bathroom will let me heal a shaving cut or something. As if on cue, I hear a rustling, like someone—something—is moving slowly toward the door. Toward us.

"Do you smell that?" It's the salty odor of seawater. My dream rushes back to me: My brother lying on the floor. Baba Yaga telling me what I can do to ease my mother's pain. The rusalka pointing up toward Viktor. *"And then you cursed me! He doesn't know what you did. But I do. I know the truth. I won't forget. I can't. I gave her up. And look where it got me."* In my dream, this is what she said. *I gave her up.* Who did she give up? Something as frightening as the prospect of opening the bathroom door begins to rise in my chest.

Ethan turns the handle and slowly pushes the door open. A cloud of steam escapes the small tiled room. The saltwater smell grows stronger. If my eyes were closed, I'd think I was at the edge of the sea.

Through the fog of steam, I can make out the water running full blast in the glassed-in shower. Fingers of mist drift into the hallway, sifting around us. "Do you see her?" My question gets swallowed up in the billows of gray steam.

It's the rusalka who answers me, rising from nowhere and sliding her way through the narrow doorway, her lilac dress hanging heavily on her, dripping water onto the floor. "Of course he sees me. But when he looks closer, perhaps he won't want to. It is as I have told you, my sweet, my dearest. I cannot do this on my own. You must see for me. You must fix what needs to be fixed. This is a burden, I know. But you must carry it. It is your destiny. It is what is coming, whether you are willing to see it or not. Look at me. Please. Do not turn away. Secrets within secrets. Life within life. Life within me, passed down to you."

Look at me. Her words spark something else from my dream. *Don't look at her*, the Ethan in my dream had told me. But why? What is it about her that I just can't see?

"*Kak vas zovut?*" Ethan asks her like he did at the pond. "What is your name? What do you want?" He's gripping my arm so tightly that he's cutting off my circulation.

She doesn't answer us. She just stands there, shoulders slumped sadly, her dress in tatters, her wild hair dotted with wet sparkles as the fog settles on it.

"*Kak vas zovut?*" Ethan repeats. "We can help you if you tell us your name."

The rusalka sighs sadly and stares at me with storm gray eyes. The shape of them looks familiar. So does the slight tilt of her full lips and something I hadn't noticed before—the sprinkling of freckles across the bridge of her nose. They stand out starkly against her pale skin and her dark hair, her sharp jawline and slender build. Confusion jolts through me. I see now why it was so easy for her to mimic my mother's appearance. Not only does she look a little like me, but if her hair had auburn streaks and her eyes were brown, she could be my mother.

"*Kak vas zovut?*" Ethan says a third time. My heart is pounding. It's so humid that each breath is like taking a sip of water.

Ever so slightly—as she had at the pond—the rusalka stands a little taller, straightens her thin shoulders. That motion again. So very much like my mother. An idea rises in my brain. Is it possible?

I'd tried to find her now and then since last fall, but not one email, not one website yielded anything. Back then, my heart had hoped that she would be looking too, still trying to find the daughter she'd given up: the woman I call mom. It was only a few weeks ago that I'd finally decided that Lily, my mother's birth mother, just didn't want to be found.

It had never once occurred to me that just when I finally stopped searching, she'd find me instead.

In my head, I see Professor Olensky in his office last fall, showing us the letter from the woman named Nadia Tauman—the one who swore her friend was descended from the Romanovs. Her friend who was my birth grandmother, who'd given up my mom for adoption.

I peer at the rusalka through the mist. And with a quick intake of breath, I finally understand.

"Oh, my God!" I shout at the rusalka. "I know who you are! You're Lily, aren't you? Oh, my God, you're Lily! You're my real grandmother! And you're a mermaid. Every single time I think my life can't get any weirder, it does. My grandmother's a Russian mermaid." I stop before I add the part about how she also tried to kill my boyfriend—correction: ex-boyfriend, even if he doesn't know it yet.

Still gripping my arm, Ethan looks at me sharply. The

141

rusalka doesn't answer. She just smooths her wild dark hair with bony fingers.

I wait for Ethan to tell me I'm crazy, that I've got it wrong. *Anne, you're an idiot. How can a crazy Russian mermaid be your grandmother? Isn't your family dysfunctional enough, what with great-great-grandfather Viktor being Tsar Nicholas's wacky illegitimate son who caused my hundred-year immortality problem and Anastasia's entrapment?* Instead, he squints at Lily through the billows of foggy steam.

"I know you," he says slowly. "I saw you once. It was only for a second on the street. But I saw you."

My pulse quickens. "Saw her when?" I glance from Ethan to the rusalka and back to Ethan. Is she really Lily, my grandmother? And he knows her? Excuse me?

"A long time ago. I don't know—it was years ago. The early sixties, I think. I was here in Chicago with Viktor." He flips his gaze back to the woman I think is Lily. "Can you tell me? Is that it? I did see you, didn't I?"

Lily—I decide to think of her as Lily now—nods her head silently. More droplets of water fall to the floor. I'm attempting not to freak out about this sudden collision with Ethan's past. I'd understood in theory that he had one. But other than that Tasha story a few minutes ago, I'd mostly ignored it. It is now officially impossible to ignore. *Where exactly had he seen her? What was she doing? How can she be a mermaid?*

"You know him?" I pry my arm from Ethan's grip and edge closer to her. Tiny scraps of seaweed adorn her hair. Is there seaweed in Lake Michigan? How did she get here anyway? By swimming across the Bering Strait with other Russian rusalkas and sort of magically migrating from Alaska to Chicago? Was she a mermaid when she had my mother? Even for me, this is way too twisted.

"He was one of the last to see me alive." Her voice echoes everywhere, bouncing through the swirling fog. "Did you know that, Ethan? Did you know? I like to believe that you did not. That you were unaware of what your friend was up to. But I'd seen you with him, and so I ran, and only when it was too late, when there was no going back for me, did I stop to think that perhaps he had not involved you."

Lily tilts back her head and laughs.

"You know my name?" Ethan moves next to me again, and we both step even closer to Lily.

"You know mine," she tells him. "It is only fair I tell you that I know yours. He killed me, you know. Oh, not in the way you might think. Not like he killed Misha. Even *that* he didn't do on his own. He sent men after us, but they were fools. They did not care who they shot, as long as they shot someone, and so they shot my Misha. My darling, darling Misha. The father of the baby that was heavy in my belly. Do you know the pain I felt that day? A girl like me? Alone with a child in her womb? Not even a ring on my finger to prove that I belonged to someone? It was too much for me. I was not strong like this girl here. And I did not really understand who had wanted me dead. My sisters explained it later. This was something they understood. To be a rusalka is to grieve. It is to know how men see us. It is to have everything and nothing. The power to seduce and the pain of never knowing love."

"The baby?" I ask her. My voice shakes, and I concentrate to steady it. "That was my mother, right? Is that what you're telling us?"

For one crazy second, I imagine myself trying to explain this to my mother—along with everything else about our family history that she doesn't know.

"I am telling you many things. But I do not know if you are ready to listen." In that instant, she's gone—just a faded shimmering outline in the fog, and then nothing.

We wait. I count off the seconds and try to even out my breathing. "Is she telling the truth?" I ask Ethan. "Did you know her?" *Can she even tell the truth?*

He rubs a hand through his hair. His face is damp from the fog. "Each time we've seen her, she's seemed familiar somehow. But it was a long time ago, Anne. There was no reason to think—it was downtown here. Viktor and I had been—searching. He'd been sure the girl we needed was here. But then late that afternoon, he'd met me at the coffee shop where we usually ate our meals and told me he'd been wrong, that he'd seen the girl, and he knew she was not the one. I had no cause then not to believe him."

"Yeah, and that turned out great, huh?" He smiles grimly at my lame attempt at humor.

"Here's the thing." He walks into the bathroom, reaches into the shower, and turns off the water. I walk in behind and catch a glimpse of the two of us in the foggy mirror: Ethan—tall, lanky, and brown-haired, his blue eyes wary. Me—shorter and very pale. My shirt is plastered to my chest, and my hair is frizzing crazily. I reach up to smooth it, but I know it's pointless.

Ethan sighs. "I never connected that with what I saw later. Viktor said he was meeting someone, and I headed back to my hotel room. It was dark, and some of the streetlights were out. I remember passing a little bookshop, and then as I walked past the alley near the end of the block, there she was, so close that we almost collided. But she stopped short just in time and looked at me. It's her eyes that I really remember. That's what I saw when I was in the pool with her yesterday—those gray eyes. And what I've never forgotten is that when she looked at me, she sort of froze—just stood there staring—and then she turned and ran. It didn't occur to me go after her. I was a stranger, and it was dark, and I assumed she was afraid I was going to rob her or something. She ran around the corner, and that was the last I saw of her. Until yesterday."

"So that's what she means? When she said *your friend*, she meant Viktor? Is it true, do you think? That he's the one who had her husband killed? That he tried to kill her? Because that would mean—"

Ethan sighs again. He takes my hand, and we walk out of the bathroom. We stand there in the hall, both barefoot on the wooden floor. "That would mean that Viktor knew who she was—that he had figured out somehow that she was potentially the one we were looking for."

"So he tries to get rid of her. But they shoot her husband instead, and she somehow gives her baby—my mother—up for adoption. Then at some point later, she sees you, knows you're friends with Viktor, and runs—and then what? She jumps or falls into a river and gets adopted by a band of rusalkas, where she waits until she figures out how to haunt me so I can somehow help her? I'd say it was impossible, but obviously, nothing is impossible anymore."

"Even if it's all true, I don't know what it means. I don't know why she's appearing to you, or what she really wants, or why she's chosen now to ask for it."

He pulls me to him, and I wrap my arms around him. He tucks a stray strand of my hair behind my ear. "If Viktor went after her, it's possible that he knew everything, even then. That somehow he knew she was connected to him. The daughter of—well, what would she be? The daughter of his daughter, most likely." He shakes his head. I can feel the shiver of disbelief travel through his body. But I realize we're both thinking that it was probably true—Viktor's desire for immortality had outweighed everything else in his world.

I'm sorry for the words that blurt out next, but there's no pulling them back in. "You really didn't know? But then why did she run from you? If you didn't know who she was—if you'd never seen her—then why did she look at you like that and run?"

It's as though I've slapped him again.

"You think that I knew what he was up to and just ignored it? That I let her die or become a rusalka or whatever it is that happened to her?"

"No. Well—no. I just want to understand, that's all." *Is that what I think?* I wonder. I said it, but that doesn't mean that I really think it. It just means I'm confused.

"So do I, Anne. And you know what? The man who has the answers isn't about to tell us anytime soon."

I feel a twinge of anger rise. "Well, that's easy, isn't it? Viktor's the one who's trapped now, so that's the end of it, huh? Lily will just hang around trying to off my boyfriends, and you'll just say it isn't your fault, and then what? Hey, maybe next year she can just come to college with me. She can live in the shower in my dorm like some sort of creepy mascot or something. Because you told her that we'd help her, but you don't have a clue how we're going to do that, do you?"

Before he can answer me, the fog thickens again, and Lily—her hair a wild tangle—shimmers back into view. She steps into the hallway with us and reaches out one thin arm to me, palm up. In the center of her palm is a tiny hair clip shaped like a little fan with seed pearls and what look like rubies. It's the kind of thing I see in the Jewel Box all the time, the kind of piece Mrs. Benson loves to bring back from estate sales: small and delicate with lots of pretty detail.

"Take it," she says. "You will know what to do with it when the time is right."

I don't answer her. I'm not about to take anything from her either, grandmother or not.

When I don't reach for the pin, she turns to Ethan. "You must help her understand. She has been to the witch, and she can go back. So much was promised me, and so much was taken. My child. I want her to see me. I want her to hear me. But she cannot until this is over. That is my curse. I gave up what I held most dear, and only when his blood is shed can I have peace. Only then can I rest. I will swim and swim until it is broken. When you saved Anastasia, I thought it would be over. He would become mortal, and somehow his blood could be taken. But he escaped that destiny at the last moment. You thought he sacrificed for her so she could have the ending she deserved. But I think he did not. His sacrifice was a lie."

I'm positive I don't even see her hand reach out, but it does, and the pin is lying in my palm before I can even protest. Lily's fingers are ice cold. So is the palm of her hand as she presses it against mine, the jeweled hair clip between our hands. The clip part digs into my palm hard enough that I wince.

"You must go to the witch and do what I cannot. I cannot cross the witch's stream. I cannot enter her forest. You must promise. I cannot rest until you do. I will not ask you to do the rest. That will come when it will come. But this—this you must do for me."

"Do what?" What could she possibly want me to do?

"Free Viktor."

Oh.

"No way," I begin. But she's gone.

Friday, 8:45 am

Ethan

You know"—Anne flops into a chair at the coffee shop near my apartment—"I really have to find a way for everyone to stop telling me what is or isn't my destiny. It's getting old. And even if this mermaid really is somehow my birth grandmother, does she really think that I'm going to head back to Baba Yaga's and let Viktor go? Because I'm thinking that's not going to happen anytime soon."

I try to formulate an answer. But it's hard to do that when every mistake I've made over the decades has chosen this moment to haunt me—including the one I've made by letting myself love her. Anne Michaelson—the girl sitting across from me, auburn hair tucked behind her ears, face a little too thin, hands clasped together as she talks—the one who gave me back my life. What I feel for her is more than I've felt for anyone— even Tasha Levin, who's buried in a small cemetery in the Lake District outside London and whose grave I've quietly visited over the years. To have this chance to love again—it's more than I deserve. But there's no time to ponder. If the woman I saw for those few seconds so many years ago really was Lily, then Viktor knew more than I ever understood. And I have been a *zalupa* for a very long time.

Anne rests her chin in her hand, and for a moment I think about how it felt to kiss her—about the feel of her body against mine. "You were on the right track earlier when you asked why now," I tell her. "Why has she appeared to you now with this request and not any other time since last fall?"

"So what's your answer to that one? Everything that goes bump in the night just decided to get together and meddle with my life?"

"Don't be flippant about it."

"How else am I supposed to be? What *I* want is to be like that girl over there." She points at a girl in jogging shorts and a T-shirt who's drinking an iced tea and laughing about something with a guy eating a muffin. "Just living my life. Maybe actually going to the movies with you on a normal date, or bowling, or anything that doesn't involve danger and magic and running for our lives. But no. Not going to happen, is it? You and I couldn't even just—oh, never mind." She flushes and then looks down at the table.

Bowling? She wants me to take her bowling?

"Took you long enough to call me. I've got the clothes you asked to borrow." This is how Tess greets us as she breezes into the Coffee Spot, thrusts a plastic drawstring Gap bag into Anne's hands—some spare clothes—and drags another chair to our table. She looks from me to Anne and then back to me, then narrows her eyes. "I really can't leave you two alone for a second, can I?"

It hasn't been my idea to include her—yet again—in this whole mess, but I have yet to come up with a way of keeping her out of it. And as her question doesn't seem to require an answer, we place our coffee orders while Anne brings Tess up to speed about the rusalka.

"So she just materializes right there in Ethan's bathroom in this cloud of steam," Anne tells Tess as I place the drinks on the table. "It was freaky. I mean, one minute we're kissing, and the next—boom, there's a mermaid in the bathroom. And she looks so familiar that I ask her—and this is the part I told you on the phone—if she's Lily. Because that's what she's been hinting about. And then she looks at Ethan and tells him that he should remember her because she's the woman he saw on the street back in the sixties. And that Viktor was the one who killed her Misha. Then she started talking about—"

"Whoa." Tess's eyes narrow even more.

"Anne," I begin, hoping to deflect what's obviously coming next. "You know, we really need to talk about our plan of action. We don't have time to—"

"Whoa," Tess repeats. "You were making out with someone who knew your grandmother when she was young? Doesn't that, like, bother you at all?" She grins. "On the other hand, your grandmother's a mermaid, and she tried to kill Ben. I guess it's all relative, huh?" She snorts out a loud laugh. "*Relative*. Get it? Funny, huh?"

The very long silence that follows indicates that just possibly, it's not that amusing. I take a sip of my swiftly cooling black coffee and think about all the many things that I've done in my very long life that have led to this particular moment. The list seems endless.

"Well, one thing's for sure," Tess adds. "I'm never going to complain about my family again. Because compared to yours, we're really functional. And you thought your Grandma Ellen was a pain. I guess this puts that in perspective too, huh?"

"What's there to complain about?" Anne tastes her latte, then rips open a sugar packet and stirs in the contents. "Your grandmother lives in Lake Forest and gardens and makes needlepoint pillows. She doesn't stalk you when you're kissing someone and tell you about yet another destiny that you don't want."

Tess shrugs. "I guess. Since you brought it up"—Tess shifts her gaze from Anne to me—"here's what I think we should do. Let's finish our coffee, then we'll let you deal with the mermaids, and I'll take Anne to work. What we *won't* do right now is repeat the craziness from last fall. You know—the part where you dropped me off at my house and then took her home, after which the two of you almost killed each other in your dreams, and while you were busy lusting after each other in fantasyland, the professor got murdered. That kind of thing."

I remind myself that she is only seventeen. But the mention of Alex is a low blow.

Anne scowls at her friend. "Do you really think all this is Ethan's fault? I know I say that sometimes too, but—"

"Come on, Anne. It's one thing to have some mermaid haunting you—and I can't stress enough how freakish it is for me to admit that's business as usual. But it's another to have her attacking Ben and giving you gifts and hanging out in Ethan's shower. And you absolutely can't make me believe that this somehow isn't all because he's back." She glowers at me again. "Seriously. Explain to me how this isn't your fault."

I open my mouth to do just that. I'm tired of listening to her and tired in general and—

"Wait." My brain shifts from annoyance—its usual mode around Tess—into actual thought. "As much as I hate to admit it, I think you're right."

"Of course I'm right. I wouldn't have said it if I wasn't right. I'm always—wait a second. How am I right?" Tess manages to look curious and self-satisfied at the same time.

Suddenly, my head is racing with possible connections. "You've been saying that the rusalka's behavior has intensified since I've been back. But it didn't make any sense to me. What did my return have to do with her? Did I really set something else into motion by being near Anne again? And why would that be?"

"Okay. I'm with you, but so?" Tess's tone is still cautious.

I grab a napkin and spread it out. "Give me something to write with." I take the pen that Anne produces from the chaos of her purse. Finally, things are beginning to make sense. There's a pattern we can work from.

"Think about it. This won't answer everything, but I think it's a start." On the napkin, I scrawl the word *rusalka*. "Okay. I need to know every time you've seen her and what exactly she did—what, if anything, seemed to trigger her behavior."

We make the list. There were silent appearances first. At the pond near Anne's house. On the sand near the lake a few days later. Standing by a tree in a rainstorm one afternoon. Always with water nearby. Always wearing the same dress.

"She would just stare at me," Anne says, "then she'd disappear."

"But yesterday," I prompt her. "Yesterday was different."

"Yeah."

"Different how?" Tess frowns, but her tone finally shifts to something less hostile.

"Well, she talked to me, for one. I've told you that. About me and Anastasia and her doll. About how something's coming. And—men. She talked about men."

"She should have talked to me about *that* subject." Tess takes a long slurp from her coffee. "So what was her opinion? Wait, let me guess—it's not good."

"She said someone loves me, but that it wasn't easy. She said it never is for men." Red rises in Anne's cheeks as she glances over at me. "I guess I assumed she meant you. Or maybe Ben, to be honest. No offense, but what she said fits a lot of guys—the whole inability to commit thing. It was really kind of general."

"Yeah," Tess adds, "but it makes sense if the rusalka is Lily, since her boyfriend was killed before they even got married. She had to give up her baby for adoption, so if she thinks it's partly your fault somehow, Ethan, then of course she'd be sort of bitter toward men."

I force myself not to sigh. "Let's go on. So she talks to Anne about men and love. Then she appears at the bottom of the pool, but when Ben dives in to save what he thinks is someone drowning, she pulls him down and tries to hold him there. And the question is, why? Was it only to get Anne's attention?"

"Or was it because it was Ben?" I hear the alarm in Anne's voice. "If that's the case, was it because he's a guy? Or is it specifically because it was Ben?"

"What would that mean?" Tess asks. "That your mermaid grandmother has a grudge against Ben? But why? She doesn't even know him. It doesn't make sense. Or maybe it does. If she's your grandmother, she probably feels like she should have an opinion."

"Hmm. Maybe that's *exactly* what it means." Anne grabs the napkin and pen and scribbles a few more ideas. "I was so freaked when I left Ben's last night that I didn't really think about it. But Ben—okay, no one judge me here; it's been a confusing day or so—Ben kissed me. And that's exactly when the rusalka appeared again. But he couldn't hear her, I don't think. Only I could. And she was talking about men again. How Ben would get over something. And how men forget so easily. Not like women. She said she tried to show me something, but that her body doesn't always do what she wants it to do."

This I understand. At least, in part. "It's a spell," I tell the girls. "It's got to be some sort of spell. Maybe specific to her condition as a rusalka. Maybe something else. But there's a force controlling her will. If she's telling the truth."

"That's a big *if*, Ethan." Anne blows out a breath. "A huge *if*. What if she's not? What if she's just lying? I mean, how do we really know?"

"We don't." I put my hand on hers again and hold it there because I like the way she smiles at me when I do. "Not yet. But let's go on. There was nothing else until she appeared to the two of us earlier this morning?"

Anne shakes her head. "No."

"So let's focus on this morning. She didn't appear in the evening. Even when our magic combined, we didn't see her."

"You mean when we flew?"

"You *flew?*" Tess shakes her head. "You know, if you want me to back off, telling me stuff like this isn't going to cut it."

"We hovered," I correct Anne. "It was hovering."

"Whatever." Anne shrugs. "The point is, we didn't see her—not until later. But after we—well, after we kissed, that's when she appeared. Not randomly. She appeared because the two of us were together. That changed things for her somehow."

I nod. "I agree. But in folklore, rusalkas are seductresses. That's their curse. They can't have what they want—maybe they've been scorned or murdered by a lover or lost a child or just lost hope and walked into some body of water hoping to end it all. So they seduce instead. Except Lily doesn't seem to fit that pattern exactly. Maybe because you're not the one who's hurt her. Or maybe she's just so desperate for you to help her that what she wants overrides what she's become."

"So she does stuff in spite of herself? Is that what you're saying?" Tess furrows her brow. "That even though she might not want to act like rusalkas are supposed to, she does rusalka stuff anyway? She lures Ben to the bottom of the pool and makes herself look like Anne's mom so we'll follow her to the water. And goes all *Fatal Attraction* every time Anne locks lips with someone?" Tess turns and angles her chin at me. "Except—wait a second. What about you in this whole scenario, Ethan? You'd be the perfect one for her to go after. But she really hasn't, has she? As far as I can tell, she hasn't tried to lure you to do anything."

"That's not the point, Tess." Anne shakes her head.

"Actually, I think it *is* kind of the point. She wants you to find a way to let Viktor go. She doesn't seem to like Ben, although that might be just because he's a guy and she thinks guys suck. And if what she says is true, she wants to see your mother again, which makes sense if your mom is really her daughter. But what about Ethan? What does he want from him? Let's face it, Anne. All this stuff—all the way back to Baba Yaga, Viktor, and Anastasia—it all ties in to you, but it ties in to him too. So why not this also? Which means that even though we might not know what it is, she's got to want *something* from Ethan."

As always, I hesitate to admit she's right. But she is.

"See?" Tess adds when neither Anne nor I respond immediately. "You agree." She turns to Anne. "He agrees."

"Do you?" Anne pulls her hand away from mine. "Why? She hasn't followed you anywhere. She hasn't pulled you into the water. She hasn't offered you anything. Not like she did to me." She grabs her purse and extracts the rusalka's fan-shaped hair clip, places it on the table. "She made me take this. Told me I'd know what to do with it when the time was right. But if you agree with Tess, Ethan, then what does she want from you?"

I don't answer. I have no answer to give. Unbidden, the image of the girl from my village—so many years ago—returns to me. How old was I then? Seven? Eight, maybe? While Anne and Tess sip their coffees, I tell them my rusalka story.

Her name was Lena. For the longest time, I told myself that I'd only imagined what I saw that day down by the stream—and what I saw a few days later, and a few days after that. Maybe that was why I was so open to learning magic later on—once that veil is lifted, there really is no putting it back. I'd been hungry that day—not enough food in our house, and a lot of mouths to feed—and so I was down at the river trying to catch a fish or two when Lena's father found her.

I didn't see him walk to the water's edge. There was a small curve in the shoreline there, and he was just out of my range of vision. I'd been concentrating on spearing a small fish with a stick when I heard him cry out—a deep, ragged wailing that startled me and made me drop my stick. What I remember most is that I was angry. I was hungry, and whoever it was had made me lose my potential supper. And then I saw them. Lena's father was kneeling at the water's edge, his face ashen. And Lena—she was floating in the water, her long blond hair fanning out around her like pale snakes. She was dead. Peter, the blacksmith's son, had the bad fortune to get her pregnant and then die of influenza when she was about three months along. I'd seen Lena muttering to herself the past few weeks—her face streaked with tears, her hair often uncombed and matted, her clothes dirty. But there she was, floating dead, her father weeping uncontrollably on the shore.

I also remember what happened next. He stood up—this huge bear of a man who I knew was responsible for the purple bruise on Lena's cheekbone, because in a small village, not much goes unnoticed—and began to wade into the stream to retrieve his daughter's body. Even now, I don't think he ever really knew I was there, watching. So he didn't know that I witnessed the rest of it. How Lena sat up in the shallow water, her blond hair dripping. How she grinned at him with sharp teeth. Or how the creatures that I later learned were rusalkas reached up their hands and pulled her under and away. I turned and ran, heart pounding crazily in my chest, until I'd reached home, where I might be hungry, but at least I felt safer.

I never told my family what I'd seen. I was too afraid that it would come find me. It was the first time I knew that there were things beyond the regular world. It was the first time I wondered if there was something other than death. Maybe, I think now, that really was the beginning of my own journey. Not my parents' death. Not meeting Viktor. But my sight of this nineteen-year-old girl whose body never made it to a grave.

Later, the story was that wolves had dragged her off—that she had drowned herself, and when her father pulled her from the water, the wolves had come from the forest and taken her. But the women in the village—the ones who sometimes drank tea at our kitchen table with my mother—they whispered otherwise. Rusalkas, they said. "The water sisters have taken *her. Perhaps it is for the best." No one talked much about the rest of it—about the series of drownings that happened for months afterward. Always men. Always of the same height and build as Lena's poor dead Peter. And then one day, they found Lena's father floating facedown in a shallow stream at the edge of his land. No one ever knew how it happened. A huge man like that, dying in a stream? But it doesn't take much to drown.*

"Do you really think she wants something from you, Ethan? This rusalka, Lily?" Anne asks again.

"I don't know." I run my fingers over the little hair clip lying on the table. "I think Tess is right. I think there are connections within connections, like Lily told you—stories within stories. Some will be true, but not all of them. I think it comes down to two things—she blames Viktor for what's happened to her and for the loss of her daughter, and she seems protective of you, especially when it comes to men, including me. What she'll do about either of those, I don't know."

"And yet she hasn't lured you into Lake Michigan." Tess grins at me. Anne flashes her a look of annoyance.

"So what now?" Anne's annoyance shows in the tone of her voice. "Do we just wait until she makes an appearance again? And if she does come back, then what? Go back to the forest and help Viktor escape so she can get vengeance on him? Why would I do that? Maybe he did what she said he did. Maybe she's lying. You're the only other one who was there, and you don't even know. Maybe what she really wants is to hurt you somehow. Or hurt my family. Or me."

She picks up her cup, then puts it back on the table

without drinking. Her voice gets softer. "There's something else. Let's say Viktor was responsible for her death. Okay. But I'm sitting here right now because of him. Because when your Brotherhood's stupid spell still compelled her to take a Romanov, he offered himself to Baba Yaga. That means he not only let Anastasia go back to die with her family, it means he went with the witch instead of me. Baba Yaga could have taken me, Ethan. We never talk about that, you and I. But it's the truth. Viktor's trapped there now, and I'm here living my life. So maybe I don't care what she's asking me to do. Maybe I don't want to know if it's true or a lie. Because even if Viktor did everything the rusalka said he did, the way I see it, he still sacrificed himself for me. I can't forget that part. I just can't."

"You can't feel guilty about that," I tell her softly. But I know that she does.

Over at the counter, the baristas call out some more orders and loudly steam milk for lattes. The hiss and chug of the cappuccino machines is background noise. A tall, slim, gray-haired woman chats with the barista at the register. Other customers have continued to come and go while the three of us have sat here, the rusalka's hair clip on the table between us.

Anne rests her elbows on the table and holds out her hands. Slowly, a shimmering of blue and white appears on her palms, flickering and sparking just beneath the surface. "Lily keeps telling me I'm supposed to heal someone. What if she's lying? What if that's not what I'm really supposed to do with all this power? What if I heal the wrong person and end up hurting someone else? I can't do that again, Ethan. I saved you, but I helped Anastasia go back to die. I can't do something like that again. It's too much. It hurts too much."

She places the hair clip in the palm of her hand. The rubies and pearls sparkle in the glow of the fading energy beneath her skin. "Maybe we should just leave this here when we go—let someone else have it. Lily told me I'd know what to do with it when the time was right, but maybe we'd all be better off if I just left it here."

Hair clip in hand, Anne pushes from the chair, strides over to the couple we'd noticed earlier—the girl in the jogging shorts and her boyfriend. "Here." Anne sets the little jeweled fan on their table. "It's your lucky day. Wear it. Sell it. Give it to someone. Your choice. I'm done with it."

I move in behind her and scoop the clip off the table. "Excuse her. She's not quite herself today."

"I absolutely *am* myself. And this is what I want to do. Just because you and I—well, it doesn't mean that you're suddenly the boss of me."

Keeping my hand on the small of her back, I nudge Anne back to our table, collect her things and Tess, and head to the door. She protests only slightly.

"Great. Now I'm beginning to sound like a two-year-old. Did I actually just say, 'You're not the boss of me'?" Anne mutters once we're outside. She swipes at her hair, pushing it behind her ears. "Plus, my hair is really gross, isn't it? On top of everything else, I couldn't wash my hair because I was afraid the mermaid would pop in again while I was taking a shower."

When I laugh, she punches me in the arm. Hard. But still she lets me pull her into a hug. I ignore the fact that Tess is still standing on the sidewalk next to us and press my lips to Anne's hair. "Your hair is fine," I whisper to her as I hold her against me. "And you'll be fine. We'll be fine. I'm in this with you, Anne. Whatever it is that you have to do, I'm here. Know it. Believe it. You need to believe it'll be okay."

Her humorous tone disappears. "Promise me," she says. "Ethan, you have to promise. Maybe last fall, I just didn't know enough to be really scared. But this time, I am. Promise me that it will be okay, that you won't leave again before it's over—even if you have to lie right now. Promise."

"I promise," I tell her. "I promise." And I wonder—even as I tell her that I've got some things to do, but I'll call to check on her in a couple of hours—how it is possible to mean something and still feel like I'm not telling the truth.

Friday, 10:16 am

Anne

It's Tess who drops me off at the Jewel Box. My mother and I are scheduled to work the same hours today, and she thinks I've spent the night with Tess. Correction: she thinks I've spent the night with Ben but lied to her. She is, of course, right about the last part.

"So." Tess pulls up to the curb. She slams on the brakes hard enough that I lurch forward and the seat belt tightens. The little pine tree air freshener she insists on dangling from the rearview mirror rocks back and forth. Either she's in a hurry to get rid of me, or she's got some kind of agenda. "No more Ben? For real?"

"I think so."

"You good with that?"

I nod. "Yeah. Weirdly I am. I like Ben so much, Tess. I really do. You know that. But Ethan's just—I don't know. But there's something different there, and I—yes. Done with Ben. Just need to tell him, obviously. Which is so not going to be easy. Am I horrible? Crazy? Wait, don't answer that."

"Crazy, maybe. Horrible? Never. But it *is* weird, you know, right? You macking on this guy who's old enough to be—well, whatever he's old enough to be, even if he is undeniably hot and starting over again at eighteen."

"He's not just some guy. He's Ethan. He's—"

Tess puffs out an impatient breath and taps her fingers on the steering wheel. "Yeah, yeah. He's Russian perfection. I get it. He's back two seconds, and suddenly, you're breaking up with Ben, getting chased by a mermaid and making spreadsheets so you can track the crazies. Business as usual."

There's an edge to her tone that worries me. Not that she's incorrect on some level. Things have unfolded quickly between Ethan and me. Maybe too quickly. Maybe so quickly that it's possibly a good thing that Lily popped out of the bathroom when she did. But there's something else under her comment—except it's Tess, so I know better than to push her. I just roll my eyes and wait. I don't have to wait long.

"I broke up again with Neal last night. I texted him while I was at the movies with my brother." She says it like it's no big deal, but I know it is. Some of her blond hair has come loose from the single braid that's hanging down her back, and she twists the strand around one finger.

"Why?"

"It was just time. I'm better than that. I can't keep taking him back and worrying that he's cheating or whatever."

I stay quiet—partly to let her say what she needs to, and partly because her words remind me of what I'm doing to Ben.

But Tess isn't my best friend for nothing. "You know I didn't mean it like that," she says. "I didn't mean to imply that—"

I lean over the gearshift and hug her. "I know. But it's true. I just cheated on Ben. When I break things off, he's going to be hurt. And angry. And for good reason. But if you're sure you need to break up, then that's what you should do." Said by the girl who isn't really sure what she's feeling anymore.

Tess nods. "Very sure."

"Okay, then. We'll talk more later. Or sooner, if Mrs. Benson fires me this morning for cutting out on her. I'll let you know how it goes."

I grab my purse. I'm already ten minutes late for work, and after yesterday's little disappearing act, I'm really pushing things if I want to keep this job.

Tess puts her hand on my arm. "I don't want you to get hurt. And I think you're going to."

I know she means well, but the words still cut deep. Why does she assume that something will go wrong? Worse yet, why do I think she might be right?

"Ethan won't hurt me, Tess."

"Maybe not on purpose. But c'mon, Anne. Think about it. He's back one day, and already you're dumping Ben for him. One day, Anne. I know it feels like longer when he's around. I know that. It's like whatever happens between the two of you happens in some sort of overdrive. God knows, I can't judge people's choices in guys. But—well, when it comes to Ethan, you don't think straight. And that *isn't* like you. That's why I love you so much. You always think straight. Me—I'm a mess. You're not. You're way stronger than I am—than anybody I know, especially about the whole guy thing. Don't make a face when I say it. It's true. If I was like you, then I wouldn't have ever gone back with Neal. So maybe Ethan won't hurt you. But that doesn't mean you won't get hurt."

She's got her pit bull expression going, and I know better than to argue with her. "Did you notice that I'm not commenting on how you broke up by text?"

Tess laughs. "It was easier that way. Definitely limited his response to just a few choice words. And I don't want to argue. I just want you to be careful."

"I will. You'll see. *Careful* will be my middle name."

Tess shakes her head. I pretend not to see. I just say goodbye and hoist myself out of the car. I nod when she says she'll come check on me at noon after teaching her ballet class.

She's right, of course. But what does that mean? Lily loved her Misha, but that didn't stop them both from being hurt. My family loved David, but that didn't stop him from dying. Ethan loved the girl named Tasha, but he had to leave her. Ben loved me, but I've never loved him back—I just pretended to love him because he makes me feel secure, which isn't the same as love at all. People love each other, and people get hurt. It's just the way things are. But what Tess has said to me lingers in my brain. Is acting on what I feel for Ethan something I normally wouldn't do? It's a scary thought and not one I'd like to examine too carefully right now.

My mother—dressed in a white three-quarter-length-sleeved blouse and khaki skirt, her auburn hair hanging loose to her shoulders—is setting up a display of vintage gemstone bracelets when I walk in the door. Her face breaks into a smile when she looks up and sees me, then turns serious before I've crossed the room to the counter where she's standing. I realize that I haven't changed clothes; I'm holding the bag Tess brought me and still wearing the jeans and tank from last night. Mrs. Benson has not yet arrived. Suddenly, I'm thinking that it might be easier dealing with stalker mermaids and my confused feelings for a certain formerly immortal Russian than it will be to deal with my mother.

"You're late."

"Sorry. Just a little. Tess dropped me off." I say this like it will explain everything. It doesn't. "And I'm sorry about how I left yesterday," I add because I realize that I am. "I'm sorry I yelled at you and Daddy."

My mother presses her lips together. "I'm sorry you did too," she tells me after a few beats of silence. I watch her scan me and resist the impulse to smooth my less than stellar hair. "What's that?" She points to the bag.

"Tess loaned me some clothes so I didn't have to take the time to go home. We wanted to go for coffee." *And some of that is even the truth.*

"You and Tess? At Java Joe's?" She gestures across the street to the place Tess and I normally meet.

"Yes, Mother. Me and Tess. And, um, Ethan, actually. We went to that place over in Evanston—Coffee Spot. The one off Orrington near NU." So what if I'm leaving out a few crucial details?

My mother tilts her head and observes me. She's still holding a topaz and silver bracelet in her hand, but she seems unaware of that at the moment. "And Ben? You left last night with Ben." She's clearly not leaving interrogation mode anytime soon.

"Yeah, but Ben—well, I don't know what's going to happen with Ben and me."

"Meaning?"

"Meaning I don't know. Meaning I'll let you know when I do." If there's some middle ground between guilt and annoyance, I'm standing in it.

A million years ago, I was the person who told my mother almost everything. We were one happy tell-it-all family. Even last fall, when my world had turned upside-down, she'd sat on my bed and asked me what was wrong. Now we do this dance instead. Tell a little; withhold the rest. Not just me, but her too. To prove my point, I ask her, "So where were *you* yesterday? When you weren't here?"

With a slow precision of motion, Mom arranges the topaz bracelet with the others on a royal blue velvet display cloth, then tucks them all into the glassed-in showcase under the counter. She pulls the stretchy key chain off her wrist and locks the display door. Only the less expensive costume pieces ever sit out. The real stuff stays under lock and key.

"I needed a day. I went into the city. Walked Michigan Avenue. Did a little window-shopping. Actually bought your father a tie for his birthday. I know he's told us he doesn't want any more ties, but this one—I'll show it to you. It's silk and—"

I don't want to be angry with her, but the anger rises in me anyway, which is totally hypocritical, since she's definitely not the only one in the room with secrets.

"You know what, Mom? I don't care about the tie. You could have bought a tie half a mile from here at the mall. Daddy won't know the difference, and you know it. This is not about your need to go tie shopping when you're supposed to be at work."

"I don't appreciate your tone, Anne." She slips out from behind the counter. The heels of her peep-toe pumps click on the shiny wooden floor as she walks around to me.

"I didn't realize I had one." I stare at my mother and think about how very much she looks like Lily. Can I believe that? Or is it just a trick, a magical shifting of molecules meant to confuse me? She stares back. Her eyes are brown, not rusalka gray, but the shape really is the same.

Mom reaches out and pushes some stray strands of my unwashed hair off my face. "Sweetie, did Ben do something?" It's the oldest mom trick in the world. Change the subject from her own issues to mine. Still, the concern in her voice is real. "Is that what this is about?"

"Ben didn't do anything, Mom. Ben is just fine."

"Because if he's—or if you two are thinking about… Well, if you're ready to—um, if that's what this about, then—"

Fabulous. We're about to embark on the safe sex talk, or possibly the "Are you still a virgin?" conversation. Ironically, either would be easier territory than, *Hey, Mom, did you know your birth mother is now a mermaid?*

"God, no. I mean—no, Mom. Ben and I aren't—well, it's not that I haven't thought about it…"

"Well, of course I know you've thought about it. You're seventeen. I just wanted to—"

"Mom. I promise I'll tell you if I decide to have sex, okay?" I sigh. I actually don't know that at all, but it sounds better than anything else I can come up with. My mother's a whiz at diverting me anytime I poke too hard at her own issues, which are always the same: David died. She feels guilty. She's grieving. She's going through the motions and not moving on. Of the things she's done lately that haven't been predictable, this part always is.

"So now tell me." I glance at the clock. It's almost ten-thirty, but there's not a customer in sight—nothing to interrupt our little mother-daughter mini-drama. "What's going on with you? All this cutting out of work and shopping or whatever. You don't even like shopping, Mom."

My mother shrugs and rubs a finger over an imaginary spot on the pristine counter. "I've been having these dreams," she says, and my stomach does an unexpected flip. I think of last fall—of her telling me how she used to dream she was Anastasia.

"Oh?" It's so not what I expected to hear that my voice quavers on that one tiny word.

"It's silly, Anne. Really, it's nothing."

I could leave it at that. She's given me an out. But I don't. I can't. "Dreams aren't silly. At least not to me."

"Well, that's sweet, honey, but it's just so—I'm underwater. And there's a woman with long black hair, and she's holding my hand and swimming with me. When I look into her face, I feel like I should know her. We swim deeper and deeper, and I keep thinking she wants to tell me something. But she never does. And just when I think I'm going to run out of breath, she lets me go, and I wake up. I know it's just a dream—but it feels so real. Crazy, huh?"

The connection between my brain and my tongue feels severed.

"I just keep thinking it's a message or something," Mom goes on. "I know that sounds absolutely out there, Anne. My God, don't ever tell your father. He's worried enough about me these days. To tell the truth, I don't even know why I'm telling *you*."

The last part hurts. Is this how it is now? Me not telling her my secrets, and her feeling that she can't talk to me?

"You can tell me stuff, Mom. Believe me when I say you can tell me. I am seriously the perfect audience for weird."

Mom's brow wrinkles. "Oh? And what is it exactly that gives you all this weirdness experience?"

Gosh, Mom, where do I begin? Oh, that's right. I don't. But I have

to say something about the dream, something that might—
"Who do you think she is?" I blurt out. "The woman in the dream?" The one who's clearly your mermaid birth mother.

I can see my mother hesitate, like what she wants to say will sound so odd that she doesn't feel comfortable saying it.

"Someone you know?" I prompt her.

Mom looks startled. "Now why would you—? Yes. Well, sort of. That's the strange thing. When I dream it, I'm absolutely convinced that she's someone close to me—like a relative. Someone who knows all about me. And she's in such pain. It's hard to explain. I just know that she cares about me somehow. I know it's ridiculous to let a dream upset me, but it just brings up all sorts of emotions. David's death…and other things."

"Things like Lily, right?" I go ahead and blurt that out too. We haven't talked about Lily since that night I'd come back from Professor Olensky's—the night I'd learned our line of descent and how it connected through my mom.

Mom looks at me with a combination of relief and nervousness. She nods. "Okay, maybe you *do* understand more than I was giving you credit for. But I'm a grown woman. I've known I was adopted all my life. Why would I suddenly now be dreaming about some woman who makes me think about my birth mother?"

"Maybe she's thinking about you too. Did you ever think of that?" Suddenly, my mouth seems to have developed a mind of its own. *I'll tell her everything*, I think, *just get it over with and tell her.* "Maybe she wonders how you are. Maybe she wants to know. Stuff like that happens, Mom. I mean, have you ever tried to find her? Do you want to find her? People do that all the time now. Maybe the dream means that you should—"

Tears well up in my mother's eyes. "How in the world did you know that I've started looking? I haven't even told your father. How did you know that? I need a tissue." She sniffles loudly in case I need some encouragement in getting one for her.

I grab my purse from the counter and unearth a crumpled tissue, but when I pull it out, Lily's hair clip comes with it. One of the sharp edges has stuck to the tissue, and I have to pry it off.

"What's that?" Mom blows her nose noisily, then runs her fingers over the hair clip that's now resting in the palm of my hand. "It's beautiful, Anne. Where did you get it?"

I ponder some kind of answer—*It fell from the sky?*—when Mrs. Benson saunters in through the back of the store. "Hey-ho," she calls to us and then stops dead still a few inches from us, the color draining swiftly from her face. She smacks both hands against the cameo pin she almost always wears and clutches it. A tiny *eep* sound escapes her throat.

Behind me, the front door opens, and the bell above gives its distinctive, happy jingle. I turn. It's Ben. He smiles at me, but even from the middle of the store, I can see an anxious wariness in his eyes. The three red welts on his cheekbone— one for each of my fingers that touched him—are faded but still visible. My breath catches in my chest. *Maybe I have it all wrong*, I think. *Ben is steady and kind. How can I break up with a guy who smiles at me like that?*

"Hey," he says quietly. "Hey, Mrs. Michaelson, Mrs. Benson. Can I borrow Anne for just a few minutes? If it's okay?"

Mom looks a little iffy about this. We're in the middle of a moment here that Ben knows nothing about. But it's Mrs. Benson who suddenly looks oddly pale—pale enough to distract me from all things Ben and Mom.

"Are you okay?" I plop the clip on the counter and angle around Mom to Mrs. Benson. "Do you need to sit down or something?"

"Where did you get that?" Her hand shakes as she points to Lily's fan-shaped clip. Her voice trembles. Her face has gone so pale that it's almost bloodless.

My pulse kicks up a notch or two. Make that three or four. Without warning, my hands begin their familiar under-the-skin buzz. The light from the plate glass window behind me dims. I whip around in time to see the sky darken. The wind picks up enough that even inside I can hear it whooshing.

"Was it supposed to rain?" my mother asks. "Look at that sky." And then her voice trails off as she turns her gaze to Mrs. Benson.

"Amelia, what is it?"

"Where did you get that hair clip?" Mrs. Benson asks again. She's looking at me very strangely.

"You really need to sit down." Ben's next to us now, his hand on my boss's shoulder. He guides her to a stool over by the counter, his voice calm but insistent—it's his lifeguard voice. "Your color doesn't look good."

"I—someone gave it to me," I say. It's true. Lily had handed the pin to me, hadn't she? I pluck the thing from the counter, pull back a few strands of my gunky hair, and use it to clip them back. Maybe if I show ownership, she'll calm down. Why is she freaking out about this anyway?

"This is impossible." Mrs. Benson shakes off Ben's hand and rushes back over to me. "Who gave this to you, Anne? Who was it?"

Outside, there's a crack of thunder. Next to me, I feel my mother tense. Since that horrible day last fall, she doesn't do well in thunderstorms. I'm not so good with them myself. The rain starts to pound from the sky—huge drops slamming against the plate glass window so heavily that at first I think it must be hail.

The four of us stand in the middle of the Jewel Box—a triangle of women and Ben in the middle.

The look on Mrs. Benson's face is part intense focus, part shock, and part wonder. "I gave that to her," she says, really more to herself than to the rest of us. "When she told me she was pregnant. Rubies and pearls. Passion and creation. Fire and water. I pinned it into her hair myself."

Overhead, thunder booms so loudly that I clasp my hands over my ears. The store shakes. My pulse is racing; my stomach feels like I'm on a roller coaster. What's forming in my brain makes no sense. Or maybe it makes perfect sense.

"Gave it to who?" I squeak out the question in a voice pitched higher than I want it to be.

"What are talking about, Amelia?" My mother looks from Mrs. Benson to me to Ben. Outside, the sky is almost totally black. Above us, the recessed ceiling lights of the Jewel Box flicker wildly.

"How can *you* have it?" Mrs. Benson is in full-blown freak-out. She points at the fan-shaped pin with its rubies and pearls—right now, I'm pretty sure I shouldn't have taken it, even though Lily insisted. *Take it*, she told me. *You will know what to do with it when the time is right.*

"She drowned herself," Mrs. Benson whispers. "I ran after her, but I didn't get there in time. Her coat was heavy. Her hair got caught. And then—oh, God. I told her it would be okay. I promised her. *Give her up*, I said. *We both know it's the only way to*

174

keep her safe. He won't be able to find her. I told her not to listen to the witch. That it was only lies. She shifts her wild gaze to my mother. I try to swallow, but my throat's gone totally dry.

"What are you saying, Amelia?" My mother's voice is shrill. "What kind of crazy story are you telling? Who are you talking about?"

The sky goes even blacker. The thunder keeps shaking the Jewel Box. A flash of lightning illuminates Mrs. Benson's face—it's pale as death.

"I searched for years for you, Laura," she says to my mother, and for a second, I think my heart actually stops. That's what it feels like—my breath's jammed up and my heart stops beating, and I wonder how it is that I'm still standing. *People without breath or heartbeats should fall down, shouldn't they?*

"I had to make it right. I had to find you. I'd promised Lily that you'd be okay—that it was the right thing to do. I didn't understand until it was too late what was really going on. But then she was gone and you were gone and I had to make it right. I had to find you."

Lily? She knows Lily? How is that possible?

"Find me?" my mother says slowly, her voice still sharp. "Find me? Lily? You mean *my* Lily? My birth mother? How do you know about that? I've never talked to you about that. You knew Lily? Amelia, what is this? Some kind of joke?"

Ben moves to stand next to me. "What's going on?" he whispers. He takes my hand in his, and I let him, because right this second I need something—someone—to anchor me. It's like last fall all over again. I'm tumbling into something that up until this moment, I hadn't even known existed.

"Not sure," I whisper back. It's not even a lie this time.

I don't understand what's happening or how it is that Mrs. Benson is saying all these things.

Ben links his fingers with mine. Would he do that if he knew that I'd been kissing Ethan? And what does it say about me that I'm still so willing to hold his hand? But I can't focus on that right now.

"She was my friend," Mrs. Benson says. "Lily was my friend. Always just a little different. That's how your mother was, Laura." Mom stiffens visibly. Her eyes are wide, and her mouth is open a little, like it wants to form words but doesn't know which ones they should be.

"She knew things. I don't know how she knew, but she always did. She said her mother was like that too. At first, I thought she was just one of those sensitive types—good at reading people, that kind of thing. But it was more than that. Little things happened that were easy to overlook. A dying houseplant that grew stronger after she'd touched it. A breeze that would pick up on a summer day when we were sweltering at the park. I'd see her smile, but I never questioned it. I should have, but I didn't. I just listened and nodded when she'd talk about her mother and her grand-mother. About family secrets. And once—after we'd both had too much wine one night—about how her mother had whispered to her about the Old Ones. About powers. About the old ways of Russia—deep secrets that went back so far that no one really knew their source. And about how her grandmother had told her that nothing was ever as simple as it seemed."

"You knew my mother?" Mom's eyes are huge. "You knew my mother? How can that be? Amelia, do you understand what you're saying? And what does any of this have to do with Anne? Or the hair clip?"

"You need to listen!" Mrs. Benson is shouting now, competing with the thunder—this is not a woman who's ever shouted as long as I've known her. She yanks the cameo and chain off her neck. I see for the first time that the cameo itself is not just flat. It's a locket with a hinge that opens.

"Your mother was pregnant. She and Misha were supposed to marry before anyone found out. It happens, you know. We love who we love, and sometimes it happens. I told her it would be okay. But she kept saying that she had a bad feeling—that something was coming. She'd look behind her when we were out walking, like she expected something to pop up. And I'd turn, and nothing would be there. I thought it was just the pregnancy. Just hormones talking and setting her off. But I should have paid better attention. I should have believed her when she told me something was wrong."

Mrs. Benson's hands shake as she struggles to open the cameo. She's talking so fast that I can barely keep up.

"She was four months along with you when Misha was shot. It was horrible. Lily kept raving about how he was shot because of her. The police said it was a robbery, but Lily kept saying no. Month after month—even the day you were born—she kept telling me that she knew differently. That men had come after Misha because of her, because of who she was. She didn't know what they wanted. She didn't know why. You were just a few hours old, and she was mad with it all by then. I didn't know how to help her, and I still couldn't believe what I was hearing. Even after those things I'd seen her do, I still didn't believe—not really. Who could believe it?

My grandfather had been Russian too, but I'd never heard of things like this. But she was so sure. That's why I gave her the hair clip. Your mother's hair was so lovely—so long and lovely. Her crowning grace, I always told her. I was so foolish. I told her it would protect her. Rubies for her passion and pearls for her pure heart. *Wear it*, I told her. *Wear it for me.*"

Ben reaches up his free hand and touches the clip in my hair. "Is she talking about this? What's this all about, Anne? Does this have to do with what happened last night? When you ran out of my house like that?" I can hear fear in his voice. This unnerves me as much as anything.

The lights above us flicker madly again, and for a moment, the room goes pitch black. When the lights blink on again, I can see Ben searching my face for answers.

Every piece of my crazy world is colliding at once. Well, almost every piece. Ethan's not here—only right now, I wish he was.

"Your mother was certain she was in danger. That you were in danger. You were just hours old, and she was nursing you. You were such a beautiful little baby, Laura. So tiny and pretty! You looked just like her. She kept going on and on about how you weren't safe. *I've tried to go to the witch*, she kept saying. *But I couldn't get there. I couldn't find the forest. I couldn't cross the river. There's a way. I know there's a way. The Old Ones told my mother's mother, and her mother, and the ones who came before her. This is what my own mother told me. If I'm willing to give up what my heart desires most, then I can save her. The witch could help me. But I can't get to her.* It was craziness…but she was so certain. And so I told her the only thing I knew to tell her: give the baby up for adoption. No one will know where she is. It seemed the only solution anyway. I offered to take you myself, but she kept telling me no, that it wouldn't be enough—that I was her friend, and they would find you with me. So there we were. Lily couldn't have taken care of you. She could barely take care of herself. She agreed to the adoption, and the hospital took care of the rest of it. Two days later, they'd placed you in your family and closed the records."

My mother's gone totally silent. Ben is still holding my hand, so tightly now that he's cutting off the circulation to my fingers. Mrs. Benson manages to open the locket's clasp. Inside, there's a tiny picture.

"I didn't believe her," she says to my mom. "Who would believe such things? I thought you were safer gone, and I still think you were. But it ripped her to pieces, and me along with her. My lovely Lily—her husband gone, her baby daughter gone, her mind filled with crazy talk of witches and Old Ones and secret forests that no one could find. I thought that time would heal her. A month passed. Two. Three. I gave her the hair clip. I thought it might remind her that she was still Lily— still beautiful and kind and special."

"You were friends with my mother? Amelia—all this time I've been working for you, and you didn't tell me this?" My mother's forming her words slowly, like she's working all of it out in her head as she talks. "This is what you want me to believe? That my mother talked about witches and was scared that I was in danger—and that's why she gave me up for adoption? And you knew this and never told me? In danger from who? From who-ever killed her lover during a robbery? What the hell is this all about? Why are you saying these things to me? How could you possibly think that Anne is involved in this somehow?"

"It's okay, Mom," I say softly, or as softly as I can and still be heard over the pounding rain, thunder, and lightning. Except it's not okay. Maybe it's never been okay. *Stories within stories,* Lily had said to me. *Secrets within secrets.* Is it really possible that Lily—the human Lily—knew about Baba Yaga? Is that the witch she was talking about to Mrs. Benson back then? If that's so, then did she know? Did she have powers like I do? How did she get them? Was she told that *she* was supposed to save Anastasia? What about her mother? Did she know, too? Did I not know at first only because my mother was taken out of the loop? And how much of this is Ethan aware of? The knot of fear inside me tightens and grows larger. My skin feels cold and clammy.

My mother looks at me sharply, and I think she's about to say something else, but Mrs. Benson doesn't give her a chance.

"I know it all sounds crazy, Laura. Oh, how I know. That's what I thought, too. That's what I'm trying to explain. It was that last day, the day your mother—oh, Laura—the day your mother died."

"Died?" Mom's voice cracks over the word. "When? How? I've tried for years to find out what happened to her. You know that, Amelia. After David's death, I wanted to—well, you know I talked about trying to find her. Are you honestly saying that you listened to me talk about this, and you said nothing? Why? Why would you do that?"

Mrs. Benson is almost shouting now, her gaze flicking wildly from Mom to me to Ben. "Because she was right! Because I saw him that night—the man she was afraid of. It was all those years ago, but I won't ever forget it. I won't ever forget him. I couldn't forget him. Because Lily had given me his picture."

She jabs her finger at the photo in the cameo. "I thought

it was just another of her ravings. She made me swear that I would keep the photo with me—so I would know him when I saw him. Told me some story about a Brotherhood. About men who didn't age. About how her own mother and her mother's mother had whispered stories: a curse on the Romanov family that was somehow connected to her. A secret beyond what even that Brotherhood of men could understand. That they were destined for something that was yet to come. That one of their own blood would betray them and use them, but that even *he* wouldn't really know the truth of who they were, of what they were. She said the witch had warned her mother, and her mother had warned her. That the gift of power came with a price—and she couldn't allow her daughter to pay it."

"Amelia." My mother's voice is urgent. She grasps Mrs. Benson's hands in her own. "You need to calm down. This is madness. All this talk of blood and Brotherhoods and witches—what's gotten into you? How do you even know these things?"

My first impulse is to run. I've been pretending for so long that I can handle all this—the magic and the secrets and being something I never asked to be. But maybe I can't. Maybe I don't want to. My entire world feels like an enormous jigsaw puzzle that's missing a few crucial pieces, and I'm positive that once I slip them into place, everything is going to explode.

"She's crazy," Ben says, loud enough that my mother flashes her gaze on him and frowns. *No crazier than* I *am*, I think. *No crazier than what happened last night at your house.* The tendrils of fear inside me grab me even tighter. I need to say something. I *have* to say something. I can't let her stand there spilling all this stuff and not say something. But what do I dare say?

"What do *you* know?" Mrs. Benson shakes off my mother's hands and moves close to me. Too close. She yanks the fan clip from my hair, and I yelp as she takes a few strands of my hair with it. "How did this come to you? Anne, you have to tell me. We could be in danger. You have to tell me."

"Danger?" My mother's eyes are wild with confusion. She grabs me away from Mrs. Benson. My hand slips from Ben's, and he pulls me back, wedges himself between me and Mom and Mrs. Benson. I appreciate the gesture, but it only seems to make Mrs. Benson more agitated.

"There were two of them that night," she says. She's talking so fast. Word tumbles after word, and when I realize what she's saying—really understand—my heart sinks.

"They were coming out of a restaurant downtown. Lily and I were closing up shop. We both worked at Hyson's Jewelry downtown, and we were open until eight on Thursdays. Lily was still inside locking the cases, and I'd stepped outside to have a cigarette. It was windy that night, and I couldn't get the match to stay lit long enough. The taller man with the dark eyes, he walked right by me, but the other one—so handsome and with these very blue eyes—he stopped and pulled a lighter from his pocket and held it for me. *Thank you*, I told him and that was it. He walked off in the other direction while the dark-eyed man crossed the street to the newsstand. Lily came out of Hyson's, and that's when I realized I'd left my purse inside. I wasn't gone for more than a minute when I heard her screaming.

"*It's him*, she kept saying. She was pointing across the street to the newsstand, and she was pale as a ghost. When she grabbed my arm, her fingers were like ice. She let go of me and pulled at the thin gold chain she'd taken to wearing around her neck." Mrs. Benson holds out the cameo. "She was wearing this under her blouse. She shoved it into my hands, told me this was how she knew, and then she ran. In the time it took me to slip the key from the door, she was already a block ahead of me."

Mom reaches for the cameo. "This belonged to my mother?" Tears well in her eyes. "You wear this every day, and you've never told me this? How could you keep that a secret from me? How?"

Ben's arms are still wrapped around me, and I think he must be able to feel my heart pounding, my blood pulsing in my veins. Everything is unraveling so quickly that I'm dizzy from it—if it weren't for Ben, I think I might just fall. *Ethan had said he'd seen Lily, but Mrs. Benson? Had he really seen her too? Does he know that's who owns the Jewel Box?*

"Let me see." I find my voice and reach for the locket at the same time as my mother. All three of our hands meet—my mother's, Mrs. Benson's, and mine. A tingling shoots through me—my hands? The magic? Something else?—and then I curl my fingers around the cameo and pull it from Mrs. Benson's hand. The thin gold chain trails over my palm. I look at the picture inside. Viktor stares back at me—same dark eyes, dark hair. He's smiling slightly—just the edges of his mouth turned up, as though it pains him to look happy.

For a few dangerous seconds, I'm thrust back into the dreams I used to have inside Anastasia's head. I remember falling asleep on the floor of Professor Olensky's office and dreaming as Anastasia. I felt my half-brother's betrayal—how he used me to gain immortality and said I would save my family.

I remembered that moment when I realized I had trusted the wrong person—that my family was dead, and I was about to be worse than dead. Anastasia's realizations had rushed through me in the dream like they were my own.

"Is that the guy she was afraid of?" Ben asks.

My mother blinks and shakes her head. "I've seen him," she says slowly. "A long time ago, when I was little. Well, sort of." She turns to me. "We talked about that once, remember? I told you that I used to dream I was Anastasia Romanov—that I was her when she died." She points to Viktor's picture in the cameo. "This man—he was with her sometimes. Or she was thinking about him. It's hard for me to remember exactly. When I dreamed about her, I know he was there somehow. But this is all impossible! It was a dream. How can he be in this picture? Did this really come from Lily's mother? My Lily? Is that who I've been—?"

I finish her sentence in my head. *It's who you've been dreaming about. It has to be.* But if she says it aloud, then it will make it all true. Once you learn that things are different than what you always believed, there's no going back. I get it.

I get something else too—at least, I think I do. In my mind, I see Professor Olensky clicking through saved documents on his computer. His wild hair is flopping over his face and Tess, Ethan, and I are waiting for him to find whatever he's looking for. *There was a woman who contacted me a few years ago through one of my colleagues in Prague. Nadia Tauman was her name.* And then he showed us the family tree—Lily's family tree. The one that leads to my mother and stops with me. I don't believe what I'm about to ask, but I ask it anyway.

"Are you Nadia Tauman?" Mrs. Benson's head jerks sharply at

my question, and her eyes widen. "That's how you're Lily's friend. You're not just Mrs. Benson, are you? You're Nadia Tauman—the one who wrote to Professor Olensky. The one who said her friend was the great-granddaughter of Tsar Nicholas."

The expression on Mrs. Benson's face is my answer.

She's screaming at me then, shrill questions echoing over the increasing roar and thud of the thunder. The lightning is coming so fast now that it's illuminating the store with a flashing strobe effect.

"You know? How can you know? I've been so careful all these years—so cautious!" Mrs. Benson holds out her hands to my mother. "I wanted to let you know—so many times. But I couldn't. What happened that day your mother died—she was right. You weren't safe. At first, I couldn't find you, but even when I did, it was safer that you didn't know. And easier for me to believe that none of it was true. Because how could…?"

Mrs. Benson shifts her gaze back to me. "You knew Professor Olensky?" She laughs crazily. "Well, of course. Of course. This is what happens to secrets, isn't it? I told myself if I didn't talk about it, then it would stop being true. But it didn't. I tried to pull her out of the water. I saw her wrestle the coat off at the last minute. I thought I could save her then. But I couldn't. She sank out of reach. I jumped in, but I couldn't find her. There was just her coat. The police thought the current must have taken her, but there was no current. They never found her. I knew it was something else—something more than what I could see. It had to be. But I told myself over and over that it didn't matter, that none of it mattered if her baby was safe. That was the only thing."

Mrs. Benson shakes the fan-shaped clip at me. "So how can

you have her hair clip? How can that be? Because if you have it, then that would mean…"

Ben hasn't loosened his grip on me, and this both comforts me and fills me with fear. He really shouldn't be here. Something is going to happen, and it's going to be bad, and Ben is going to be in the middle of it. This is what I tried to avoid when I ran from his house last night. But it's going to happen anyway. Like when this very store collapsed and almost killed my mother. I didn't understand what I was doing then, and guess what? I still don't.

"Then last fall—it was real, wasn't it?" Mrs. Benson says. It's as though she's plucked the image out of my head. "What I thought I saw before the store collapsed? I told myself that it couldn't be real, that you weren't standing there with those same two men and the girl in the white dress, that the shadow I saw overhead wasn't what I thought. I saw a witch that day, Anne. Just like Lily told me. Baba Yaga, the witch she wanted to help her. The one she couldn't find. I thought she had gone mad from grief and fear. I knew that witch from stories. Everyone's Russian grandmother tells her the story of Baba Yaga, her iron teeth and removable hands and the hut that stands on chicken legs. They tell us to scare us. The witch in the forest who will eat up bad little girls. But it's just a story. A fairy tale."

"What shadow? What men? A girl in a white dress? A witch? Like the one on those lacquer boxes you used to stock? What are you talking about? Wasn't it lightning, freak lightning, that hit the store last fall? Professor Olensky? The one who was killed? You knew him? I thought only your friend Ethan knew him." Some of these questions come from my mother. Some come from Ben.

Everyone's talking at once, and it's hard to even think. I pry the fan-shaped hair clip back from Mrs. Benson and shove it in my pocket. My hands tingle and glow—but maybe that's just because of the strobe lightning. I thought this was all over when Anastasia went back to die. But it isn't. Maybe it never will be. If Ethan's idea is right, and this power inside me isn't from the Brotherhood's magic like everyone has always thought, then maybe this will never be over until I find the source.

That's the thing about destiny. Once it chooses you, you end up feeling like you really don't have any other choice but to follow, even if you've been hiding from it.

"We've got to get out of here," Ben says.

"I know. I know. I—wait. Ben—oh, shit, Ben. Just don't be scared, okay?" He's looking at me like I've gone totally crazy, and maybe I have. "I think I can—well, I've got to do this. I don't think there's any other way."

"Got to do what? What are waiting for? Let's bolt."

He pulls me toward the back of the store, but I shake him off and do the only thing I know to do. I stop hiding.

"Baba Yaga!" I shout over the thunder that's now so loud my body is vibrating with it. "Baba Yaga! Are you out there? Do you hear me?" I don't know if she does. She's come to me, and I've come to her in my dreams. Only for a few seconds in front of Miss Amy's last fall did she appear to me here in my world. After that, she followed us out of the forest only when the magic went wrong. Taking Viktor seems to have kept her put in her hut. Wherever those chicken legs have taken her, it hasn't been here. The forest and the river lie between us. Neither of us has crossed them in a long time.

"Baba Yaga!" I call again. I don't know why I want her—this witch that I mostly try not to think about, with her iron teeth and detachable hands. I just know that she's part of the puzzle. Dream after dream, I keep going to her. Now she needs to come to me.

I try to swallow my fear. It chokes going down, so I have to squeeze out the rest of my words around it. "I'm not compelling you! I'm not using magic! I'm just asking! Help me! Lily needs me! I need you! Will you come to me?" I almost say more, but then I don't. I won't make any bargains with the witch unless she shows herself. Even then, I don't really know what I plan on doing. In my dreams—and here's the part I haven't told Ethan—she's asked me to drink from her stream. Standing here in the Jewel Box, I'm thinking that's still not going to happen anytime soon. But we're old pals, now, aren't we? "Baba Yaga," I call over the wind again.

"What the—?" Ben says under his breath. He grips me tightly against him. I track where he's looking.

It's not Baba Yaga.

Though the rain, they're drifting: dozens of rusalkas, swirling down Second Street to the Jewel Box, their hair long, wild, and wet, their skin pale as death. One after the other, they press their faces, their dripping wet bodies, against the plate glass window of the Jewel Box.

My mother and Mrs. Benson shriek in unison.

And then—as in my dream, only this time it's real—the roof of the Jewel Box just opens up and disappears. Rain begins pouring in, buckets of water drenching us and the store. The thunder cracks, and another flash of lightning rips jaggedly through the sky. Now I'm screaming. Ben's trying to drag me somewhere. I grab for my mother's hand. Mrs. Benson clutches at her chest and sinks to her knees.

A howling cackle fills the air above us. The same voice sounds my name. I look up. Rain smacks hard against my face. And through a sky that's black as midnight, Baba Yaga streaks above us in her mortar.

Friday, 11:03 am

Ethan

THOUGHT YOU QUIT THOSE."

The unlit cigarette drops from my hand to the grass near Alex Olensky's grave. He's sitting on the little bench a few feet from where I'm standing. My toes are at the edge of the small stone plaque that bears his name—the one I'd had placed there a few months ago so the grave site wouldn't be so anonymous.

"You real?" I bend to retrieve the Marlboro. It's the last in the pack that I'd told myself I wasn't going to smoke but did anyway, and I figure if I'm going to talk to a ghost, I'll need this one. So I slide my lighter from my pocket, stick the cigarette in my mouth, and, once it's lit, inhale deeply. It does little to settle me, but old habits linger just as long as I have.

"Real as you'd like me to be, dear boy." He grins at the last word. I'm a boy now, I guess. And Alex Olensky is very, very dead, even if he doesn't look it right now.

I lower myself onto the bench, since it feels awkward standing there while he's sitting. The cold air around him hints that he's not real, but he's real enough for right now. I pull in another drag on the cigarette. It tastes far too good.

"So. You love her, eh?" Alex looks not at me but at the

cigarette that's between my fingers. I offer it to him, but he shakes his head. "Can't. Tried it, but I can't inhale. Fascinating, really. But I can smell it. At least there's that." He flares his nostrils. "You haven't answered me, have you?"

Nothing much makes sense today, so I suppose discussing my love life with the ghost of my friend is about as sensible as anything else. I've done what I told myself I'd never do and let myself love her—so completely and utterly that I know there's no going back from it. I'll be in love with Anne as long as she wants me. I'll be in love with her even if she doesn't.

"Seems that way."

"Good." Alex's ghost claps his hands together and gives them a little shake. It's a gesture I've seen him do many times. He was always a fan of the physical punctuation of an idea or comment. "But then, what are you doing here? If you love her, you should be with her—not here with an old man like me, especially in my current condition." He gestures to his gravestone. "Although I do appreciate the sentiment. Haven't seen you around for a while."

"Been away. Since everything last fall. Once it was over, I needed to—well, I don't really know what I needed. But I went looking for it anyway." I study Alex's face. The features are right. His hair is as silver and wild as always. He still smells of paper, tobacco, and ink. Still, there's something off—not that this surprises me. What *does* surprise me is that I don't feel edgy, that I don't feel the need to leave. That in the midst of everything going on—the rusalka, Anne and me, all of it—I'm sitting here talking to a ghost.

"I'm sorry." I wasn't there when Viktor murdered him. Of the many, many things in my life that I regret, this one looms painfully large. "You paid a very large price, my friend. If I could undo what happened to you, I would. You know that, don't you?"

Alex is quiet for a moment. He sniffs at my cigarette and watches it with what looks like longing as I take one last puff, then stub it out on the bench, flick away the remaining ashes, and tuck the butt into my pocket. I don't like the thought of leaving it lying here between people's graves.

"You did what you had to do. Was it right? Only you can tell. Was it worth it? Hard to say, isn't it? But you have that beautiful girl now. That's something, isn't it? A girl like that, a girl of substance—she's worth some sacrifice, wouldn't you say?"

"It wasn't about that, Alex."

"Wasn't it?" The cold seeping from him gets a little colder. My skin prickles. "Come now, Ethan. What does the world come down to really? Love? Power? Fear? Maybe a righteous cause now and then? Look at the Romanovs. Someone wanted what they had or didn't want them to have it—it all amounts to the same thing, doesn't it?—and so history played itself out. It's the way of the world, dear fellow. It's how we all behave. It's what we're made of. Nobility is quite the illusion."

In my head, I see Anne standing with Anastasia in the middle of the street and feel the wrenching sadness and regret that ripped through me when Anastasia chose to go back to die. What if the rusalka—Lily—is telling the truth? What if that's not what happened? What if there really was some other possible outcome for this whole mess that I helped create?

"Nobility isn't an illusion," I argue. "You know it was more than that. You know I thought it was more than that." But I wonder, as I say the words, if I can even believe them. What did I really hope to gain from helping Viktor save Anastasia back then? Was it an act of altruism or did I just feel indebted to him for taking me in when I had no place to go? And why am I arguing with a ghost?

Alex's ghost makes a chuckling sound. "So you're the noble hero then, Ethan? Good to know. I suppose that's why I hung on while I was bleeding to death on the floor: so I could thank you for your great sacrifices on my behalf. I get to be here," he spreads out his arms, "and you get to do it all over again—only this time with the girl. Yes, it's quite the sacrifice. I can see why you had to run off to brood in Paris."

He looks disappointed when I force myself not to react— not an easy task when some piece of me feels he's right. Every day I was in Europe, I told myself that I had done the best I knew how to do. Still, when I got on the plane to return to the States, I had yet to convince myself that this was true.

"Clever man." Ghost Alex smiles. *Can he somehow read my mind?* In the distance, there's a long peal of thunder. The breeze that's been rustling the leaves of the trees in the cemetery blows a little stronger. The air smells like rain.

"Perhaps I have underestimated you, after all." Alex rises from the bench and paces a few steps to stand in the middle of the grass that covers his grave. He bends and studies his gravestone, then straightens and turns back to face me.

"What is it that people want, Ethan? Why do we do what we do? What crafts our destiny? Did Anastasia wake up one morning and just decide that she should trust that bastard half-brother of hers? Or did she come to it slowly, day by day? Your friend, Viktor. What forces made him choose vengeance? Or you, my friend. Did you wake up one morning and just decide that you wanted to be the hero? How much would you have to lose before you chose a different path? What would it take? What would it be? Is there something that you could not bear to lose?"

Two faces float into my mind. One is Anne's. The other—perhaps not so strangely, since I was speaking of her only hours ago—is Tasha Levin. Natasha, who was lost to me long ago—that day I left her without a word. Even before that, really, because I knew that while Anastasia remained trapped, so did I. I bore the pain of that for decades, but it did not change my course. It has not altered who or what I am. Only Anne has done that—Anne who gave me back my life.

Ghost Alex tips back his head and laughs. The sound echoes in the quiet cemetery, bounces off the oak trees, with their wide branches covered in leaves, and the mausoleums, thick with the sleeping dead. He steps around his own grave and leans against a large tombstone that reads *Oberman Family*, crossing his arms and observing me with an expression of amusement. A storm cloud settles overhead, and a few small raindrops begin to sprinkle.

"Well, well," he says. "Our hero has a few secrets, eh? Does your girl know what a coward you were back then? Sad, tortured Ethan. Had to give up the one he loved. Did she feel sorry for you when you told her? Did she tell you that you didn't have a choice, like our dear Anne told you that day you brought her to see me? When she realized you'd killed one of Viktor's men before you went after her?" Alex moves his lips to speak again, but it's Anne's voice that emerges from his mouth. *You saved my life*, I hear her say. *If you killed him, it's because you had no other choice.* And in my head, I hear myself reminding her that there's always a choice.

"You're not Alex," I declare. "So let's cut to the chase here. Who the hell are you? And what do want?"

The Alex thing shakes its head. "Just when we were having such fun. I don't have much fun lately. And here you have to go and ruin it all. Perhaps your friend Viktor was right about you. Too damn virtuous for your own good. You'd really be so much more fun if you'd just let it all go once in a while. Imagine the havoc you could wreak if you did, Ethan! Women, riches, whatever you want. Like we've been discussing. Everyone wants something. And here you are, getting a second chance at it all. Why would someone who knows the way the world works not want to use it to his advantage? Shake loose, friend. Just let it all go! I did."

This isn't Alex—or his ghost. I rise from the bench and the rain starts to pelt harder, drops smacking my face, the ground, the thing that looks like Alex, the graves. A bolt of lightning shivers through the sky above us. In the brief seconds during which my gaze shifts skyward, the figure leaning against the Oberman Family tombstone changes. When I look back, it's not Alex Olensky looking at me. It's Viktor.

He's horribly, horribly aged: pale, gaunt, white-haired, with deep crevices of lines etched into the sagging flesh of his face. The skin on his hands is paper-thin, the joints huge and stiff and knotted. He looks every year of what he really is. And more.

"Ah, yes, Brother Etanovich. Look your fill. I'm not even sure what you're seeing. She keeps no mirrors in her place, our girl Baba Yaga. I can catch my reflection now and then in her eyes. But I don't want to bore you with what happens when I get too close to her. Let us just say that I should have thought twice about letting her take me in place of my half-sister. But that's the thing about sacrifice, isn't it? You don't really get to control how it all turns out. Not that I haven't been trying to find a way to fix things, although I haven't quite stumbled on it yet. But these are my concern, not yours. You've been too busy with your little girlfriend. Sweet, sweet Anne. I really would have thought she'd have better taste in men. It must really *eat* at you that she took up with the lifeguard while you were gone. Or is our friend Alex right? Perhaps you're too virtuous to think about such things."

My hands tighten into fists, but the thing shifts again before I can hit it. The rusalka stands in front of me, her lilac gown soaked to the skin, strands of her black hair twisting about her like snakes. Even as the smell of rain surrounds us, the salty scent of the sea washes over me as intensely as it had in my apartment. She smiles. Her sharp white teeth gleam in the jagged flash of lightning that bursts over us again.

"You really shouldn't listen to him." Briefly, she lifts her face to the rain. "He's never told you the truth, and I doubt that he's going to start now. Then again, you don't know whether I'm lying either, do you? But you know my kind. That girl from your village—Lena. You saw what happened to her that day. So you know."

I swallow the fear that's risen inside me. I *do* know. The memory of those other bodies flickers in my mind: the men that Lena and her rusalka sisters dragged to their doom. The body of her father, a man too big to drown in such a shallow stream.

"You planning on changing again?" I keep my voice low

and even. It's not easy over the increasing thunder. I'm as soaked as she is now, and the rain shows no sign of letting up. The sky continues to darken. A man and a woman rush past us on the little path. I see no indication that they notice me talking to a mermaid.

"No need." The rusalka grins through the downpour. "I've kept you here long enough. My sisters are taking care of the rest of it for me."

I must look confused—which I am, since I'm not sure what she means. Maybe I'm too busy trying to figure out how she's been in my head long enough to create images of Alex and Viktor that feel real to me. Or maybe I'm still not sure if this last image is the one I can believe. Is this Lily? Is this the rusalka? What does she hope to gain by her little charade here in the cemetery? If she wants vengeance on Viktor, if she thinks that will change things for her, why waste time talking to me and showing me illusions? What good will it do her?

"What does my granddaughter see in you? She's such a clever, sharp girl. So lively and amusing. I've been explaining it to you this whole time—although perhaps I went a little too far with all the impersonations. But I really needed to get your attention, make you understand. We all come to the truth in different ways. I came to mine when it was too late. So I thought I'd make things simpler for you. But I see that it's not working."

"Well, then," I say, "why don't you save us both the effort and just tell me? I've been around for longer than you have. I think I'll catch on."

She wags a bony finger at me. "Temper, temper, Ethan. I do believe that my darling granddaughter is rubbing off on you."

198

She nods her head as though considering that. Rain flies from her hair and pelts against me. I shiver violently.

"I told Anne what I wanted. But I see that she needs some extra motivation to get it for me. So I've decided to give it to her. And here you are. Her hero. Visiting your friend's grave rather than protecting her when she needs you. She and I are going to have to chat about this. My Misha wouldn't have left me in the face of danger. He knew I was strong, but he didn't make assumptions about things beyond what we understand. On the other hand, he hadn't been away from the Old Country as long as you have. He hadn't forgotten. And still, Viktor killed him."

In that moment, I understand what she wants from me. Bait for Anne.

The rusalka's spell is as fast as the lightning in the sky above us and more potent than any magic that I have left inside me. She's gripping my hand before I can move. The coldness of it shoots ice through my veins. The world around me slows to a crawl. I need to do something—conjure a spell, even though I have no real magic left. But all I can do is look at her. Every fiber of my body tells me that she's the most beautiful creature I've ever seen. Only one tiny fragment of my brain screams that it's a lie—and also reminds me that because I'm now mortal, it is quite possible that I will die.

"She's the only one who can set Viktor free," Lily says to me. "Baba Yaga is still compelled because your foolish Brotherhood didn't have any idea what they were dealing with. You thought the power came from you. But it didn't. It's her. It's always been her. I knew it all those years ago, and I know it now. I couldn't get to her then unless I went with one of you. And you had no idea what Viktor was up to—no idea that he'd found me and planned on getting rid of me. Or that he killed Misha instead. But Viktor himself didn't know everything about the witch. Not really. And Laura—my baby—she has no idea about any of this. Then there was you. You found Anne and set the rest of it motion. Only there are rules—aren't there always with magic? I can haunt her, but Anne has to know me. And she has to want to help me. And that's where you come in, Ethan."

We drift together across Alex Olensky's grave and wind our way out of the cemetery. The rain never ceases. If my feet are touching the ground, I can't feel it. Blank-brained, I keep pace with the rusalka, my hand bound to hers as though with invisible ropes. I don't have to ask where we're going. This much I understand as we move east through the rain, passing by cars and people with umbrellas as though we are both now invisible. In Chicago, heading east eventually means only one thing: Lake Michigan.

ANNE

THE PLATE GLASS WINDOW IN THE FRONT OF THE JEWEL Box cracks—one thin line down the middle, then hundreds of them all over as the rusalkas press themselves against the glass. The window shatters. Thousands and thousands of tiny shards of glass crash in a heap onto the soaked wooden floor. Rusalka after rusalka swishes inside. They move slowly toward us, their bodies soaked with rainwater, their hair long and tangled.

"Don't look at them!" Baba Yaga calls from the sky. "You know better than that, my girl. Don't look at them! Don't let them fool you!"

Oh, right. Because that's going to make a difference right now.

"One of *those*—that's what I saw yesterday," Ben says. I can hear the terror in his voice. "Carter said I was seeing things. But you knew it was real, didn't you? When you jumped in the water to help me—you knew what was down there. Your friend Ethan did too, didn't he, Anne? What is this? Last night, you—shit, Anne. Whatever this is, we need to get out of here. Now." He yanks me toward the back of the store. The rusalkas edge a little closer. The smell of seawater is overpowering. Even in the steady downpour, I feel dizzy from the heavy odor of salt and seaweed. I gag. It's filling my lungs like sludge and making me cough. It feels like drowning.

My mother's coughing, but she hooks her arms under Mrs. Benson's and pulls her up from the floor. I try to collect my thoughts, but my own fear is pounding in my veins like a crazy drumbeat. I've called Baba Yaga, and she's come to me somehow, even though she couldn't before. All the rules—did I ever understand them?—have changed again. And where's Ethan? He was supposed to call, wasn't he? The drumbeats of fear inside me pound harder.

"What have you done?" Mrs. Benson wrenches herself free from my mother and stumbles over to me. She's gasping for air that's clear of the thick scent of the rusalkas. "What are you? Why is this happening?"

"What do you mean, what is she?" My mother grabs Mrs. Benson's shoulder. "She's my daughter! She hasn't done anything here! You're the one with the secrets and the lies. You're the one who knew what happened to my mother and never told me. What kind of person are you?"

"No, no." Mrs. Benson sloshes through the water that's pooling heavily on the floor. "Oh, Laura." She coughs violently, spits what looks—impossibly—like a clump of seaweed onto the floor. "No. I wanted to find you. Do you hear me? I wanted to make sure you were safe."

"We need to move," I yell at them. My lungs feel tight. Every word hurts my chest. "Ben's right. We need to get out of here!" Baba Yaga makes another swoop above, but the rusalkas are almost on us, and it doesn't look like she's planning on stopping them. Why did I bother to call for her? Or is it part of the magic that I don't understand? Maybe she can't help us, after all. Maybe she doesn't want to. All those dreams, all those conversations—possibly all lies. But why should this surprise me?

"Ben Logan," one of the rusalkas croons to him. "Dearest Ben Logan. Take my hand. Be with me. I need you, Ben. I want you. Don't you like to be wanted? I can give you everything. More than she can. Just ask her. Ask her if she truly loves you. And when she doesn't answer, just look into my eyes."

"Shut up!" I shout at it. "Leave him alone!" But Ben is already letting go of me. His body is moving toward this thing with blond hair and eyes dark as the seaweed that's clinging to her hair.

"Pretty," he says. "You're so pretty. What's up, pretty girl?" He smiles goofily, the same sweet, half-drunk smile he'd given me right before the first time he'd kissed me—really kissed me—at a party at Carter's. We'd wandered off to the study and made out, and for the first time since Ethan had dropped into my life, I'd felt like maybe I could pretend I was still the old me. A nice illusion while I could get it.

"Don't listen to it, Ben!" I pull him back to me, gripping his arm hard. I even think about slapping him, but the faint mark where my fingers had burned his cheek stops me.

With an effort, since he's still sweet-talking the mermaid, I drag Ben toward the back of the store with one hand and grab my mother's hand with the other. She's got her other arm linked around Mrs. Benson.

"Do something!" I shout up to Baba Yaga. "Damn it! What's it going to take for you to help me?" But she still refuses to answer.

"Wonderful! You yak up a storm while I visit you in my

dreams, and now what? You're just going to hang out up there and watch the show? What kind of witch are you, anyway?"

"We're going to die!" Mrs. Benson begins to moan. Her voice is a wheeze, and I know why, because I'm choking again myself. "We're all going to die! They're coming for us the way they came for Lily! The rusalkas took her. They made her one of them. I couldn't make myself believe it. But I knew. I've always known. "

"Lily?" Ben tries to squirm away again. "Who's Lily? Is she pretty too? Like that girl over there? Isn't she pretty, Anne?"

"She's a mermaid, Ben. And no offense, but she's probably trying to kill you."

"This can't be real," my mother comments weakly. "How can this be real?"

"It's real, Mom. I'll fill you in later. But trust me, it's real."

She's about to argue with me about this—at least, that's what I figure, since she's squinched up her forehead in that way she does sometimes when she's about to launch into a rant. Except she doesn't, because that's when the back door of the Jewel Box—the same door I was trying to get us to—crashes open. Dozens of rusalkas flood into the store.

My gaze whips from mermaid to mermaid. Some are dark-haired. Others are blond. Some have light skin, others dark. There are tall rusalkas and short ones. It's a veritable buffet of mermaid madness, all moving steadily toward us. I search frantically for the one mermaid face familiar to me, but Lily isn't there. So if she's not here, then where the hell is she? Why are all these others here, but not her? I'm already beyond freaked, but the questions amp up the fear.

Tess's voice runs through my head. "*It all ties in to you, but it*

ties in to him too. So why not this also? Which means I ask again—what does she want from Ethan?"

"Think, my girl!" Baba Yaga calls to me. Could she seriously be any more useless to me at this particular moment? "Think! Have you learned nothing from me? Have I been wrong about you? Is this what you are deep down? Just a fearful little girl who asks her Baba Yaga to help her? Is this all you are?"

Still in full mermaid-induced daze, Ben asks, "Is that witch up there talking to *you*, Anne? 'Cause she is one ugly lady. You know that, right? Not pretty like you. Not like these other girls. Do you see them? You need to let me go with them and stop holding my hand so hard. You really should try out for wrestling or something this year. You've got grip like iron, baby."

"Shut up, Ben. I'm not letting you go. Just look at me, okay? Not the pretty mermaids. Mermaids are bad, Ben. Just look at me." But Ben is not a particularly good listener right now either. He continues to strain toward the rusalkas.

The air thickens even more. I start to cough again, only it just makes things worse. The air is humid and wet and almost solid, and it feels like the cough doesn't even leave my mouth.

"We're going to have to try to push through them," I say to my little group, although I don't know why I'm even bothering. Between the rusalka magic that's tempting Ben and the fact that my mother and Mrs. Benson are standing frozen with crazy fear, it's not like they're even paying attention to me. The only things that I'm sure of right now are that Baba Yaga doesn't plan on helping me anytime soon, and that in my jeans pocket, my battered cell phone has begun vibrating every few seconds.

The rain continues to soak us. Once again, because of me,

the Jewel Box is being destroyed. The water's now lapping at our ankles, and things keep crashing to the floor. We're trapped in the middle of the rusalka brigade, and if the water keeps rising, the mermaids will be the only ones equipped to survive. Already I see tails under some of their gowns, swishing heavily as they advance.

"You're really part of all this, aren't you?" My mother's still gripping my hand as hard as I'm gripping Ben's—maybe harder, since I'm suddenly registering that our palms feel like they're on fire. "Is Amelia right, Anne? When I was hurt last fall, was that part of this too?"

"Yes. Mom, yes."

"My birth mother's a mermaid?" She's gasping, but I don't know if it's from the weirdness of what she's asking, or because we are all having difficulty breathing due to the thick rusalka sea smell.

"Well, not originally. I mean, you're not from a line of sea creatures, Mom. But yes, I think so. And there's more. If we get out of here, I'll explain. I promise. I should have explained it to you before. But—well, I will. Really."

"There's more?"

"Lots more. I—it has to do with the Romanovs. And Anastasia. And this secret Brotherhood. Like Mrs. Benson just told you. It all started when Ethan—we don't have time for this right now, Mom. We need to figure out how to get out of here. Then we can talk."

"Ethan," she says. "Your friend Ethan is part of them?" Her hands aren't free, so she gestures to the rusalkas with her chin.

I snort out a crazy-sounding laugh. "A mermaid? No, Mom.

Ethan's not a mermaid. Or merman. Or—he's a guy. But he's part of that Brotherhood—or he was, only now he—"

"Ethan?" This manages to snap Ben out of his trance. "So I was right? There's something going on between the two of you?" How he's made this intuitive leap in his general condition is beyond me.

The sound of Baba Yaga's laughter echoes around us. When I glance briefly skyward, I can see her iron teeth gleaming as she tilts her head back and cackles. Terrific.

The burning of my hand against my mother's stops me from trying to come up with some sort of answer for Ben. Besides, whether I confess to him or not, if I don't figure out a way to get us all out of here, it won't matter anyway. I'll just be the dead girl who cheated on her boyfriend—the boyfriend that the crazy mermaids will drag away once I'm out of the picture. Or possibly even before that, if I don't do something soon.

Another coughing spasm hits me. I feel my hands start their glow thing and glance down— and realize that the one holding my mom's hand is shining brighter.

"What is that?" Mom's voice is shrill. She's staring at our clasped hands. They're both glowing. Not just mine, but Mom's too. My heart—already racing—zooms faster.

"You guys are all lit up," Ben comments.

It's just our hands, but he's right. In that moment, I think I understand something. Lily gave up my mom for adoption and took her out of the loop of knowledge of our line of descent. But adoption didn't undo who my mother was. She's got Romanov blood just like I do. Maybe this connects her to my power too.

Overhead, Baba Yaga calls to me. "Stories within stories,

my girl. Like your rusalka has reminded you. Like the doll that your Anastasia showed you. It is woven inside the insides. It is never what it seems. Think, Anne! I can only cross into your world so far until you open the right doors. So think!"

I don't want to think. I don't want to figure out riddles. I don't want to stand here choking to death while it washes over me that not even Ethan and Viktor really ever understood anything—that maybe we've all been used, and the answers lie so far back that I don't have a clue how we'll ever find them. I just want out.

"What am I?" I scream. "What is this all about? If you'd just tell me, then I could do something! I can't help anyone if I don't understand! Think about what happened with Anastasia! Is this just more of the same thing? Are you using me like Viktor used her? Is that all this really is?"

She doesn't answer. So I stop thinking. I hold tight to my mother's hand, because she's part of me, and this somehow makes whatever it is inside me feel that much stronger. I close my eyes, try to breathe whatever air there is to breathe. When I feel the magic build, I yank our two hands out in front of us, visualize what I want to happen, and let it all free.

We're facing the back of the store, so the power that hurtles from us—blue flashes streaming from our hands—smashes into the newer group of rusalkas first. I pivot quickly—my mother a little less willing to cooperate this time but having no real alternative—and smack the rest of the mermaids with the same thing. They scream and shriek, and some of them clutch at their heads, because even with the rain steadily pouring on all of us, their long, wild hair flickers with sparks of fire. Their hair is burning. The harsh odor of it adds to everything else in the air. Blood runs freely from my nose and down to my lips. I can taste the salt of it in the already salty sea air around us.

"Anne! Anne! What did we just do?" My mother struggles to free herself from me and so does Ben, and I know it's only a matter of time before one or the other of them is successful. Or before Mrs. Benson—who's become scarily mute in the past few minutes—does something wacky herself.

In the commotion that's started—lots of mermaids slithering here and there, lots of screaming and all that burning hair—I see my opportunity. "This way!" I yell. "We can make it out the back! But we have to be quick." My vibrating cell phone continues to beat a consistent pattern against my thigh. A loud *whoosh* from above us has me glancing skyward again. Baba Yaga motors her mortar into the thunderclouds and out of view.

"Where are you going?" I call to her. "I'm doing what you want! I'm thinking! So why did you just disappear?" I don't really expect a response, so it doesn't surprise me when I don't get one.

"You hurt them," Ben says. "You hurt the pretty girls. That's not nice, Anne. You're making them cry." At least he's not asking about Ethan anymore.

I keep dragging everyone toward the parking lot. My mother typically keeps her car keys in her pocket. If we can get out of here, maybe I can just hustle everyone into the Volvo and drive us somewhere. I have no idea if Swedish sedans can outrun pissed-off mystical Russian mermaids—some of whom are on fire—but there's no time like the present to find out.

The back door's been wrenched off the hinges, and it's half blocking the doorway, so we're going to have to climb over it to make it outside. I scan the parking lot—no rusalkas in sight—and push Ben ahead of me. "Go to Mom's car, and don't move," I order him. "I'm serious, Ben. Go. I'll be right there. Go to the car. Then Do. Not. Move." He looks longingly over my shoulder toward the horde of burning, moaning rusalkas, but he hoists himself over the broken door. One down.

I ease my grip on my mother's hand. She's still holding on to Mrs. Benson. "Go," I tell them. "I'll be right behind you. Find your keys, Mom. You need to unlock your car. Can you do that? Just focus on getting to the car. Don't think about what's behind us. If you can do that, we'll be okay." I'm lying about that last part, obviously. We're not going to be okay. But at least we're not going to be dead—or worse.

My mother nods. And then things go terribly wrong.

"This isn't my fault," Mrs. Benson wheezes out. "I'm being punished—but it isn't my fault! I tried to save her! I kept her secret! I protected her daughter! But now look. You've ruined my store. You've ruined my life!" The wheezing turns into hysterical crying. The cameo with Viktor's picture falls from her hand to the floor.

She whirls on me. "It's you," she says. "Everything was fine until you. I protected your mother from whatever Lily was afraid of. But it's found you and taken you. And now it's come back for me. I can't have it. I won't have it!"

"No, Amelia." Anger and fear mix in my mother's tone. "Are you crazy? Look around you. Do you think Anne caused all this? We—oh, my God, there's no time to argue. We need to get out of here now!" She grabs Mrs. Benson's right arm and starts to pull her toward the back door. It's only then that I see the residual glow in Mom's hands. The power surge that she just shared with me isn't gone.

"You're burning me! Your hands. Let go! Don't touch me!" Mrs. Benson wrenches her arm away with such force that my mother stumbles into me.

Unfortunately, the rusalkas take this as a threatening move.

"Sisters," one of the rusalkas cries out. "Sisters! Rouse yourselves! You know what we must do! Lily has told us. We act as one, sisters. Lily must have her vengeance! And she won't have it without the girl! Keep her safe, sisters!"

As one hugely creepy unit, the rusalkas advance on us, so swiftly this time that they surround us before I can even move. Ben's outside, and we're inside, and I think that I'm going to vomit or drown in this mucky air—or both at once.

A dark-haired rusalka, her white dress filthy, her teeth sharp as arrows, grabs Mrs. Benson and pulls her away from us.

"No!" I reach for her. My mother reaches for her. But we're not quick enough. The rusalkas, some still smoldering, circle tightly around Mrs. Benson—a cluster of crazies closing in tighter and tighter.

"Amelia!" my mother shouts. "Amelia! No!"

"I've kept your secret!" Mrs. Benson cries as a rusalka in a long gown—gray with age and ripped across the chest, so that the edges of her breasts are visible—clutches at her. "It's Anne you need! You just said so! She can help you! That's what you need, right? Someone to help you? She's right there in front of you, you stupid fools! Don't you see?"

I guess they don't. Or possibly they don't appreciate being called stupid. Or maybe they're just pissed off in general about being crazy mermaids. In the time that it takes me to process what's about to occur, the mermaids reach as one for Mrs. Benson. I hear a dull crunching sound as the mermaid in gray twists Mrs. Benson's arm in a direction it doesn't want to go.

"Help me!" she cries. Another cracking sound punctuates her scream.

We try to save her. I paw at the rusalkas and pull them aside, and I think my mother's hands burn some of them again, but more appear each time we remove one. I'm sobbing and gasping, and I barely feel it when my mother pulls me away, forcing me to climb over the fallen door and stumble into the parking lot toward the car and Ben.

"Are you satisfied now?" I scream at the clouds while my mother digs into her pocket for her car keys. "Is this what you want? Is this what makes you happy? They're killing her! Or turning her into one of them. It's all the same, isn't it? Does this make you happy? Are you done with me now? Please! Just be done with me!"

If Baba Yaga hears me, she makes no answer.

My mother thumbs the remote, and the car doors unlock. She looks too shocked to cry, and Ben is just standing where I've told him to stand, staring back at the ruins of the Jewel Box. I grab the keys from her, numbly hustle Ben into the back and my mother into the front passenger seat. I don't know what else to do. I should go back for Mrs. Benson. But it's too late. *Tess,* I think dimly. I need to make sure she's okay. And my dad. And—

I turn the key in the ignition and screech out of the little parking lot onto the street. I don't even know where I'm going. Ben and my mother are saying something to me, but I don't even hear them. I just find myself annoyed that the phone has started vibrating yet again in my pocket. I yank it out and slap it open. "What?"

"Anne! Oh, my God, Anne. Finally!" Tess's panicked voice shrieks from the cell. "You wouldn't pick up! Anne, you have to come! You have to come now!"

"What? Come where? Tess, you—I can't. Whatever it is, you need to take care of it yourself. I can't."

"You're not listening. Anne, it's Ethan! It's Ethan, Anne! You have to come now. I didn't trust him. You know I don't trust him. So I—I didn't go to work, Anne. I'm not at Miss Amy's. I followed him. I wanted to see what he was up to. I followed him to the cemetery."

"You did what? Why? Cemetery? He went to the cemetery?"

"I—it doesn't matter. Just listen to me. She's taken him. The rusalka. Lily, or whoever she is. She's taken Ethan, Anne! I'm at the lake. Right past Lighthouse Beach. She's got him, Anne. She's done something to him. She's got him! And they're headed toward the water!"

ETHAN

THE RUSALKA IS TRYING TO MAKE ME LOOK AT TASHA Levin. We're at the edge of the water. Somehow, I'm barefoot, or at least I think I am, and the sand—wet from rain—feels cold and damp and gritty under my feet. I haven't seen Tasha in so very long, and I wonder if this woman standing up to her knees in the waters of Lake Michigan is actually what she looked like. She's taller than I remember, and her hands are thin and narrow. Her dark hair—was it really that dark?—is piled atop her head in a loose bun. Did she wear her hair like that? Maybe when she was playing the piano. This is what I remember. At least, I think it is.

But here's what the rusalka does not seem to know. I may not have much magic left now that I'm mortal, but I've got enough. And I've got my years of discipline. I know what I'm looking at is a glamour. I just don't know how to break through it. And she's strong enough that I'm finding it hard to think.

"See?" the rusalka's voice whispers in my ear. Her wet breath tickles my skin. "Do you remember how she made you feel?"

"Of course," I tell her. "But that was a long time ago. I'm not quite as young as I look. But I guess you know that, because neither are you." I have to force the words out. My tongue aches to form other words—ones the mermaid wants me say. I can feel them in the back of my throat. Words of endearment for someone I no longer love try to slither their way out of my mouth. My arms tingle with the urge to reach out for Tasha, so I shove my hands in my pockets and grip the sides of my legs, digging my fingers in hard enough to make myself wince. Pain is a great focuser, and right now I need to focus. If I know Anne even a little, I know that she'll end up here at the water with me eventually. And when that happens, I damn well better be able to protect her.

Lily whips me around to face her. She bares her sharp rusalka teeth. Her breath is dank and wet. I focus on this too, use it to help me block out my desire to do what she tells me. The wind's picked up again, and it's spraying drops of lake water against my back even as the drizzle continues overhead. The rusalka's in her element. "No need for insults, Ethan. That's not really the way to win me over, now is it? And here I thought you were a fine, old-fashioned gentleman."

I shrug, work to keep my breathing even and my pulse steady. "I don't find it insulting. It's the truth. Both you and I have been around for a while. But we also both know that's not Tasha Levin. So what's your purpose in showing me her face?"

My tone is almost pleasant, but it makes no difference. Against my will, my feet propel me into the water. Tasha beckons, gestures at me with those long, graceful fingers—and in a rush of memory, I see her hands at the piano keys, feel them against my skin.

"Think. You are not that foolish." Lily's voice sounds pained. I walk deeper into the water, my jeans growing heavier with each step I take. "My granddaughter would not fall in love with a foolish man. She is smarter than that. She is better than I was—better than those who came before me."

With an enormous effort, I dig my toes into the bottom of the lake and stand still. I blink, hard—try to remove my gaze from Tasha Levin. But when I open my eyes, she's still there.

"Sister, no!" Lily says sharply, and in the tiny space of time where those words hang in the air, the image in front of me wavers. Tasha disappears. In her place stands a rusalka with long blond hair and a gown so torn and ruined that I can see most of her naked torso underneath. She looks human but only barely. She waves me toward her with pale, emaciated fingers, then submerges one hand in the water. Something thin and barbed twists and cuts at my ankles.

Behind me still, Lily grabs me around the waist, her grip impossibly strong. And in that moment, I understand my situation. I hear Lily's voice. *To be a rusalka is to grieve. It is to know how men see us. It is to have everything and nothing. The power to seduce and the pain of never knowing love.* Seducing me to drown isn't a choice. It's what she has to do as long as she is one of them—even if it means that she thwarts her own desires in the process. Back and forth we'll continue to go, neither of us really in control of the outcome.

"No!" Lily cries. But as abruptly as she's held me back, now she releases me. My traitorous legs force me even deeper into Lake Michigan. Water laps at my thighs. But my brain finally understands. Whether I manage to get myself out of here or not, no one is going to have a happy ending. If I drown, Lily will have nothing to hold over Anne's head. If Anne doesn't go into the forest, Viktor will remain where he is. Lily will be bound to the rusalkas forever. And if I don't drown, then I'm still bait. Anne will—once again—save me. Or at least attempt to. And if she agrees to free Viktor from Baba Yaga, then what? And what about the witch? What will she do?

Of course, the real question is this: if I'm face-to-face with Viktor, exactly what will I do? Lily might not have to worry about extracting vengeance herself.

"And so you see." Lily breathes into my ear. She's walking beside me, and the water's up to my waist now. "I would rather not. But it really isn't up to me, is it?"

As if to purposely contradict this, she drags me backward through the water to the shallows, and when I stumble, she pulls me by the hair. Her nails dig into my scalp. I stumble again, and my back slaps against the water, and then I'm under, struggling on the hard sand beneath. At least three rusalkas materialize from somewhere and nowhere and press their hands on my chest and arms and legs, holding me to the bottom. The memory of Lena's father flashes through my mind. The water I'm in is shallow—but it doesn't take much for a man to drown.

"She'll come for you, Ethan," I hear Lily say from above me. "Have faith in my granddaughter. She'll help you." She yanks my hair again, and for a few sweet seconds, my head surfaces long enough for me to suck in a few breaths. Then she lets the others push me under once more. My head slams against something hard and sharp, and for a few terrifying seconds, I think I'm going to black out.

I try to conjure up what little magic I've got left. I know it's there, under the skin—I saw that when Anne's power mingled with mine yesterday. If I can harness it, I can get out of here.

"Or maybe she won't," Lily calls to me. "Maybe what you had with her last night is all you're going to have. Maybe someone like you just shouldn't hope for more. Like me and my Misha. And my darling Laura. Maybe you get what you get, and then that's it. Don't be so selfish, Ethan. You've wasted at least two lives. What gives you the right to hope for more? Love? It's just an illusion. It doesn't keep you from dying, now does it? You're a man. The least you can do is die like one. Anne will get over you. She's like me. And her mother. And those that came before us. She'll go on."

I struggle to stand and manage a small protection spell. I feel a brief, grim satisfaction when the two of the rusalkas shriek in pain, let go, and thrash away. The third moans, then shifts her skeletal grip to my throat. My arms free, I attempt to wrench her hands from my neck. The blackness threatens to descend. I refuse to allow myself the fear, but it comes anyway. I've lived this long only to die here in the water. The girl I've let myself love will find my body on the beach. Or worse, never see me again. *Forgive me, Anne*, I think. *Will you forgive me for dying like this without being able to even hear you say good-bye?*

"Oh, for heaven's sake!" The voice I hear then isn't Lily's. Or the rusalka's. Or Anne's. "What kind of horrible grandmother are you? I mean, I know you're a cursed mermaid and all, but give me a break. Enough with the Russian melodrama. Everyone doesn't have to die in every story. Can't one of you get on board with living happily ever after? 'Cause Anne's my best friend. Ethan might be an idiot, but he's her idiot. So why don't you just leave him alone? Besides, you're her grandmother—so going after her boyfriend is just plain creepy. Or am I the only one who's noticed that?"

If there's real fear—and I'm sure there is—under Tess's bravado, I don't hear it in her voice. But maybe that's because

I'm still gasping for air when, clearly furious at the interruption, the remaining rusalka lets me go, whirls around, and begins advancing on Tess, who's somehow waded out into the lake, seemingly to save me. I heave myself up and suck in air.

Then so much happens at once that I find it hard to keep track. Above us, the thunderclouds split open. Baba Yaga swoops down in her mortar. Over on the beach, a tan Volvo sedan squeals to a stop at the water's edge. The doors fling open. From the driver's side, Anne hurtles herself toward us, followed in quick succession by Ben and Anne's mother.

Even the rusalkas seem startled.

"Are you going to help me now?" Anne screams up at Baba Yaga. "I mean, honestly, what kind of useless witch are you? The least you could have done was fly us all here, rather than make me drive my mother's car!"

"Laura," Lily sighs. Then more loudly, "Laura. Don't come any closer. Please, don't. I can't be with you. Not yet."

"Took you long enough!" Tess calls to them. "I thought you'd never get here! They were trying to drown him, you know. In fact, I think they still are."

"Which one?" Mrs. Michaelson says. She's shifting her gaze from rusalka to rusalka. "Which one is she?"

I look over at Lily, but she's disappeared. The rest of her rusalka spell still fogging my head disappears with her.

"Get out of the water!" I push Tess toward the beach. "Do you have any idea how dangerous it is for you to even be here?"

"Do you have any idea how dead you were about to be unless I did something?"

The words aren't even out of her mouth when the blond rusalka—the one who'd been wearing Tasha Levin's face—grabs Tess, and in a blink of an eye, pulls her through the small rush of waves. She's out of reach and beyond standing depth before I can react.

Just like that, they both slip under the water.

"No!" Anne rushes into the lake, her hair wild around her from the rain and wind. "No! Tess! Tess!"

It takes all the strength I have left to stop her from swimming after them. "You can't," I say. "Don't. You can't—"

I feel Ben race into the water before I even turn to see him. He wades swiftly to us. "What are you waiting for? Someone has to go after her. Jesus, Anne. I can't even see her anymore, but it's not that deep out there. I'll dive under. Don't worry. I can find her." He stops only to slam his fist into my jaw. "Whatever this all is, Ethan, it came with you. So what are you going to do about it? Just stand here? I'm going after Tess. One of you needs to call 911, get a boat or something. I don't know why no one's around—so call and get someone the hell out here."

He wades past us and hits the water smoothly, starts to swim with long, even strokes. The rusalkas, bobbing in the water, begin to smile at Ben in their very inhuman way.

"Ben, no! Wait! Ben! You can't fight them this way! You don't know what you're dealing with. You're not going to help Tess. You're just making it worse." Anne manages to grab his ankle, but he kicks free of her, leaving her sputtering lake water in his wake.

"They enchanted him or something. I thought it had worn off, but I don't know. Ethan, the rusalkas attacked us at the store. They took Mrs. Benson. I think they—God, Tess. Ben."

"I need to you calm down." I feel a trickle of blood oozing

from what feels like a split lip from Ben's fist. Over Anne's shoulder, I see one of the rusalkas swimming in tandem with Ben, matching him stroke for stroke. Above us, Baba Yaga continues to circle in her mortar. "I need you to breathe. I need you to focus, Anne. I can help you, but I can't do it without you. That's how it's been—you know that—and that's how it is now. So breathe. And think."

"But Ben—I can't just let him swim after her. I can't! But if he doesn't, then Tess—"

"Stop. Breathe. Think."

On the beach, Mrs. Michaelson is shouting something. Overhead, the witch laughs. "Girl!" she howls into the wind. "Girl! Your man can't help you. Only I can do that. I think you need to promise me now. Promise me that you'll drink from my stream. Promise, and then see what you can do. You are mine, girl! You've always been mine. It's been your destiny—everything and everyone leading you to this moment!"

"Don't tell *me* about my destiny! If you won't help Tess, then don't tell me anything at all!" Anne grabs my hand in hers. We stand in the water, the rain pouring on us, thunder booming, lightning flashing jagged edges through the purple sky. Her skin against mine. I feel when Anne focuses and centers, feel as she draws her power up and outward until it rests just under her skin.

"*Ya dolzhen*," I begin. And then again in English, "I must." I squeeze Anne's hand in mine. "We need to bring them all to us. Safely. Breathing. We may end up bringing the rusalkas too, but we'll deal with that when we get Tess back. Concentrate. We can—you can do this. I'm here with you. Don't look at Baba Yaga. Just hold my hand and focus. Focus, Anne. Tess needs you. Ben needs you." *I need you. And I'll lose you if I don't help you do this—maybe even if I do.*

"What if I can't?" Anne says. She tries to pull her hand from mine, but I hold tight.

"Of course you can. You know you can. You've been able to for a long time. Don't wait any longer, Anne! You can't wait! You have to act! I'm here. I love you. I'm here."

If she's heard anything I've just said, she doesn't give me a sign. Even in the freezing water and the icy downpour, her hand feels warm as I link my fingers with hers. I savor the feel of it, even though I know it's just the magic—Anne's magic now, not really mine.

"Don't let go of me," Anne says. "Do you feel it? I'm stronger with you here. Help me, Ethan. Please. Oh, my God—Tess. She could be—and Ben—we need to do this. Now!"

I close my eyes. I don't remind her how little magic I really have, or tell her that accessing it is like scooping water from a well that's almost dry. I just hold her hand and tether her to me. It isn't enough. It probably never will be. But it's all I have.

Friday, 2:28 pm

Anne

I can do this. I can do this. Both hands out in front of me, Ethan's fingers still linked with those of my left hand. Visualize what I want. But what is that? Think. Think!

In my mind, I picture Tess. Blond hair, denim skirt, footless tights, T-shirt. Tess Edwards. I say her name over and over, because names are important and powerful, and even if they aren't, it feels like the right thing to do. Then I hear myself scream without knowing that I've even made the sound, because out in the lake, one of the rusalkas edges closer to Ben.

"Ben! God, Ben! Come back!" Can he hear me? Can we save them both?

"Promise me, girl!" Baba Yaga says again. I refuse to listen. I can't listen.

"I can't. Ethan, I can't. I can't think. Help me think!"

Ethan's grip tightens. I feel him hesitate. Then he pulls me to him, cups my face with his hands and kisses me. "Whatever I have left in me, let it go to her." His voice is fierce as he speaks the words against my lips. "Ya dolzhen. I must. Ya dolzhen. I must. Ya dolzhen. Let her take what has been mine. Let it be hers."

The force of what he's just offered smacks into me like the waves crashing against us. "No, Ethan! Don't! You shouldn't!"

Before the words are out of my mouth, I feel a surge of energy course through me, rushing from toes to my scalp, more potent than when we opened the locked gate at the pool, stronger even than when I wrapped my hand around his and healed his cut.

"Shh," he says. "It's done."

I start to protest again, but he places a finger on my lips. "It's the only way I can help you."

A million thoughts race through my mind, but only one stands out. I need to save Tess and Ben. I close my eyes. There's no time to think about how I'm going to do this, so I just focus on getting it done. Picture them both coming back to me in the first image that pops into my head. Waves.

"Anne." Ethan's voice is low and steady, so low I can barely hear him above the roar of the surf that now crashes into our legs, slapping hard enough that I'm knocked off balance every few seconds. My feet shift in the sand at the bottom of the lake. "Anne," Ethan says again. "Can you control this? Anne. You need to open your eyes."

He says it like you'd tell someone to bring you a drink or pass the salt—no hint of panic or anything. Just hey, Anne, could you do this little thing for me, please?

Lake Michigan has waves. In storms, they get dangerous. The undertow can be deadly. But what I see when I open my eyes is more than deadly. It's huge. Tsunami huge. And it's chugging steadily toward us. A rusalka dances on the crest of it, her tail beating against the water, her arms fluttering in the air like she's conducting an invisible symphony.

"You need to push it back," Ethan tells me. "You need to hold it." His voice is still unnaturally calm.

I, however, am not.

"I can't! Did I do that? How the hell did I do that? I've killed them, Ethan! I know it! I've killed them! Shit! Shit! What am I supposed to do?"

"No choice, Anne. Stop talking. You need to hold that thing off and lower it. Lessen it. That's what you need to visualize."

Visualize? Everything is as wrong as it can possibly be. For the millionth time in the past few minutes, I wonder why Baba Yaga has appeared if she's doing nothing to intervene. Except maybe that's the whole point—some kind of sick challenge to see if I'm worthy of something I don't even want.

"Make her help me!" I'm crying now, clutching at Ethan. "Don't any of you understand that I don't know what I'm doing?"

"Anne. Stop! There's no time. You need to do it now."

I glance back at the beach. My mother is standing there, staring out beyond us to the impossibly large wave of doom that continues to push toward shore. Lily stands near her, but Mom seems unaware of her presence. It's just another crazy piece of this whole mess: a rusalka who wants me to give her a chance for vengeance. A witch who won't explain herself. And the rest of us out here in the water, where we'll probably die if I don't get my act together. Not exactly how I planned on spending the first week of my summer vacation.

It's the absurd humor of that last thought that actually yanks me out of the paralyzing fear that Ben and Tess might be lost forever: the ridiculous realization that other girls might spend their summer getting a tan, earning money, and hanging out with their friends. But I was never going to be one of them. Why? Because I have a destiny. And a formerly immortal guy who's given me magic and told me he loved me, possibly because he figured I was too panicked to hear him. I've just outed my magical self to my mother. My boss—the one with a secret identity—my best friend, and my almost former boyfriend have been dragged off by mermaids. And if I don't pull off a miracle in the next five seconds, we'll all be pulverized by the humongous wave I've conjured up while trying to save everyone.

"Ah." Baba Yaga is still above me, but her voice feels like it's inside my head. "That's my girl."

This time, I ignore her.

"*Ya dolzhen!*" I call to the wave. I have no earthly idea if I need to start like Ethan did or if I'm even saying it correctly, but I figure it can't hurt. The words feel potent, and I need to feel strong. "I must."

I force myself past my main desire right now—which is to squeeze my eyes shut and just pretend this all isn't happening.

"*Ya dolzhen!*" I shout into the wave that's riding toward us, impossibly tall. And then, because it feels more like me, "You need to listen to me, wave. You will do what I say. You will not kill my friends. You will not let the rusalkas take them. Whatever I have—whatever it is that I've been given—it's mine now. I am not Baba Yaga. And I am not Lily. I'm Anne. And you will listen to me. You will give me back my friends."

"Keep going," Ethan says. I risk a quick glance at him. His blue eyes are as intense as I've ever seen them. His jaw is set tightly, and his thick brown hair is blowing in the wind. "I'm here. I won't leave you, no matter what happens. I'm here, Anne. Keep visualizing what you want." He nods at me, then sloshes through the water to stand hip to hip with me.

My own hair whips around my face, and because it distracts

me, I pull Lily's hair clip from where it's still shoved into my pocket. I snap it into my hair so quickly and clumsily that I scrape my temple—hard—as I do so. But it's not just to keep my hair out of my eyes. I need Lily to think that I'm on her side. If she and the witch are both unpredictable, then maybe that's what I need to be too. Let her think that I'll do her bidding, that when this is over, I'll go back to Baba Yaga's hut and let Viktor free. If they can be cagey about everything, well, so can I.

I stare down the wave. It's so close now that I don't have time to think about anything else except what I want. Tess and Ben. Tess and Ben. A smaller wave that does no harm. A wave that won't kill us all. Keep me safe. And Ethan. And my mother, whose life just got as crazy as mine and who—I realize with a sharp pang of fear—has just waded into the water next to me and Ethan.

Mom's hair is plastered to her head. Her white blouse is ripped and splattered with mud from the rain and blood is oozing from a cut on her forehead. She pulls on my arm. "You can't stay out here, Anne! Look at that! What are you doing? It's going to kill you! It's going to kill us all! Please, get out of the water!"

"Mom, no. I can't talk right now. It's going to be okay. You need to let me do this." My fingers suddenly ache to press themselves to my mother's forehead, to heal that cut, which wouldn't be there if it wasn't for all this mess.

"Do what? What is it that you think you can do?"

Ethan moves around from the other side of me. "Mrs. Michaelson. Laura. She can't listen to you right now. You're not helping her. You have to believe me."

I tell myself to block out whatever else they say to each

other. I can't block out my mother's presence next to me, though, so I use it to intensify my focus. If I don't finish this right now, then my father will lose both of us. Our family has lost enough. I can't let that happen to him.

So I take all of it: the pain and the fear and my magic mingle inside me with Ethan's. With whatever it is that connects me now to something greater than myself. "Let me do this," I say. "Please. Please! Please let me do this!" The wave is so close now that its own power crashes against me as I fight to control it.

I force myself to imagine a calm day at the beach. I'm walking along the shoreline with Ethan and Tess and Ben. Other people sun themselves on towels. A guy in board shorts, hooked up to his iPod, jogs at the water's edge. A boy about six is building a sand castle. The sun is shining, and in my mind's eye, I see a school of silver fish darting through the water. In the distance, a sailboat steers south. Farther out, a couple of tankers chug along slowly. I can make out the water pumping station in the distance, the red buoys bobbing peacefully. A lifeguard sits atop his tall white stand, his nose covered in zinc oxide. The old lighthouse sits behind us, and farther west, on Sheridan Road, traffic moves steadily.

I force myself not to doubt. *I can do this. I can stop this. I have the power in me.*

This time, when the magic flies from my hands, it's so powerful that it sends me stumbling backward in the water. Everything is churning around me, and I can't look at anything but the wave. I sense rather than see Ethan holding my mother. But he stays next to me, just as he's promised.

"*Ya dolzhen!*" I say again. "I must control the water. The wave must do what I want. I must bring back my friends."

230

I'm hurtled backward again, and again I struggle up from the water. I dig my feet into the sand and push the wave back and down. Back and down—again and again. I don't know how long it takes. It feels like hours.

"I knew you had it in you, girl!" Baba Yaga shouts to me.

What's strange is that, somehow, I knew I did, too.

The sky grows blue. The wave shrinks, lowers itself so quickly that I don't even see it all happen. My body vibrates with the power that's streaming out of me and into the wave. When it hits me, it's still big enough to wash over me completely. My eyes are open as I lose my balance again, and inside the wave, I see rusalkas tumbling about. And then it's over. Ethan drags me to the surface.

My mother is pale as death and crying. "You're bleeding," she says. "Anne. You're bleeding. Oh, sweetheart. Thank God it stopped. You're okay."

"Where are they?" I look wildly around me. The magic is still racing through my veins, my blood, my everything. Have I failed? Was I too late?

"Look!" Ethan points out into the lake that's still choppy but slowly settling.

Lily wades toward us gracefully, like it's no effort at all for her to make her way through the surf. In her arms, she carries Tess's limp body.

"Tess. Tess!" Half wading, half swimming, I make my way out to them. "Tess. Oh, Tess."

"Anne. Oh, my dear Anne. I'm so sorry." This is what Lily says to me as I approach her—as I look at my friend's arm trailing lifeless against the water. Her face is white. Her eyes are closed.

But Lily isn't looking at Tess. Her gaze is fixed to her right. I track where she's looking, see the body floating facedown in the water.

Ben.

I don't really know what I do or say after that. Ethan swims swiftly to Ben, and somehow, we're all on the beach except Lily, who stays in the shallows, watching silently, and Baba Yaga, who has momentarily disappeared into the clouds.

My mother and Ethan kneel over Ben and Tess. I stand there, numb. They can't be dead. They just can't be. How could I have brought them back and not have them be alive?

Ethan starts chest compressions on Tess. I think fuzzily that we really should try to revive Ben first. Ben's a lifeguard, isn't he? He's trained in CPR. He'd know what to do. He'd be working on Tess right now. Except he's not. Because he's lying there dead.

Ethan lifts Tess's wrist. Presses his fingers to her wrist. Dips his head to her chest. "There's a faint pulse," he says grimly. "She's alive. But just barely." He rolls her to her side and pats her gently on the back. She coughs—the barest of sounds.

I look out into the lake at Lily. Other rusalkas have joined her now, but they make no move to come to shore. Is she controlling them? Could she have stopped them from attacking us, from taking Tess, if she had wanted to?

"Is this what you wanted?" I scream. "Does this make you happy? Do you think I'll help you with your vengeance plan now?"

I sink to my knees, place one hand on Tess and the other on Ben. Their bodies are cold from the water but still warm with life. Tess is clinging to a thread and Ben—Ben is strong.

I know this. He's strong and good and doesn't deserve to be mixed up in my stupid world.

"Move." Mom edges me over in the sand. She places her hands on Ben's chest, and like Ethan with Tess, begins CPR.

How useless am I? Magic girl. Destiny girl. But it's Mom who took the CPR class when David was first diagnosed with cancer. It's Mom who said that if something happened and the ambulance was delayed, at least if she was there, she could try to do something. How stupid have I been for keeping my secrets from her? Thinking what? That she's too fragile to handle them?

"Anne." Mom continues her rhythmic compressions. "Pinch Ben's nose closed, and when I stop, you need to breathe into his mouth. Like this." She mimes what she wants me to do.

I do as she directs. Tears sting the backs of my eyes as I press my mouth to Ben's and try to breathe life back into him. Ben, who I've probably killed. Ben, who I've betrayed in every way possible.

Ethan stays with Tess. Mom and I work on Ben.

"It'll be okay," my mother says each time she presses against Ben's chest. "It'll be okay." Like a prayer. A mantra. I watch her hands. And then I think I understand something else.

Lily. My mother. Me. The women who came before us. Lily's mother and her mother. I remember the way Mom's hand gripped mine at the Jewel Box. The way the magic seemed to flow from both of us. But Mrs. Benson's story was about more than that, wasn't it? About more than just our line of descent from Viktor. I hear her words in my head again…*her mother had whispered to her about the Old Ones. About powers. About the old ways of Russia. Deep secrets that went back so far that no one really knew their source. About how her grandmother had told her that nothing was ever as simple as it seemed.*

If the source was unknown, if Lily's story is true, then would that mean that my power isn't really from Viktor and the Brotherhood? Would that explain what's been happening inside me?

I don't know what to believe. But I know what I saw back at the Jewel Box. I know what we did.

"Mom," I say. She pauses from her chest compressions. Ben's eyes flutter, just a little. "I need you to help me. I need you to do what I say. Please. Just for a few seconds. If it doesn't work, then we'll go back to the CPR. But please. Please, Mom."

I will be forever grateful that she doesn't argue with me. Ethan doesn't either, but I can see the quizzical look in his blue eyes. He wasn't at the Jewel Box with us. He didn't see what I did.

So I tell my mother what to do. She places her hands on top of mine as I press one palm to Tess's forehead and the other to Ben's. I visualize myself healing the cut on Ethan's thumb, try to access the magic that allowed me to that—the magic I've been toying with since last fall.

Nothing.

"No." I know I've spoken the word, but my voice is so soft, I don't hear myself. It isn't enough. Whatever I have isn't enough for this. I need more.

"Don't," Ethan says sharply. I wonder if he's read my mind. Or does he just know that there's finally no other option?

I don't raise my palms from Tess's and Ben's foreheads. My mother's hands remain pressed over mine.

"Baba Yaga," I say slowly and firmly. "If I promise to drink from your stream, will you help me?"

"No," Ethan is saying. "No, Anne. No. You can't. Don't."

But it's already done. She stands over us, huge and imposing, her hands impossibly large in the sleeves of her coarse brown dress. Her iron teeth gleam as she grins at me. A red kerchief is wound around her head. Her skin is wrinkled and ancient.

"You really shouldn't trust me, daughter."

"I'm not your daughter. My mother's right here. And I don't trust you. But I don't really have a choice anymore, do I?" My mom's hands tighten over mine. My gaze is fixed on Baba Yaga, but out of the corner of my eye, I see Mom's mouth move silently. I wish I had the time to tell her not to panic.

"Perhaps. Perhaps not." Slowly, she slides her tongue over those horrible metal teeth like she's shining them. Stares at me in a way that's strange and familiar at the same time. Like there's a link between us that I just need to understand. I try to pull the pieces of this crazy puzzle together before it's too late.

More of Mrs. Benson's raving story echoes in my head. *A secret beyond what even that Brotherhood of men could understand. They were destined for something that was yet to come. One of their own blood would betray them and use them, but even he wouldn't really know the truth of who they were, of what they were.*

"It's not just Viktor's bloodline is it?" I ask. "I'm connected to him, but it's more than that, isn't it? This has never been only about Anastasia, either, has it? That's what I still don't get. I dreamed about Anastasia. I dreamed her dreams. Her life. Her death. Saving her was supposed to be my destiny. But it's always been more than that, hasn't it?"

She cocks her head to the side and observes me. Next to me, I feel Ethan move. The witch's reaction is lightning speed. She flicks out a finger from one of those enormous hands, and by the time I turn my head, she's somehow blocked him.

"Don't touch her," he manages, and then clutches at his throat in silence. It's like Baba Yaga has hit his mute button. My mother's too. Her eyes are huge with fear, but there's nothing I can do but just let her keep holding my hands until the witch and I are finished.

"Leave them out of it," I tell her. "Haven't enough people been hurt already?"

"Their silence pleases me, daughter, nothing more. As for your destiny, that will be up to you."

"I never wanted all this."

"Girl, you've already taken it."

"Then let me give it back. Just help me save my friends, and I'll give it back."

I glance at Tess and Ben. Tess's eyes are still closed, but I can see her chest flutter up and down slowly. Ben's eyes twitch again, but his skin is gray. Whatever bargain I'm about to make, I need to do it now.

"Daughter Anne, this is no trifle." Baba Yaga's voice booms so loudly that my ears feel like I'm right in front of one of the giant speakers at a concert. She reaches out with one huge hand and touches her horribly wrinkled, brown finger to Lily's shell-shaped ruby and pearl clip, still tangled in my hair. I'd forgotten it was even there. "No mermaid's frippery. This power has been your destiny forever." Her fingernail grazes my temple where the clip had scratched me while I was putting it back in my hair. My skin stings, and I feel blood start to ooze and trickle down the side of my face.

"Whatever."

She smiles again. I really wish she'd stop it because each grin forces me to think about what those iron teeth can do. She stares at me, her eyes dark as night, a skull glowing inside each pupil. I start to shiver.

"Here's what I did not expect, my girl," she tells me. "I did not expect you to love him."

She shifts her gaze to Ethan, still sitting in forced silence on the sand. "You—you I was more sure of. Oh, not that I didn't meddle a little. When one wants a certain outcome, one must tinker a bit. But it does add another element to the story, does it not? You transferring over your power to this girl, leaving yourself helpless. Such wonderful heroics, Ethan. Viktor will be delighted when he hears. I will have to tell him when I return to the hut. Some days he listens to my stories. Others, he is less—well, less able. But eventually, he'll hear. And I'm sure he'll find it quite in character."

"You know, all this rambling is great and all, but we don't have much time left here. Are you going to bargain with me or not?" My mouth spits out the words while my brain busies itself digesting what she's just said. Did she really know that Ethan would love me? Did she really think that I wouldn't love him? "What is it exactly that you really want?"

Baba Yaga's skull-eyed gaze burns into mine. "What I want is to undo the harm that has been done to me. What I want is to take back my rightful legacy. I am the Death Crone, girl. I have been weakened. I have been used. And I will take back what is mine. This is what I want—what I need. This is what your destiny leads you to. This and only this is the true source of your power. It is a story you do not yet know. But you will learn. You will do. You will listen. And in the end, more choices. But it's choice that makes you strong. Oh, girl, what I have in store for you! Quite the adventure."

"But what do you need me for? You're the big bad witch. I'm just a girl. That's what you keep saying. So what do you need from me? Whatever it is, just tell me. I said I'd drink, I'll drink. But help me save my friends." How can she talk about choice when it always feels like I don't really have one?

"I am what I am, my girl," Baba Yaga says. Above us, a seagull cries out. I risk a glance at the lake. Lily and her band of rusalkas are still lurking at the water's edge.

"I cannot be otherwise." Baba Yaga grins at me. "But I know this. It is you who doesn't know. I have come to you. Now you must come to me. See what is really in my hut—what it really means to go to Baba Yaga's. Not in a dream. Not to save a girl who is beyond saving. But for yourself. Like Vasilisa in the fairy tale. You will go on your own terms and return on your own terms. And then we will see what you truly want. If you are to take what I am about to give you, if you are to be worthy, then you must know. You must know the desires of others. If you cannot look into people's hearts, then you will never know your own. Does it not concern you that I am surprised you might love this man?"

"What do you care about that? What are you saying? You're a witch. What do you care whether or not I fall in love?"

Baba Yaga doesn't respond. She just reaches out one enormous hand again and strokes it across my cheek. The blood from the cut she's made on my temple has dripped there, and when she pulls back her ancient, wrinkled hand, some of my blood is on her fingertips. I shudder violently when she flicks out her tongue and licks her fingers clean, then rubs her tongue over her creepy iron teeth.

"You have offered. I accept."

She presses one giant hand over mine and my mother's. Our three hands are on Tess. Our three hands are on Ben. Her power courses through me from feet to scalp. My body thrums and vibrates with it. I see stars. My pulse pounds in my ears. Underneath my hand, Ben's heart begins to beat firmly and steadily. His chest begins to rise and fall. I look down. He opens his eyes.

"Did I save Tess?" Ben coughs. I ease my hand off his chest. My mother and Baba Yaga do the same. Mom sucks in a loud breath—a heavy wheezing sound—but her voice is back.

Ben looks only at me. "God. I can't think. My mind's a mess. There was a woman in the water again. Like the one at the—I was swimming to Tess when she grabbed me. She kept saying that you don't love me. Then she pulled me under the water. You know it's really beautiful down there, Anne. You have no idea—"

"Anne." Her voice is weaker than Ben's, but it's Tess. My Tess. "Anne," she says again. She clears her throat, turns her head sideways, and spits out some water. We all remove our hands from her as well. Baba Yaga steps away. In less than a blink, she's back in her mortar in the sky. But my attention stays on my best friend.

"Am I dead?"

I'm laughing then, on top of my tears. Classic Tess.

"No, really," she rasps. "Am I? Because maybe you just don't want to tell me. You know, because you're my best friend and all. Maybe you—"

"Idiot." I stroke my hand over her wet, tangled blond hair. "You're alive. Do you think I'd let you die? Who would be here to annoy me?"

"You saved me? Where's Ben?" She looks over at him. Ben

reaches for her weakly. His hand pats her shoulder and then rests itself there. "Did you get hurt trying to save me, Ben?"

"Tess." Ethan too has his voice back. "Tess. Oh, Anne. What have you—?"

Tess—because she's still Tess—interrupts him. "Ethan!" She clutches at his arm. "You're okay! Thank God. I was so worried. I didn't know what was going to happen with all those mermaids, and you were acting drugged or something, and then…what did happen out there? Everything's so fuzzy. I just can't remember."

"It's okay, Tess," I tell her. I stroke her matted hair. "It's okay." I lean over to wrap her in my arms. As I do, the cut on the side of my face—the one that Baba Yaga etched into my skin with her sharp nail—begins to drip blood. One drop falls onto Tess's arm. Another falls onto the sand between her and Ben. The third drops onto Ben's hand, still resting on Tess's shoulder.

"Destiny has a mind of its own, girl!" Baba Yaga calls to me.

"No, Anne," Ethan says. "Oh, no."

The beach and the lake beyond it shimmer and flicker and disappear. Baba Yaga's forest flashes into view just inches from us. Her three horsemen gallop through the trees. I recognize my mistake—and the truth behind it—too late to stop what begins. Ethan and I had been wrong. Our entrance ticket into the forest last fall had never been about the lacquer box. It was always about me. About my blood.

"Whoa," says Ben. "Horses." He reaches out and sticks his free hand into the forest.

And then, just like that, Ben, Tess, and Ethan are gone.

My mother starts to scream. The shock of what's just

happened careens into me, a runaway El train colliding full force with my heart.

"You made your choice, Anne." Baba Yaga's voice is everywhere. "You promised. And now you will have to act. In the end, girl, each of us is always alone. Didn't you know?"

"Anne!" Mom's voice is totally panicked. Suddenly, I can feel the enormous pain her heart, in her soul. I need to tell her something, anything.

But it's all too late. I'm reaching out for her, calling her name, telling her it will be okay when Baba Yaga's giant hands swoop down from the sky, grab me, and pull me up and into the mortar.

Friday, in the Forest

Ethan

My head slams against the ground in Baba Yaga's forest hard enough to make me see double. I squeeze my eyes shut and try to quell the nausea rising in my throat. Something wet and rough flicks against my eyelids, followed by a puff of fetid breath. I open my eyes, then manage to sit up. Baba Yaga's black cat, her koshka, watches me with his gold-flecked stare.

Behind me, someone groans. Ben sits slumped against a thick tree, rubbing his head. No more spell-induced giddiness—just confusion and fear mingling on his face.

"Ethan." From the opposite direction, Tess stumbles toward me. She's barefoot, as are Ben and I. Her blond hair is matted with blood on one side, and she's sporting a cut over her left eye. "Where are we? What the hell just happened?"

I stick to the basics. No sense panicking anyone more than necessary. "Baba Yaga's forest. Anne's blood was the key. I guess it's always been Anne's blood, only we didn't know it. Some dropped on each of you, then Ben put his hand in the forest, and—well, here we are."

"We're in a witch's forest?" Ben looks at me as though I've gone insane. I have no idea how much he remembers of what's just occurred.

Tess doesn't comment. She just holds out a hand and hoists Ben off the ground. The koshka narrows his gold eyes to thin slits and draws his ears back. Around us, the forest feels close and heavy, so thick with trees and vines that only the barest trickle of sunlight slips through the heavy canopy of leaves and branches.

"It'll be okay," I say idiotically. My hand sinks momentarily into a slimy mass of dead leaves and dirt as I push myself up. "We'll get out of here. We just need to—"

"To what, dude?" Ben snaps out of his shock. "Who are you, anyway? And where's Anne?"

"She—she's not with us?" Tess's voice quavers, then steadies.

"I don't think so. She wasn't—we were all connected, all touching. But not Anne." I sound more positive about the explanation than I really am.

Tess puts her hand to her mouth. "She saved me. I almost drowned back there, didn't I? Anne saved me and now—it was all so fast. The rusalka dragged me under. Oh, my God. I really was dead, wasn't I?"

"Yes." I see no point in lying to her. "Yes, I think you were—mostly, anyway. Both of you, actually. Anne brought you back. She—" My heart sinks. Do I explain the bargain that Anne just made—do I even understand it? What we really need to do right now is figure out if we can get out of here.

"She what? What did she do?" Ben looks from Tess to me. His tone borders on dangerous, with a little crazy thrown in for good measure. "And where is she? If you did something to her—"

He lunges toward me, but the cat has other ideas. It swipes at his bare foot with one paw, razor-sharp claws drawing blood.

Ben yelps in real pain. The cat flees before any of us can stop it. "Shit! Ow!" Blood drips from the long scratch on the top of Ben's foot, and when he steps backward, he leaves a dripping trail of blood in the dead leaves. A few feet away, something stirs under the detritus. I see a flash of eyes, a thin, furry body. And I hear the skittering sound of small feet. The smell of dead things around us gets a little stronger.

"She made a bargain with the witch." I say it slowly, as though it's a matter of simple fact, but my pulse kicks in my veins and my heart tightens. "I don't know exactly what Baba Yaga wants from her in return. But she—she helped Anne save you. It happened very fast. I had no idea that Anne was going to—"

"She did *what?* Are you kidding me?" Tess smacks a hand against her forehead. "Oh, Ethan. This is bad. Really bad. How could you let that happen? You came back to help her, and this is what you let happen? How could you? You have some magic left, Ethan. You could have done something. You could have—"

"I did what I could." I place a hand gently on Tess's shoulder, but she shakes it off. "I gave her everything left in me. That's what brought both of you back from the rusalkas. I gave her all I had. But I didn't think that she—" I stop. What else is there really to add?

"You mean we're here in this place, and you don't have any magic? Is that what you're telling me?" She makes a sound that's part laughing and part crying at the same time.

"Well, I—"

"Thank you for not letting me croak, I guess. But seriously, Ethan. We're in big trouble, aren't we?"

I believe we both understand the answer.

"We need to stop your foot from bleeding." Cautiously, I approach Ben. The last thing we need right now is for him to—

His fist slams into my face harder than it had at the lake. "Son of a—"

He hits me again. This time, I punch him back. My fist plows into his solar plexus, and the force of it sends him stumbling backward. But he keeps his balance and runs at me again, barely deterred.

"Stop it!" Tess shoves herself between us. "Stop it. This isn't getting us anywhere. And I think there's something really creepy under those leaves." She points to her right, and I see the small furry creature again—a rat of some sort?—its eyes glowing red, and its feet making a scuttling, scratching sound as it dives back under cover, kicking up a residue of dirt and what look like tiny bones as it goes.

"She's my girlfriend," Ben says. "Mine. Not yours. Get it, dude? Whatever all this is, wherever we are, when we get out of here, you need to stay away from her. Wherever the hell it is you came from and whatever the hell it is you think you want from her—well, forget it. She's mine. I love her, and she loves me. I don't care what happened before. You left. She started going out with me. Whatever you've done to make her head all crazy, you're going to stop doing it. And you're going to leave us alone."

"That's up to Anne, Ben. Not you. And I suggest you calm yourself down. We need to get moving. Anne's going to end up here somehow. That much I'm sure of. Baba Yaga wouldn't have it any other way. So we need to find her hut, and I think we need to do it before it gets any darker in here. We can talk about this later."

This doesn't make Ben any happier. He shoves himself nose to nose with me.

Tess yanks his soggy shirt and pulls him back. "Stop it, Ben. Ethan's right. We don't have time for this. And he's right about the rest of it too. It's not up to you. It's up to Anne. And she's not here."

"She's with *him* now? She was at my freakin' house last night, Tess. Well, till something happened with her hand. It got all hot—shit, I don't really know what happened. She was so upset. So what are you saying? She ran out of my place and went to him? Why?"

Ben looks back at me. I deem it safer to neither deny nor confirm.

"She can be with anyone she wants to, Ben. Like I said, it's not up to you. Things happen. Deal with it." Clearly, Tess doesn't feel that saying nothing is the way to go.

"Are you serious? She wouldn't—there is no way."

Ben stalks off, but not far. We can't see much beyond this small clearing and the shafts of light making it through the canopy of trees are dimming quickly. Night seems to be rapidly approaching—or something that's mimicking night. The dark will only make things worse.

"Do you love her?" Tess whispers the question to me, but this doesn't hide the intensity of her tone. "You better, you know. Because—"

I'm about to tell her that yes, of course, yes. I do. I love Anne Michaelson beyond all reason. I have no assurance that she loves me back, but I'm a patient man. I'm used to waiting a long time for things I believe in. I'll wait as long as it takes. She is not someone I will ever give up on.

247

Only then I hear the all too familiar *whoosh*ing sound overhead. Thunder rumbles, followed by the crack of lightning hitting something not too far from us.

I look up. The canopy shifts in the wind, and through the opening, I catch a brief glimpse of Baba Yaga's mortar. But the canopy moves again before I can see if anyone—Baba Yaga? Anne?—is in it.

"Hey!" The ground underneath Ben shifts. He stumbles but stays standing. The rat-like creature I'd seen earlier scurries from under the leaves and opens its mouth wider than should be possible for a rodent that small and slender. Its tongue—impossibly long and thin—flicks out toward Ben's injured foot.

It's the koshka that intervenes. The cat dashes from whatever dark corner he's been hiding in, hisses at the rat creature, and bares his teeth. The rat freezes in mid-attack on Ben's foot, then retreats into the leaves. Ben shudders.

"Gross." Tess wrinkles her nose. "This place is seriously disgusting. But I think that cat likes you, Ben. That's good, right?" She directs the last part to me.

I nod, remembering how Anastasia had thanked the cat when it helped us last fall. Even here—especially here—maybe certain manners still apply. I kneel carefully, holding my hand out, palm up. An offering. A gesture of submission. "*Spasiba*," I say softly. "Thank you." The cat stares, then blinks. Maybe it's enough.

Ben gapes at me. "Are you talking to the damn cat? This is nuts. Attacking mermaids and crazy forests and what else? My girlfriend is some kind witch? Are you guys really saying that Anne has some sort of magical power? Shit. This is just a mass hallucination or something."

Tess ignores his ranting. "So what now? I really don't want

to stick around here and wait for more creepy rat things to attack us. Eventually, the cat's going to get bored, and then what? If Anne's here, we need to find her. I'm not leaving without her. So that means finding the witch's hut, doesn't it?"

Ben rubs his arms with his hands. The air is getting colder. "You really think that's where Anne is?" he asks. "Because whatever she is and whatever you are, if something's happened to her—"

"She can handle herself. She's really strong, Ben. I know this is all confusing, but trust me—no matter what else happens, Anne's strong. We'll find her. And then we'll all find a way to get out of here." Tess punctuates her series of pronouncements with a sharp nod.

"It's getting darker," I tell them. "At least it will make it easier to see the lights from Baba Yaga's hut. That's what we saw last time—the glow from the skulls on pikes around her hut. We didn't know that's what it was, but—the cat helped us. I know it all sounds crazy, but everything works by its own rules and time here. You have to just accept it. C'mon. Let's see if we can do this. Tess is right. We can't just keep standing here. We need to move."

So we do. The three of us start our trek through the forest. For a while, Tess and Ben keep up a constant patter of conversation.

"She's related to the Romanovs," Tess tells Ben. "Really. Her mom doesn't know—well, I guess she sort of knows now because of everything—but they are. And Ethan—it's okay if I tell now, isn't it, Ethan? I mean, since we're all stuck here and everything? Ethan was a member of this Brotherhood thing. And he didn't age for, like, decades, because of this magical spell thing that kept Anastasia—the real Anastasia Romanov—here in Baba Yaga's. This guy Viktor—he was in the Brotherhood too, and he's Anne's great-great-grandfather—well, he found a way to trick everyone and stay immortal if only Anastasia remained in the hut. But Ethan kept trying to find her. And he needed Anne to help him. That was part of the magic. Anne was the one the Brotherhood been looking for. And Ethan found her, and then they used this magic lacquer box to get into the forest and rescue Anastasia, but she wanted to go back and die like she was supposed to, and—"

"Just stop," Ben says. He pushes through a clump of small trees and low-lying prickly bushes. His foot has stopped bleeding, but there's a fresh cut on his arm from pushing aside a branch of a strange-looking tree with sharp burrs along every piece of it. "I don't want to know. I can't know this. You guys are insane. That's all this is. I'm in some kind of crazy nightmare, and you're all here with me. If I can just wake up, I'll be back in my room with Anne."

Tess shrugs. "I'm just trying to help and—hey, Ethan." She stops short, sweat running freely down her face, her hair tangled now with burrs and pieces of dead twigs. The light is almost gone, but I can still see the real fear in her face. "Viktor. What about Viktor? He's here, right? I mean, isn't that what's messing with mermaid Lily's head? That Viktor's here, and she wants Anne to get him out so she can kill him or something? But is he really here?"

I push another low-lying branch out of our way and wince as I step on something that feels like gravel and crushed bone.

"I think so. If she was still compelled to protect a Romanov, then she's been protecting him. Except I don't think it's gone very well."

"But he's not immortal anymore, is he? Like you're not?"

"No."

"So if Anne does choose—or is forced—to let him out, he can die." She makes it a statement rather than another question.

"Yes. He can die. We both can. The rusalka could have her vengeance, if that's what she really wants. And Baba Yaga—well, I don't know that part. I guess I've never known that part. That's the problem. Everything I thought was true isn't necessarily the way I understood it. But I'm thinking that's the case for Viktor too. He would never have gone into this without thinking he could control it somehow. So if he really can't…" The thought is unfinished.

We're not making much progress. The light is growing even dimmer, and it's still thundering in the distance. The cat—the koshka—has long since disappeared. I try not to think about what will happen to us if we don't find Baba Yaga's hut.

Eventually, Tess speaks again. "Why *do* you think Viktor offered himself to Baba Yaga? To make up for what he'd done? I mean, in theory, he's stuck there forever, isn't he? Do you think he knew that when he sacrificed himself?"

I ponder this. Hell, I've been pondering it for months now. I think back to the skeletal figure that I saw in the cemetery just a few hours ago—about what he told me. *But that's the thing about sacrifice, isn't it? You don't really get to control how it all turns out. You have what I wanted, and I've got this, and if there's a way to fix things—well, I haven't quite stumbled on it yet. Not that I haven't been trying.*

"If there's one thing I know about Viktor," I say finally, "it's that he always has a plan. And he always has a reason. Except right now, I'm not sure what it is."

Tess sighs and shakes her head. "Typical."

I choose not to argue with her. Correction: I don't have time to argue with her, because from in front of us, behind us, and to our right, the sound of galloping horses fills the air.

Baba Yaga's three horsemen thunder upon us in absolute unison—one white, one red, one black, each with a matching steed—the ground heaving and shaking with their approach. The branches and vines that we've struggled around seem to float away to give the horsemen space.

"Hey!" Ben points to the red horse and rider. "I saw you back on the beach. That's what I saw."

The horsemen don't speak. They just circle around us. Once. Twice. Three times.

"What do you," says the horseman in black.

"Most love," says the horseman in red.

"And desire?" finishes the horseman in white.

"You will tell us," they chant in unison, their voices resounding so deeply that they fill my chest, my ears, and my head, impossibly loud. The canopy of trees above us quivers and parts. Baba Yaga's mortar flies swiftly into view. Her enormous hands slide over the edge, and with a strange gracefulness, they plummet down to the forest floor.

Ben makes a choking sound in the back of his throat. Tess emits a small, high-pitched scream. A bolt of lightning hits a nearby tree, rides its jagged way down the bark, and sets the dead leaves around us on fire. Before any of us can even react, we're encircled in the rising flames. Ben, Tess, me, and the horsemen. The flames grow higher—a wall of fire trapping us. Heat billows into the air.

"What would you die for?" asks the horseman in black.

"What could you not live without?" asks the one in red.

"What truly lies in your heart?" asks the horseman dressed in white.

"You must answer. You must tell our mistress. You must not lie." Their voices boom again, even louder than before. My head is filled with the sound—so much sound that it's painful. Tess presses her hands to her ears. Ben does the same.

"You must tell us. The girl is to learn. Our mistress says you have lessons to teach her."

Around us, the flames burn hotter. Baba Yaga's hands skitter closer to us, rushing around on their ancient, brown, and wrinkled fingertips. The horsemen repeat their words three times. After the third time, they reach for us.

Friday, in the Forest

Anne

L ET THEM GO!" WE'RE FLYING THROUGH THE DARKNESS IN
Baba Yaga's mortar, and I can't take my gaze off hers.
"You have to let them go. This is about you and me, not them.
You have me. Why do you need them?"

I want to look over the side of the mortar. I want to jump
down and do something. But I can't. I push every bit of power
that I know is inside me to fight her. With my vision trapped, I
reach blindly and place my hands on her arms. Then I shudder
as I feel the empty flapping of her sleeves where her hands have
detached. I know I'm burning her. I know I'm hurting her. But it
isn't helping. Her eyes bore into mine, each pupil a tiny white skull
through which I'm being forced to watch Tess, Ethan, and Ben.

"You must learn. I have told you, daughter. True power
comes from knowing. You cannot leave this forest as you are.
You have hidden from it for too long. If you will not learn on
your own, then you will learn through them—these people you
love, the ones in your thoughts, the ones you believe you would
do anything for. Would you? You must know. You cannot take
what is about to come to you if you do not."

I slam my fists against her chest. Her breath is as hot as
fire against my face. "I keep telling you. I don't want it! I've

never wanted it. I promised you I'd drink, but only to save my friends. So why did you take them? Just let them go."

She says nothing. Around us, the air is thick and heavy. Exhaustion washes over me. *I need to fight it. If I don't, I'll never help them.* In the vision I see in Baba Yaga's eyes, the horseman in black grabs Ben and lifts him up onto his horse. *I have to stop this.* But my head is drooping, and against my will, my eyes flutter shut.

I drift swiftly into dreaming.

"Auntie Yaga," I say. Baba Yaga sits in her hut by the fire. I've been there with her. I know what this place looks like, this small wooden hut that may be larger than it seems, that may have twists and turns and hidden corners where things lurk that I don't want to see. Auntie Yaga rests in her chair. Her huge gnarled hands—each knuckle the size of a small egg—hold a cup of sweet tea. Her long brown dress brushes against the smooth wooden floor as she rocks. Not far away sits the wooden table where she held my hand in another dream, cut the palm and watched the blood drip. Once, twice, three times.

The dream morphs. For a few precious seconds, the two realities exist as one. I know that I'm not me anymore. I'm Anastasia. But that can't be. I saved Anastasia. Well, I tried to anyway. But I took her from the hut and let her choose her own path. I brought her back with me and watched her choose to die. She can't be here anymore. I can't be dreaming as her. I'm me. I'm Anne. I'm—

I'm sitting on my small bed with its red and blue quilt. My *matroyshka* doll lays next to me on the soft, goose-down pillow. I hear it whisper in a voice so tiny that at first, I almost don't notice it.

Secrets within secrets, it tells me. *When you wake, you must re-member this. Even the witch doesn't know. She has given you this dream, and she has lent you her magic, but there are secrets beyond what even she knows. I am the* matroyshka. *The little mother. And so I ask you this: Where would you hide something that you didn't want anyone to find? Where could you place something and still have it be in plain sight?*

"My journal," I whisper back to her. "It's inside you. Hidden away like I am. Tucked inside this hut in the forest where no one can find me." I feel tears start to well in my eyes and squeeze them shut. I will not cry in front of the witch. I have not cried here for a very long time.

No, my dearest. It is more than that. There is always something more. Didn't the rusalka tell you?

"Rusalka? Like in the stories my mother used to tell? The ones she'd heard from the women who worked for us? She used to tell me tales of village women scorned and lost and turned into something that took them beyond death. Women who met their destiny in the water and were never able to move on." Even as I say this, I'm confused. Is this something I should know?

Ah, the *matroyshka* whispers. Across the room from us, Auntie Yaga stirs, turns, and stares into her fire. Inside it floats a skull, its bones bleached white, the fire gleaming through each eye socket. She holds out her huge hands toward it and hums a wordless tune. *I have forgotten that you are more than one today. Both my girls inside the other. The one you are not will know what to do with this story. If she can remember it.*

I hear a tapping sound then. Someone is at the hut's door. Odd, I think. No one visits us here in this strange house that rests on chicken legs, ready to move if strangers approach. I hold my breath, expecting to hear the familiar sound of claws scrabbling for purchase in the dirt. But nothing moves.

"Go answer the door, girl," Auntie Yaga tells me. "See who is there."

This too is new. How can she let me do this? Does she not know that I will try to flee? Then again, where will I go? I have long since understood that everyone I love is dead and gone—long since understood how I was betrayed by my own foolish heart.

"Oh, my God," says a girl about my age with long blond hair and a cut on her cheek. "You're Anastasia, right? I mean, I guess you are. Shit. I'm sorry. I'm supposed to tell you something, I guess. I'm not really sure."

I stare at her, wondering how this can really be and why Auntie Yaga doesn't move. She just rocks in her chair by the fire, the koshka resting now at her feet but watching me at the door. Is this one of my dreams? Where will I be when I wake up? And inside my head right now, inside my heart, something feels different.

"Will you come inside?" I ask her, because I don't know what else to say. She is not here to save me. I am in no position to save her.

"I don't think I can. I think I'm stuck here. Are those real skulls on that fence? I keep hearing them scream. Do you know they're screaming? Oh, Anastasia. I'm sorry you had to live like this. I seriously didn't think—I'm Anne's friend. I don't know if you know who Anne is yet, but I'm her best friend. I love her like a sister. So if I don't get out of here, and somehow you see her, tell her that I tried to help. Tell her that I tried to stay brave. And tell her that Ethan loves her. I think she needs to know that. He didn't actually say it—mainly because we all got dragged away by those horsemen guys—but I could tell anyway. Ethan loves her—and even if I think he's kind of an idiot, that doesn't matter. Most guys are, anyway. And—I'm babbling, aren't I? Sorry. I'm just pretty freaked right now, and I'm not really sure if any of this is real because Anne already got you out of here. I know it didn't go well after that, but she did. It's Viktor who's supposed to be here now, not you. I guess if none of this is real, then it doesn't matter, but—"

"I don't understand," I tell the blond-haired girl. "Who are you again?"

"Tess. Sorry. Tess Edwards. And I—oh, crap. I forgot. I have to tell you something else. You have to listen carefully. Baba Yaga is going to ask you what I said, and you have to repeat it exactly. That's what the guy on the horse told me. He said he'd know if I lied."

The blond girl—Tess—reaches up to push her hair out of her eyes, and I see that her hand is shaking. Her face is very pale. I think of offering her some water, or perhaps some of Auntie's tea, but she is intent on telling me her story. Stories are something I understand. Auntie Yaga tells me many of them. Sometimes, they are even nice.

I open the door a little wider. It is a mistake. Although she sits behind me, I feel Auntie rise from her rocking chair, hear the koshka pad off to some dark corner.

Tess Edwards' breath catches in her throat, but still she speaks to Baba Yaga. And when she does, her voice is strong. I think I could like this girl if she were my friend.

"You helped save me. That's what Ethan just told me before all the rest of this happened. I know you probably did it for some reason other than helping me, but you did it. I'm alive because you helped Anne save me. So even though you're scaring the crap out of me right now, I guess what I need to say is thank you. Because no matter why you did it, it got done. I'm here and talking to you because you let me be here."

Auntie Yaga's laughter spills into the air. It is not often that she is amused. I turn to look at her. She is smiling, and her iron teeth gleam in the firelight. Her mouth gapes hugely as she laughs.

"It seems," she says, and her voice is deep and smooth as the wooden floor on which we stand, "that my girl has chosen her friends wisely. But I am an old, old woman, Tess Edwards. So could you please finish what you have come to say? That heart of yours is quite large. It will be tasty if I choose to sample it." Auntie Yaga licks her tongue over her cracked lips, rubs it against her iron teeth.

It's that gesture that does it, that pulls me up and out of Anastasia's head. It's the same thing she'd just done after she'd wiped the blood off my face. I'm still seeing things through her eyes, but Tess is right. This is all some sort of illusion because Anastasia is dead. Or maybe she's not. Maybe she's somewhere else now. But I'm not her. I'm me, Anne. And no matter what else happens, no matter what else I am, my best friend in the world is standing here and has just managed somehow to save my ass.

I close my eyes and concentrate as hard as I ever have. When I open them and look down, I see me: plain old Anne Michaelson in my filthy jeans and tank top, my bare feet standing on Baba Yaga's wooden floor.

"I might have promised to drink from your stream," I say to Baba Yaga, "but I absolutely do not give you permission to eat my friends."

I turn back to Tess. She still looks totally terrified, but she's grinning.

"Is that you, Anne? Really?"

The hut door is open. I grab her hand. "Run!" I tell her.

"Are we dreaming?" Tess yells as we push through the gate and ignore the screaming of the skulls. One of them opens its mouth and attempts to nip at my elbow. It grazes my arm, and I smack it with the back of my hand. It howls louder, then spits out broken shards of what used to be teeth. This is not only frightening but seriously gross.

"Maybe. But I don't think so. I can't believe you thanked her. You're crazy, Tess. Have I mentioned that?"

"It is no dream now, Anne Michaelson." Baba Yaga's voice echoes around us. "You are a clever girl. And perhaps you are worthy. Your friend has told you without telling you. She would lose many things, but she would not lose you. It is your first lesson. Let's see what you make of the others. Is your heart as big as hers? Would it be as tasty?"

And then we're back in the forest. I glance behind us, above us. Only Baba Yaga's laughter follows us. I sense this is not a good thing, but what option do we really have except to run? Hang out and have tea with her? I think not.

In the trees to my right, I catch a glimpse of something black, its gold eyes glinting in the shadows. The koshka is staying close, watching what we do. This only makes it clearer to me that we haven't really escaped. She's just let us go.

"Where did you leave them? Ethan and Ben? Do you know where they are?"

Tess shakes her head. "The horsemen grabbed us. There was this huge fire. But they rode through it with us behind them on the horses' backs like it was nothing. My guy brought me here. Said he had different plans for Ben and Ethan, but I was going to have to say what it was I'd die for, what I couldn't live without. So I'm sitting on the back of this red horse, holding on to this creepy guy in a red outfit and thinking, 'Hell if I know.' I'm seventeen. I don't plan on dying for a long time. And then he's asking me what's in my heart. So what am I supposed to tell him? I just broke up with Neal in a text message, for God's sake. But I love my family. And I love you. That's what I thought. I thought about how ridiculously brave you've been. Well, you've been kind of stupid too. And pig-headed. Making a bargain with a witch—are you kidding me? But he's asking me, and I'm thinking that I'd be there for you no matter what. I can't say I'd die for you—no offense or anything—but I'd be there as long as I could. Because who else would put up with me? I'm pretty high maintenance, you know."

I try to stop myself from laughing, but I can't. It's funny and it's not funny all at the same time.

"Did Ethan really say he loved me?"

"Do you really think we have time to talk about that now?"

"Yes. Did he?"

"Well, yes. He's crazy about you. He'd do anything for you. Have you not caught on to that? I think he's nuts, if you ask me, but yes, he loves you. If we get out of this, I'm going to have a serious talk with him. And you, for that matter. Because speaking as your best friend, I'm thinking you still might not know how you really feel about the whole Ethan thing. At least, in *my* humble opinion."

I don't respond. We continue running through the thick forest, the koshka keeping pace with us. But no matter what direction we move, we end up back in the same little clearing in the woods. The smoke from Baba Yaga's chimney is still visible through the trees, and we're still only steps away from the hut.

"Wait." I pull Tess to a stop. "We're not getting anywhere. I don't think we're going to unless Baba Yaga lets us."

"Well, great. So now what?"

The question isn't even out of Tess's mouth when a woman enters the clearing. She's tall and slim and wearing a long, gauzy saffron-colored dress that reaches to her ankles. Around her neck hangs a chain of flowers. She's barefoot, and another ringlet of flowers circles one of her ankles. A crown of leaves rests in her long brown hair.

"She's beautiful," Tess whispers. "So graceful."

Tess is right. Every step this woman takes is like a dance.

She raises one slender arm and beckons to us. "Come, daughters," Her voice is full and throaty, like a bird singing. "It is time for another story."

I catch her gaze then, and my heart stops in my throat. Her hair is long and lush, and her body is young and firm, but in each of her eyes, there's tiny glowing skull.

"C'mon." Tess pulls on my arm. "We need to follow her, right? Or should we try to keep running?"

I can barely make myself say the words. "It's her, Tess. It's Baba Yaga. Look at her eyes. See?"

I don't want to follow her, but my feet move without my permission. The same happens to Tess. We shuffle behind the woman in saffron to the middle of the clearing. Our knees bend of their own accord, and we sit on the ground.

"You have chosen without understanding," the woman who might be Baba Yaga says. "So now you must know. There really is no more time, even here where time is fluid. Come back with me, Anne. Your friend too. She has earned this for you. Her gratitude has made me generous. But do not worry. It will not last. Still, this is what I am, and I do not question my moods. So I will tell you a little secret. Sometimes, I grant favors. Sometimes, I do not. Today, I am of a mood to do so. I can heal, or I can destroy. This is the nature of my power. Both please me. But beware. Favors like this—they come only once. And only of my free will. As you are well aware, no one likes to be commanded. No one likes to be used. Nothing good comes of that kind of power or that kind of magic. And nothing—absolutely nothing, daughter Anne—comes without a price. There are no simple answers. But there is, as always, a story."

And the rest of the story unfolds as if we're in a movie. Somehow, in my head, there's a voice narrating—slow and gentle and mesmerizing. I couldn't stop listening even if I tried. I catch myself smiling. It's like a fairy tale, even in the way it begins.

Once upon a time, the voice tells us, *I was young and beautiful. You see the woman before you now. I loved, and I lived. But I cursed my beauty, because I knew it was fleeting. Beauty is power if you're a woman, but for me, it was not enough. To have the life I wanted, to have the power I wanted, I needed to be more. But how? So long ago, this was, so long that the Old Ones still roamed among us—goddesses who granted boons to foolish girls and wise girls and some of us who were both. I had seen what happened to women whose only power was physical. Nature changed them as nature does, and then their power faded. Still, I did not believe it could happen to me. I was lithe. Young. I would live and love forever.*

But then one day, the man I loved told me that he loved another—a common story until it happens to you. Then it is not so common at all. Pain is unique to each of us, and mine was unbearable. Perhaps the

Old Ones were listening that day. Perhaps it was my destiny. That part I do not know. But I made a bargain. I would give up my youth, and I would give up my beauty. No longer would I be governed by how someone perceived my face. In return, I would have the power I craved. I did not ponder the choice for long. I knew the whims of the Old Ones, how swiftly they might cancel an offer such as this. "Are you sure?" they asked me, although later, I knew that they had already made their choice. I answered yes. Oh, yes. Beauty is power, but I wanted to be feared on my own terms—to help or hurt as it pleased me. No predictability, even if the cost was a heart of stone.

But hearts are strange things. Even when they've stopped beating, sometimes they still feel.

Her name was Marina. I had been Baba Yaga for a very long time when she came to me for help here in this forest. I no longer counted my time by days or years. Such markers are of no consequence to one who lives as I do. The world had changed around me, but the midwives and the herbalists and those who still secretly followed the ways of the Old Ones—they still knew what I was, what I could do. Their mothers and grandmothers had passed the secrets down to them, and thus to the woman named Marina.

"Help me," she said. I can still see her now, half hidden behind one of my birch trees. "I love him. I gave him his precious son even before he became the tsar. Even before he married. But my Nicholas has eyes now only for Alexandra. My son should have everything, but he has nothing. Alexandra has borne him girl after girl. Only I have given him a son. What can I do? If you do not help me, I will have nothing left. There will be nothing left for me but the river. Or worse."

This is what she told me. And because—like today—I was feeling generous, I listened. Or rather, I almost always listened. But I had not chosen to act in a very long time.

"I am not afraid of you," she said. "I am too desperate to be afraid. I should have known that Nicholas would not stay with me and with the boy. But my heart could not give up hope. My darling boy, Viktor. Do you know that his name means "champion"? Nothing will give me happiness if he cannot have what is rightfully his."

It was this last part that intrigued me: the absolute certainty with which she believed her son deserved the legacy of his bloodline. How deliciously perfect! I could both reward and punish her arrogance with one single spell. Heal and harm with the flick of a finger.

I placed my hands on her shoulders and sent forth my will into her. "Go home and hug your son," I told her. "Tell him that Baba Yaga gives him her blessing. If you do this, he will get what he deserves. He will have the legacy of a tsar. Your son, and his children, and his children's children."

She thanked me over and over. And that very evening, when she returned home, she clasped her son Viktor to her, held him tight, and whispered my words in his ear. "Thank you, Mother," he told her. "Thank you."

The woman in saffron dances closer to Tess and me, presses one slender hand against my cheek. "Power has a price. It is the way of things—not only here in my forest, but in all places, in all things. A balance. I had willed Viktor a legacy, a passing down. We do not own the magic, not even witches as ancient and skilled as I. Just as I paid the price of my beauty, Viktor would pay for what he craved, even if he did not know he was paying, did not understand that his blood would allow the Brotherhood its strongest of magics. My power passed down through his blood from child to child to child. And then the best price of all for his arrogance. Each of those children would be female."

She smiles at me and Tess like we're supposed to applaud or something. I mean, it's fitting in a girl-power kind of way, but honestly, she's as full of herself as Viktor is. And even though I'm still terrified, it just makes me angry.

I push her hand away. "With all due respect, he *did* manage to trap you here, didn't he? Compelled you to save Anastasia? And now, since the spell's still gone all wonky, you're stuck with him, right? That's gotta suck."

Tess elbows me in the ribs. "Isn't she ticked off enough at us?" she whispers.

Saffron-dress Baba Yaga arches an eyebrow but otherwise ignores our interruption. "He did not believe that a mere *girl* could ever defeat him. He was the tsar's first son. How could a sixteen-year-old schoolgirl find a way to undo what he had managed? The ancient prophecies were for fools like his protégé, Brother Ethan."

The mention of Ethan's name jolts me, makes me realize that we can't sit here having story time much longer. We need to find Ethan and Ben. We need to get ourselves out of here.

The witch doesn't seem to have such a pressing agenda. She keeps rambling. "It is the perfect circle, you see. My power passed through Viktor to a daughter that he never even knew existed. And then to that daughter's daughter. And down the line to you. His own desire for power would defeat him, and in turn, would lead you to me—to a destiny that Viktor could not even have imagined."

Won't anyone ever let go of the whole destiny thing? She stops talking—finally—and begins to whirl and twirl and dance around the clearing. She may be done, but I'm not.

"What about the rest of it?" I call to her. "What about the rusalka? Lily? She tried to come to you too, didn't she? But you didn't help her. If you helped Marina, then why not Lily? Lily's part of Viktor's bloodline, just like I am. Why did you let her become such a horrible thing if you could have stopped it?" Or could she have? Maybe her help would have just trapped Lily in a different way.

She doesn't answer. She just raises her arms to the sky. The dense forest spreads open. We move suddenly and without any warning. We're no longer in the clearing, but in front of Baba Yaga's hut. In the distance, like it's behind a gauzy curtain, I see the beach at Lake Michigan. My mother's still kneeling on the sand, her arms outstretched like she's reaching for me.

To my right, the stream appears. Had it been there when we arrived? But now it is, winding through the forest, disappearing into the trees. Ben sits next to it, staring into the water. But where's Ethan?

"Ben!" I run to him. Tess follows at my heels. "Ben! Get up, Ben. Get away from there!"

"I've got a really bad feeling about this," Tess says. "Really bad."

Ben's face is as pale as I've ever seen it. He looks up at me and Tess as we skid to a stop next to him. "Can't move," he says. "I can't feel my legs. The horseman—the one in black—I think he put some of kind of spell on me. I've been sitting here trying and trying to move. But I can't. He kept asking me what I really wanted. What I most desired. And I kept telling him that I just want to wake up from whatever this is. I just want to go home."

"Oh, crap," Tess says. "Ben, is that really what you said?"

As if on cue, Saffron Dress Baba Yaga begins to laugh. "An interesting twist, isn't it, child? Are you still so torn? Hasn't the rusalka you seem to care about so much taught you anything?"

"He doesn't mean it!" I scream at her. "He doesn't

understand all these tricks and games. Just leave him alone! He didn't ask to be part of this!"

"Neither did you, girl. Is he worth saving? Is he worth the power you have, the power you are yet to receive?"

"Is that what this is about? I can only help people who are worthy of it? Is that what you think? Is that why you didn't help Lily? Because she wasn't worth it to you, and somehow, I am? Why?"

"Because you're stronger. Because you're like me. You picked this boy because you could live with the thought of him leaving you. And you haven't truly given your heart to Ethan because you couldn't live if he left you again. You are the perfect girl for my legacy: true only to yourself."

"You really don't know her, do you?" Tess pulls my hand into hers, holds tight. "She's not like you. Not at all."

"Ignore her. Help me get Ben up." Tess and I each link a hand under his arms and pull. We lift him, but his legs just buckle underneath him, and he slips out of our grip and flops to the ground.

Baba Yaga morphs. The good old original stands next to us again—long brown dress, huge horrible hands, gross iron teeth. The black koshka winds around her ankles. He flicks his pink tongue in and out of its mouth, looks at me, and hisses.

"I like you better this way," I tell her. "At least now, you look like what you are. And Tess is right. I'm not you. I never was. I never will be."

"Do you give your promises so lightly, girl? Will you dare tempt me by refusing to keep true to your word?"

"So what exactly is drinking from the stream going to do? Let you take little vacations to Maui or something? You and the cat planning on hanging out at the beach and sipping umbrella drinks? I know what I wanted from the bargain. I wanted to save my friends. But what do you want? You've given me your little history lesson, so now I think it's only fair that you tell me. Since you think I'm so worthy and all."

"Drink." Baba Yaga points one wrinkled finger at the stream. "Then you will know."

"Not until I see Ethan. Not until my friends are safe."

I realize that I'm furious. At Baba Yaga. At Viktor and the rusalka. Even at myself for ending up here with everyone's lives hanging in the balance. Everything has been manipulated for so long. Maybe even Baba Yaga doesn't know the truth anymore. But I'm tired of this crazy game we've been playing. I don't want her to ask me any more questions. I refuse to tell her that I'd pick one thing over another. She thinks that I'm like her, but I'm not. I don't know what I am yet, but I know I'm not that.

Horse hooves sound through the woods. The horseman dressed in white gallops up and dumps Ethan on the ground in front of me. One of his eyes is swollen shut, and there's an ugly purple bruise on his cheekbone.

I fall to my knees next to him. "Ethan! Oh, Ethan." I touch my fingertips to his eye. "I'm so sorry. Are you okay?"

He squints and glances around us, then whispers in my ear. "The horseman's on our side. Just be ready."

Friday, in the Forest

Ethan

"Be ready for what?" Anne grabs my elbow as I stagger to my feet.

I try to clear my vision. One of my eyes is closed to a slit. *Easier if Mistress continues to believe you are weak*, the horseman had said. Did his fist hit me? Or just magic? I don't know. I don't even know for sure if I can trust him.

But it's the horsemen who helped us get out of here last time, and it's this horseman who's helping us now. They are still not bound in the same ways as Baba Yaga. The Brotherhood's magic never took them into consideration. It's our only loophole.

"I think I can get us out of here. But we won't have much time. We're going to have to move quickly."

"We can't! Ben. He can't move his legs, Ethan. It's some kind of spell. Baba Yaga's paralyzed him or something."

I turn, horrified, and see that she's right.

A scrim will appear, the horseman had whispered to me in the forest. *Mistress will let them see their world. She doesn't mean to let them go, just to play with them. To let Anne see her mother, force her to consider everyone who might be hurt by what she does or doesn't do. As it rises, the magic is at its weakest. You can break through then. But you must act quickly. Before the witch realizes what you are doing.*

It appears just beyond the stream now, just as he's described it. A division between where we want to be and where we are. Anne's mother kneels on the sand, still reaching for her. Lake Michigan is behind her, blue and deep.

"Look." Tess points toward the lake.

"Oh crap," Anne says.

And I know in that instant that it no longer matters whether the horseman had been lying or telling the truth. After that, there's no time to think at all.

In those few seconds as the scrim settles, Lily rises from the lake and walks swiftly toward the stream. Her hair snakes around her. Her dress is soaked and tattered. She presses her hands against the magic that has kept her from us. And in those few seconds, crosses from the real world to the forest and glides into the stream.

"Well, my dear girl. Your Ethan has made quite the error in judgment. Even I don't trust my horsemen. But it seems that your mermaid grandmother has finally found her way to me. Drink, Anne." Baba Yaga looms over us, taller than I've ever seen her. "You have promised. Once you drink, then you can make all this go away."

In the middle of the water now, Lily starts to weep. Ben starts to drag himself back toward the stream.

"Stop me," he says. "Anne, please. Make it stop."

FRIDAY, IN THE FOREST

ANNE

THIS IS *so* NOT GOOD," TESS SAYS. "WHAT ARE WE GOING to do?"

The sound of Lily's pain washes through me and over me and around me and ties itself up with the overriding certainty that if I don't do something—anything—Ben is going to die again. Only this time, I won't be able to bring him back because I have no intention of doing what Baba Yaga wants, and once she realizes that, it's all over.

Unless I find a way to change the odds. The plan hatches quickly—too quickly to be sensible. But what other choice do I have? I won't let Ben die. I can't let Ben die. The words loop over and over in my head.

"Help Ben." I gesture to Tess and Ethan. "Please. Don't let her touch him."

"No!" Ethan holds out a hand as if to stop me. "We need to stay together."

But I can't listen to him. If I listen to him, Ben might die. So with the sound Lily's keening cries echoing everywhere, I run.

Behind me, Lily's voice cracks with tears. "You wouldn't help me, witch. You wouldn't let me come to you. But now, here I am."

I make it across the little clearing, ignore the skulls on the pikes, and dash to the hut door. All I can think is that Lily will kill Ben because she can't have what she wants. And Baba Yaga—well, she doesn't want Viktor either, does she? In my dreams, I've felt her desire to kill him. It's what they both want, and I'm just so very tired of being in the middle of it all. All these people have such fierce desires to live forever, but all that ever seems to come of it is death.

If there's anything left of him, I'll let Viktor out, do what the rusalka wanted me to do anyway—my crazy birth grandmother, so filled with grief at what she's lost. If anyone gets that, it's me. If I really can release him, then that's what I'll do. Let the witch and the mermaid fight over him. And while my two highly dysfunctional ancestors duke it out with Baba Yaga, the rest of us can find our way back home.

Like that first time, the hut heaves in and out, in and out, like it's breathing. The chicken legs scrabble at the ground, and my hand misses the doorknob over and over. I lunge again, grab it, and start to turn. I needed the lacquer box key the last time, but I'm not the same as I was the last time. There's more inside me, and I hope that whatever it is, it's enough.

Behind me, Ethan shouts. "Anne! Watch out!"

And then I'm hurtling through the air. I slam to the ground so hard that my breath stops dead in my chest. Baba Yaga stands over me laughing, her sleeves flapping empty in the wind. I gasp. She's sent her hands to stop me, and they've done their job. I only turned the handle halfway. Not enough. Her huge, wrinkled brown hands slide under my body, lift me, and throw me like I weigh nothing at all. I land in the stream facedown. Somewhere above me or maybe behind me, I hear

Tess and Ethan and Ben calling my name as I sink beneath the surface of the water.

It's not real. It's not real. This is what I keep telling myself as the water filters over me. The stream is shallow. I can't be sinking this far under. But it feels real—just like drowning.

Somehow, impossibly, Lily is next to me under the water. We are far, far under. I hold my breath. I don't want to drown, and I don't want to drink. Either way, if I open my mouth, I'm screwed. I'll be dead—or I'll be doing what Baba Yaga wants from me. Will I become her? Take on her powers? But I'll bound to her somehow, because that's what I promised, and that's what she expects to collect. She doesn't care that Ethan's told me he loves me. Or that I might like a little time to figure out if I love him back. Or that my mother might have just watched me fall facedown into the water and might now think I'm dead.

"You have no idea," Lily says softly. She floats in front of me, so close that as her dark hair fans out, it twists itself with mine. "I was no good for your mother. I could think of nothing but Misha—nothing but what I didn't have. I had gone to find Baba Yaga, and I did not come back the same. She had not granted my wish, and I did not know what else to do. How could you know that kind of loss?"

But I do, I tell her. I can't say it aloud, but somehow, I think she hears me anyway. I've watched my mother suffer. We all have. It's different, I know. But I think it feels the same. Like a wave my mom and I saw that winter David died, not far from where Mom is still kneeling on the beach right now. It was a wave in winter, frozen near the shore, unable to move.

Lily reaches out one thin arm and strokes it across my hair. Her ruby and pearl fan hair clip slips from my hair and drifts through the water. She lowers her hand and catches it, fastens it into her own hair and leans in very close to me.

"It was only for a second. Just one second. Just one thought as they swam toward me, as I understood what they were. Just one thought that perhaps this was what I wanted, this was better. That I had no choice but to accept. I wanted to take it back as soon as it leaped into my head, but it was too late. The words were on my tongue, and then I opened my mouth, and it all rushed in. The water. The rusalkas' enchantment. Once I accepted, there was no turning back. Not for me."

Then fight against it, I tell her with my thoughts. *Just this once. Help me. If you hate the witch, then piss her off by pulling me out of here. You've lost so much, and I know you don't have control. But maybe you could control this one thing. And then I can tell Mom what you did. That you did this one last thing for her. That you helped your daughter's daughter when she needed it.*

I'm in her head then, seeing what she sees, feeling what she feels: a tiny, dark-haired baby in her arms. The softness of the child's delicate skin as she caresses her daughter's cheek. Her daughter. My mother. She presses her lips to the baby's head. Tears well in her eyes, fall onto her daughter's face. I feel the pain—sharp as a thousand knives cutting into my skin—as she hands her daughter to the nurse. The loss is enormous, and for a few seconds, it presses me deeper into the water. Lily clutches at me. Lily, me, the infant that was my own mother years ago— all floating here on the edge of something that none of us can ever truly control.

In that instant, we're standing together in the shallow water. Lily's hand is clasped in mine. Ethan and Tess are standing in the grass, holding Ben between them. They jolt forward like statues brought to life when Lily and I appear. Had some magic stopped them from moving?

When Tess lets go of Ben to run to me, he slumps, and Ethan has to pull him up again to keep him from falling.

"Enough," Ethan says to Baba Yaga. He moves closer to her, dragging Ben with him. "Enough already."

"Has your mentor taught you nothing?" she says to him. "Viktor can't ever have enough of anything. But you tell me to stop. You have no more magic, Ethan. You will not win."

Baba Yaga's hands skitter about in front of us, splashing the water toward me with their fingers. The witch herself tilts her head and observes me. "Clever girl," she says slowly. "More clever than I even thought. Blood may be thicker than my water, after all. I am feeling generous again. Although not much." She nods, and her right hand skitters backward, then turns and flicks one leathery finger in Ben's direction.

The effect is immediate. "My legs," Ben says. "My legs!" He pulls from Ethan and walks a few unsteady steps. "The feeling's coming back."

This time, I don't thank her. Correction: I might have thanked her. But then the skulls around the hut start screeching.

We all look toward the hut. Maybe I'd turned that door handle enough after all. And maybe that's not a good thing after all.

Viktor—the ragged remains of his black leather jacket and expensive trousers hanging loosely—emerges from Baba Yaga's door. His hair is pure white, his body so thin that I wonder how he's actually standing, much less walking. He shields his eyes with one hand and surveys the scene in front of him. Then he begins to move. He doesn't speak, just walks away from the hut and through the fence, steadier with each step. One of the skulls nips at Viktor's arm, its petrified teeth gripping his elbow. He doesn't even cry out—he just wrenches his arm away and keeps moving.

"What did you do, girl?" Baba Yaga's voice slices through me. "It is impossible. I sent my hands! I am still compelled! This cannot be!"

Ethan curses under his breath, Russian, then English, then something else I can't identify.

The rest happens very fast.

Lily lets go of my hand and walks out of the water. She reaches one thin, pale arm inside the ripped bodice of her gown and pulls out a pistol.

"Do you recognize this?" she calls to Viktor. "It's what you used to kill my Misha. You destroyed everything. You took all I had—even what was yet to be mine."

She shoots. The bullet plows into the left side of Viktor's chest. He staggers. If he screams, I don't hear it. Clutching his heart, he falls to the ground, then lies very still. Blood oozes out from under his hand. For a long few seconds, everything goes white. No sight. No sound. Just the pounding thought that Lily has taken her vengeance, and I have helped her do so.

"Is he dead?" Tess screams while Ethan pulls me out of the water.

Ben's voice edges on total panic. "She shot him. She shot him. And she still has the gun."

Baba Yaga howls in what sounds like true pain. She stands between Lily and Viktor, her head turning toward one and then the other like she's really not sure which direction she needs to go.

Lily rocks back and forth, the gun still in her hand. Her eyes close, and she begins to weep. "Can I see her now?" she says to no one in particular. "Have I earned her back? He's gone. He's gone." She continues blindly rocking. Her finger's still on the trigger. "She wouldn't help me. Look at me. Look at what I've become. I was a mother. And now I am only this." Eyes still squeezed shut as if in pain, she waves the gun.

Which is when I realize it's pointed at me.

"No," Ethan says. He's running before I can even move. Tess screams.

And Ben—well, Ben's a lifeguard. Even with everything that's been happening, Ben is quick. It's what he's trained to do: save people. Keep them from dying. He moves with Ethan, both of them blocking me as they run.

Lily shoots. Does she mean to? I don't know. She's not looking at me, so I will always think she didn't know what she was doing. That it is only what happens, and not what she means, this creature who used to be human—her grief and pain still are.

I hear a crack as the bullet leaves the gun.

"Anne!" Is it Ethan's voice or Ben's? I'm not sure of that either. I only know that they're both flying through the air to block me, and that in that last second, as everything shifts into slow motion, Ethan shoves Ben sideways. Ben tumbles into me, and we both hit the ground at the same time as Lily's bullet drives its way into Ethan's chest. Blood sprays everywhere—on him, on me, on Ben.

Ethan crumbles to the ground. "Anne," he says. He looks at me with those crazy blue eyes, and then his gaze goes blank.

The gun drops from Lily's hand. Tess grabs it and throws it into the stream. It floats there for a moment, then sinks quickly to the bottom.

"Are you hurt? Anne? Anne, are you hurt?" Ben wipes his hand across my face, and when he pulls it back, it's red with blood. "Let me look. Stay still. I need to make sure you're okay."

"I'm fine. I'm okay. Ethan—Ben, I'm not hurt. It's Ethan. Ben, you have to help him. Ben! Please!" On the ground next to us, Ethan makes a horrible gurgling sound and tries to sit up.

"Get the horseman to help you," he says so softly that I can barely hear him. Blood trickles out of his mouth. "He promised me. He…" Ethan's eyes flutter closed. His chest heaves, and then it's barely moving.

"Shit." Ben presses his hand to Ethan's chest. "We need a doctor, Anne. I think the bullet went right into his heart."

I hear Baba Yaga chuckle, a deep ugly sound. But she isn't looking at us. She's looking at Viktor. I watch in horror and amazement as the first bullet rises out of his chest, the blood trickles back inside him, the wound heals over, and he sits up— very much alive.

He stares at Ethan's body, then shifts his gaze to me. "Well, well. An interesting turn of events, eh? I see your *zalupa* has taken a bullet for you. But I do thank you for setting me free, whatever your motivations. Obviously, I've had time to learn a trick or two during my captivity. Perhaps I have you to thank for that as well. If you hadn't rescued my darling stepsister, I wouldn't have had the chance to play the hero, and I wouldn't have been able to—well, as you can see, there is more than one way to cheat death, is there not? Fascinating, no? And your darling Ethan? I see he still likes to throw himself to the lions. Couldn't let your lifeguard take the bullet, now could he?"

He makes a low clicking sound with his tongue. The

horseman in white gallops to us, reaches down his hand, and pulls Viktor up behind him.

"You can't!" Baba Yaga stretches out her arms. Lightning sizzles through the air. My brain is thinking, *Ethan, Ethan, Ethan.* Everything is moving too slow and too fast, and I can't take it all in.

"Ah, Yaga." Viktor smiles. "You forget. You've given the girl part of you. Your power is diminished. And she has no idea how to stop me, does she? Secrets within secrets, eh, Yaga? Isn't that what you've whispered to me? Well, I have a few secrets of my own. Did you think I would sit there with you until I was just another rotting piece of flesh?"

He gives a sharp nod, and the horseman flicks his finger at the stream. The sky tears in two, rips and opens. The horse gallops to the edge, bucks, and Viktor is simply gone.

My head clears. I push Ben aside, press my hand on Ethan's chest. I will the bullet to come out like Viktor's did. For a second, I think I feel it happening. Then, nothing. I try again. And again. But it's as useless as what happened on the beach. My hands are red with Ethan's blood. And then I know that I don't have a choice anymore.

Somehow, Lily sees into my head.

"Don't do it, granddaughter." She's in front of me then, her thin fingers gripping my arms.

"Shut up! Just shut the hell up! Don't call me that! How dare you even talk to me right now! Look at him! You killed him! He loves me, and you killed him! Isn't there some part of you that understands that? There has to be, Lily. Some tiny part of you realizes what you just did. You wanted vengeance, so I let you have it. But you took it out on me instead!"

I turn my back on her and face Baba Yaga. "Is this what you wanted too? Ethan dead? Does this make me worthier now?"

She shrugs, her expression unreadable. Those black skull eyes dig into mine. "Time will tell, daughter. Time will tell. But let us get to the matter at hand. You want your man alive. And Viktor is not dead. Lily did not get her vengeance. She cannot have what she wants. And I am still not certain what you will do—what you are truly capable of. So it seems that none of us has what we want. Not yet."

Stretching out her arm—all parts attached this time—she dips one ancient hand in the stream, cups a small handful of water, and holds it out to me.

"First, you must drink. Not as much as you will later. But enough to bind you to me. To indebt you. Hurry, now. There is no time. His life force ebbs, and there is no healing in my forest without a price. It is the way it is. Even I cannot break that rule."

"Don't, Anne! You're crazy. Don't!" Ben grabs my hands. "He's dead. He's got a bullet in him, for God's sake. What good do you think this is going to do? I don't care what's happened, whatever's gone on between the two of you. I love you, Anne. I've told you that. How can you not know how I feel about you? Look around you, Anne. Look where we are. Is this how you want things to end up? Don't do this."

"Stop, Ben," Tess says. "You're making it worse." Tears tumble from her eyes as she kneels down next to Ethan, clasps her hands, and presses them to her lips. Then she turns her head to look at me. "Do what you have to. But be absolutely sure."

I'm shaking all over. In the end, it's always the same for me. I'm never sure, not really. Is that just a character flaw? Or is that the way life is at its truest? We never really know until it's done. Anastasia believed she was doing the right thing when she listened to Viktor. But her heart told her a lie. Lily believed she had no choice but the river. Now she's a monster, even to herself. Maybe that's the secret. We never know. We just leap in and hope for the best. Maybe that's all we can do.

Gently, even though there's really no time to be gentle, I pull away from Ben, stand in front of Baba Yaga, and open my mouth. She tips her hand. The icy stream water trickles down my throat. Everything inside me trembles. My hands flicker blue, then white. It's more than I've felt by myself before. But still not what I felt when Baba Yaga's hands pressed against mine on the beach. Perhaps there is hope in that. Maybe I've gone only far enough.

"Okay," I tell her. "I drank. Now let Ben and Tess go. And save Ethan, if you can."

"Perhaps. But first, listen. Viktor is not dead. And yet he came to me as mortal as Ethan. How has this come to be? This is what you must find out. If I give you back your Ethan, this will be part of your price. But there is more."

"More? Isn't that enough?" I glance down at Ethan, pale as death, the blood from his wound pooling around him on the forest floor.

Baba Yaga laughs. The sound of it—bitter and metallic—hurts my ears. "You gave him his life back once, and he has given you yours. That should be enough for many lifetimes. But still you ask for favors. So let me ask you what I have asked your two friends here. What is it really that you desire? I know what I want—to be what I was, to have no holds over me or my power. It is worth much to me to have this back—worth enough to give a greedy girl like you what she thinks she wants. So tell me what it is."

And there it is—the basic problem. What do I want? Ethan? Ben? Or something else entirely?

The answer comes as I catch a glimpse of my mother, still alone on the beach. Maybe Ben's response wasn't so wrong, after all. Maybe it's just because I'm still only seventeen, and I want a summer before senior year, and I want to go to homecoming and prom, and I want to take my SAT again so maybe this time I'll get a decent score. I want to lay out at the beach and buy a new lip gloss at Sephora. I want to dance at Miss Amy's a few more times, and yes, I'd like to play Clara in the Nutcracker rather than my usual role as one of the sugarplum fairies. I want to lace up my pointe shoes and work my toes ragged performing. I haven't danced—not really—in months. I want to eat my weight in pizza and kiss someone I love on a blanket listening to music at Ravinia.

More than all that, I just want to go home. I want to hug my mother. We can't go on any longer, she and I, with all these secrets between us. I want her to know who she is—even if it means convincing her that, yes, her birth mother really is a very crazy Russian mermaid. If I'm becoming something else because of this bargain I've just made with Baba Yaga, I want to remind myself of what I'm giving up. So much gets taken from us in the blink of an eye. If I have time to know what I might lose, then at least I can say I know the worth of what I've lost. And in the deepest corner of my heart, I think something that I don't even dare say aloud. If taking what Baba Yaga offers means that somehow I can heal my family's hearts over my brother's death, then maybe that's what I should do.

Thinking it surprises me, because until this moment, I've thought this was all about a different kind of love. Not that it isn't. I'm not ready to give up what I've felt with Ethan. I want that kind of love so much that it hurts. I'm filled with wanting, actually. But there's more to this story, and I guess what I desire most of all is to be able to understand what it is. All the freaky weirdness and magic and witches and mermaids and immortal Russian hotties aside, I want time to figure out how we choose who we are. How we become what we're destined to be. Moments like these that change everything—can they be undone? And I think if I understand that, I'll know how to solve the riddle that is Viktor. I'll have what it takes to help Lily—help her without hurting the rest of us. I'll find my heart's true north, and I'll face the witch on equal terms. If I'm destined to return to this forest, then I need to leave it first.

These are the thoughts that race through my mind.

"Ah, girl," Baba Yaga says "Oh, how you surprise me. And here I thought that we were done for today. It seems we are not." She places her palm on my forehead. The heat of it spreads through my body like fire.

"Kiss him," she directs me. "We could do it another way, but I do like a classic tale. So kiss him before I change my mind."

So I do. I kneel next to Ethan. Tess is still there, but Ben stands apart, looking scared and miserable, and I hate that this next journey has begun by hurting him. But I do what I have to do.

I press my lips to Ethan's, relieved that his are still warm. Then I place my hand over his heart. This time, the bullet comes out in my hand. The hole in his chest closes. His skin warms against my palm. Color floods back into his cheeks and lips.

He sits up. Smiles.

"Hi," I say.

"Time works differently here," Baba Yaga comments oddly. "And so it will for you. An extension of my forest, if you will. You have chosen your journey well. The past, the present, the future—all mingle to solve what needs solving. Your path will wind through them all. But that is yet to come. You have promised me, girl. You are bound. Stories within stories. Secrets within secrets. You will open them all—bring all to light. This is the price you have set. This is the price you will pay. So I will it. So let it be."

We stand in front of the destroyed Jewel Box—my mother, Tess, Ben, Ethan, and me. There's no trace of Mrs. Benson. Or of Lily. Nothing is certain except for one thing: we're all alive.

"You know it's not over," Ethan says. "She won't let you go until you do what you've offered."

I nod. I know.

But I also know the people I care about most have gotten another chance. We've made it out of the forest yet another time.

Forward and backward and all in between. Baba Yaga's voice echoes in the now clear blue sky above us. I'm not sure exactly what she means, but I know I'll find out soon enough.

For now, it's enough to be home.

A Few Weeks Later

Anne

Show me again," my mother says. "Go on."

I frown at her. "This is seriously so weird, Mom."

"Please? Pretty please?" She grins at me, and I give in because it's good to see her smile.

I raise one hand in the air, point a finger at the first leaf on the lowest branch on the elm tree in our backyard. I feel the now familiar buzz in my fingertip as the leaf pulls silently from the branch and flutters gracefully to the ground.

"You did that? Really?"

"Well, yeah," I tell her. "You just asked me to, remember?"

"It was more of a rhetorical question, Anne. It's just that it's so—"

"I told you. It's weird. Both that I can do this stuff and that you seem okay with it."

My mother shrugs. She tips her head back so the sun is shining on her face. "Better to know than how it was," she says quietly. "Not easier. But better."

We're sitting in the grass in our yard, playing with my magic. We both know it's not a game, not something to take lightly. But we haven't shared much in a long, long time, so this is a place to start.

There's a scraggly looking tomato plant drooping in the tiny garden plot Dad's attempted this year. The ones around it are lush with little cherry tomatoes, but this one just hasn't taken hold. I took a leaf from a tree in full bloom. Now the tomato plant will compensate, I decide.

"Watch," I tell Mom. This time I don't even hold out my hands. I just tilt my head and focus on the sad tomato plant. The magic bubbles and pulses inside me. "Poor little guy," I say. "Let's show your buddies what you really look like."

The plant bends to my will. Its stem grows thicker, sturdier. The leaves turn green and full. Tiny tomatoes sprout with abandon. Beautiful.

I stand up, walk to the plant, pluck two tomatoes. I feel the weight of them in my hand. I pop one in my mouth and hand the other to Mom, who does the same. It's juicy and sweet as candy. We sit in silence, chewing meditatively, letting the sun shine some more on our faces.

I've told my mother a lot of things since I came back from Baba Yaga's forest. The truth hasn't been easy, but like she's just said, it's better than the lies. At least, mostly. That neither of us has yet to tell any of these truths to my father sits heavily on us. But my mother and I are talking again. Really talking.

She knows about Viktor now, and about our line of descent that leads back to the Romanovs. About Baba Yaga and her forest, and Ethan and the Brotherhood. About her birth mother, Lily, who became something horrible to save her child. That part has been the hardest for Mom—knowing that Lily is still out there, still a rusalka, still grieving. My mother had wished for so long to know the truth, but the truth about Lily isn't easy on any level. We've talked about it some, just as we've talked about Anastasia now, and about the magic that's taken hold inside me. Baba Yaga's magic. My magic. Ethan's magic. I'm a pretty powerful girl these days. This too isn't easy. I guess I didn't expect it to be.

I don't know what's coming next, or when it will start. Soon, I think. The magic pulsing in my veins seems stronger lately, like it's readying itself for something big. This doesn't surprise me. I made my bargain with Baba Yaga. Viktor is roaming free somewhere. Lily's still a mermaid. The journey is far from over.

Behind us, the back gate creaks open. I turn. Ethan steps into the yard, looking ridiculously handsome in dark-wash jeans and a plain navy T-shirt. He smiles at us. I smile back, pushing away the darker thought that I wouldn't be sitting here bonding with Mom and he wouldn't be standing there smiling if we both hadn't saved each other's lives in the forest. Today, I don't feel like thinking about that. Today, I'd like to be just Anne.

"Hey, Ethan," my mother greets him. "Come join us. We're doing a little gardening."

She shrugs her shoulders when I laugh. "I'm allowed a sense of humor, aren't I?"

"Well, yeah. But it freaks me out a little, okay?"

Ethan stays quiet while Mom and I banter back and forth. "You ready?" he asks eventually.

I nod, stand up, and brush a few stray pieces of grass off my jeans. We're going on real date, Ethan and I. Lincoln Park Zoo. Pizza at Pequod's. Maybe a walk on Oak Street Beach, although we both feel a little edgy about that. Last time we were at the beach, we both almost died. Correction: one of us did die, and I had to save his ass by making my bargain with Baba Yaga. Maybe we'll just stop after the pizza.

Mom stands too. She smiles at Ethan. "Have fun," she says. Then, "Call if you're going to be late." There's just the slightest edge to her tone. This doesn't surprise me. I'm dating a guy who's on his second lifetime. She's got due cause to be a little touchy about the whole thing. On the other hand, her boss, Mrs. Benson is still MIA—and possibly now a rusalka. Her birth mother's a mermaid. Her daughter has magic powers. And she's seen a witch named Baba Yaga. My relationship with Ethan probably gets lost in the shuffle of crazy.

"I want to start with the monkeys," I tell Ethan as we settle ourselves in his car. "Then maybe the lions."

"Penguins," Ethan adds as he pulls out of my driveway. "And those meerkats. Do you like meerkats?"

"Who doesn't?" I lean back in the passenger seat, happy to be making small talk with him here on our first official date that, as yet, doesn't involve mortal peril. In the back of my mind, I know we're just pretending at normal. Nothing's settled yet in my world, not even in the romance department, since Ben continues to call me—how can I not talk to him when he almost died a couple weeks ago because of me?

My cell buzzes in my pocket. It's a text from Tess.

Beware of Russian hotties. Have fun in the bear habitat.

I choose not to text her back. For now, I'll play at normal.

Ethan reaches over and squeezes my hand. I entwine my fingers with his. The magic inside me still feels different when we're together. Is that love? Or something I don't yet understand? I guess I'll find out soon enough.

"Polar bears," I say. "And otters. I love the otters."

"Otters it is," Ethan agrees.

We drive toward the city. Destiny can wait a while.

Acknowledgments

Once again, it took a village—possibly two or three.

To Jen Rofe, for absolutely everything, but especially your cowgirl wisdom. Yeehaw!

To Dan "Mr. Tiger Beat" Ehrenhaft, for knowing I could do it and making sure I had the opportunity to prove it.

To the Sourcebooks team, especially Paul, who masterminded the *Dreaming Anastasia* blog tour that ate the world; Kelly, who leaped to my editorial rescue, and with whom I had many lively debates about the best Chicago pizza and hot dogs; Kristin and Matt for lively copyedit commentary—I have no earthly idea what I would do without you. I see many cupcakes in your future.

To Cathleen Elliott for hitting another fabulous cover out of the ball park! Your artistic vision inspires and awes.

To my dearest tribe of friends, colleagues, physicians, writers, editors, and assorted wandering minstrels who stuck by me when the trenches got a little, um, trenchier—I thank you with every molecule.

And to Rick and Jake—what can I say? Guess you're stuck with me.

About the Author

Joy Preble grew up in Chicago and moved to Texas where she learned to use the phrase "y'all" without any hint of irony and developed a passion for country music and barbecue. Joy has an English degree from Northwestern University, teaches high school students when she's not busy writing, and is married to the guy she met her first week in college when she mistakenly served a volleyball into his stomach rather than over the net. *Haunted*, the sequel to *Dreaming Anastasia*, is her second novel. Visit her at www.joypreble.com.